PRAISE FOR *IN A DARK MIRROR*

"*In a Dark Mirror* is a riveting, unsettling thriller that sticks to your bones. There are hints of Megan Abbott in the way Davis writes the lush, obsessive beats of girlhood, but this story has a rhythm and a twist all its own. I couldn't put it down."

—Jess Lourey, Edgar Award–nominated author of *The Taken Ones*

"At once terrifying and thought-provoking, *In a Dark Mirror* is a haunting exploration into the tight clutch of childhood friendship. Even more frightening than the violence itself is the blurred line between what is real and what is imagined, and the dark power of a secret shared between friends. Pitch-black, multilayered, and deeply unsettling . . . prepare to read this with an almost fevered need to find out how it ends."

—Laurie Elizabeth Flynn, author of *The Girls Are All So Nice Here*

"*In a Dark Mirror* combines true crime and urban legend into something entirely, achingly human. It's a testament to Kat Davis's remarkable storytelling that she brings out new facets of the lonely girls who seek refuge in the supernatural, but perhaps her most powerful feat is in following those girls into adulthood, examining the grown women forced to grapple with the real-life consequences. Bold, haunting, and incredibly difficult to put down, this astonishingly confident debut will have you looking into every face you encounter and wondering about the secret darkness we all hold within."

—Sara Flannery Murphy, author of *The Wonder State*

"*In a Dark Mirror* is a propulsive and twisty thriller that explores girlhood and friendship, obsession and horror. Kat Davis captures the desperation of adolescence with observations so sharp they will take your breath away. Once you start reading this book, you won't be able to stop!"

—Jennifer Close, author of *Girls in White Dresses*

"Get your nightlight ready—*In a Dark Mirror* is the kind of book you stay up all night to read, and then you'll spend the rest of the week thinking about it. It's a mesmerizing, creepy, original and deeply compelling novel about adolescent girls and the darkness that lurks within, and I gobbled it whole. Kat Davis is a star."

—Annie Hartnett, author of *Unlikely Animals*

"Kat Davis mines a sensational true crime story for something unsettling and deeply human in this potent novel about girls searching for their places in the world and finding something sinister instead. *In a Dark Mirror* asks uncomfortable questions about the paper-thin boundaries between our best and worst selves, and it paints a picture of adolescence so tender I had to look away at times. Davis's prose is gorgeous and unflinching. She deftly weaves timelines and perspectives to examine the way lives, families, and entire communities are affected by horrors big and small. I tore through *In a Dark Mirror* in under twenty-four hours, but I know it will linger in the shadows of my mind for a long time to come."

—Kate Brody, author of *Rabbit Hole*

IN A

DARK

MIRROR

IN A

DARK

MIRROR

KAT DAVIS

THOMAS & MERCER

Published by Thomas & Mercer, Seattle

www.apub.com

Amazon, the Amazon logo, and Thomas & Mercer are trademarks of Amazon.com, Inc., or its affiliates.

ISBN-13: 9781662518638 (paperback)
ISBN-13: 9781662518621 (digital)

Cover design by Ploy Siripant
Cover image: © Sol Vazquez / ArcAngel

Printed in the United States of America

For A. K. D. and I. H. S.

Oh, I've been so afraid! It was so dark inside the wolf!

—Brothers Grimm, "Little Red Riding Hood"

What are little girls made of?

Sugar and spice,

And all that's nice;

That's what little girls are made of.

—English nursery rhyme

PROLOGUE

August 11, 2007

It was a little past two in the afternoon when the patrol car stopped them. The two girls were walking along the side of the road in a part of suburban Maryland where no one walks, in a wasteland between two shopping centers, stepping along the line where uneven asphalt met brown grass. The summer heat shimmered off the black pavement. Both girls were sweaty, their cheeks flushed. They wore backpacks, their heads bowed toward the ground. Lana was a little shorter than Maddie, with dark hair and glittering dark eyes. Maddie's hair was a mousy brown, and her cheeks and forehead were spotted with acne. Lana had the knife in her backpack, wrapped in a T-shirt. They had stopped at a Walmart several miles back to use the bathroom, where they had both washed their hands and faces, but Lana still had splotches of red on her shirt and lines of dried blood under the rough-bitten edges of her nails.

When the police car pulled over in front of them, Maddie felt a moment of fear, followed by relief. She was hot and could already imagine the cool of the air-conditioned car. The two men who stepped out wore uniforms and an air of authority, but when they saw the girls up close, neither of them could wipe the confusion off their faces. The officers took them both in, their eyes lingering over the stains on Lana's shirt.

One of the officers cleared his throat. "What are you girls up to?"

"We're going to the Bay Bridge. To the Eastern Shore," Lana said, and she smiled. It was the sort of smile a child gives an adult to win them over, and it was incongruous coming from a girl covered in blood.

"You're walking to the Bay Bridge? It's over twenty miles."

The girls nodded. "We brought granola bars," Maddie explained, motioning to her backpack, "and water."

The first officer looked again at the stains on Lana's shirt. "Do you know why we stopped you?"

Lana looked him straight in the eye. "I think so. Because we killed a girl."

I

2017

When twenty-two-year-old Madeline Thompson steps through the front entrance of the Needmore Mental Health Center, it's the first time she's been outside an institution since not long after her twelfth birthday.

It is a sunless day in early September. The concrete walkway leading to the door of the brick building is lined with planters filled with overly cheerful flowers. Needmore is by far the nicest of the places she's been, the sort of place that bothers to have flowers in plastic vases, even if they are fake. The director has a personal philosophy, likes to give lectures about the role of art and beauty in the healing of mental illness. This was fine for the others, an assortment of anorexics, cutters, and would-be suicides—girls who only ever tried to hurt themselves. Needmore was a major step up from the state hospital where she'd spent nearly seven years, where patients talked freely to the open air and Haldol was given out like candy. At Needmore, she was the only criminal.

Maddie follows her mother silently to the car, a gleaming Honda that she doesn't recognize. She doesn't know why she expected to see the old station wagon, which her mother must have traded in years ago.

In the car, Mom fumbles as she puts the keys into the ignition. She turns to Maddie next to her in the front seat.

"Well," she says, and she reaches out to clasp Maddie's shoulder, as if making sure she's really there. "You're out," she says. "You're home."

Maddie nods. She pushes a tendril of light-brown hair off her face. In the last ten years, her mother has touched her only a handful of times. The hand feels light, insignificant.

She's not really going home. Her mother sold the house a few years back, after Gran died, after she married Steve. Mom met Steve at a support group for people like her, parents whose children had done awful things and ended up incarcerated. Steve's son was in year five of a twenty-five-year sentence for raping a woman in an alley behind a bar. When she first started seeing Steve, her mother liked to talk about how much they had in common, how he understood so much of her own experience. As she listened to her on the phone, Maddie's lips puckered, her gaze wandering over the ugly yellow tile of the wall beyond the receiver, her thoughts suspended, waiting for the girl behind her in line to tell her that her time was up.

"How does that make you feel?" the psychiatrist at the state hospital asked when she told him about her conversations with her mother.

"It's stupid," she said. "I'm not a rapist."

The psychiatrist looked at her, waiting.

"He was a grown man in his twenties. I was twelve. And I wasn't the one with the knife."

The psychiatrist nodded gravely, then paused to scribble a note in his spider handwriting. Later, when her petition for early release was denied, she remembered this conversation and knew she'd blown it. There was only ever one correct answer: *I am guilty, guilty, guilty.*

Her mother pulls out of the parking lot and merges onto the highway, her fingers thrumming against the steering wheel. Next to her, Maddie is immobile. During the years in juvie and then the state hospital, she learned to keep her body still. People find sudden movements startling. When she went in, she was a skinny kid, an easy target. Back when she first started putting on weight, it was because she spent most of her commissary money on candy. Chocolate bars were the only sensual pleasure available in a place where she once found a cockroach floating in her cup of fruit cocktail. But as she got larger, she found that she was safer, a more imposing target. By the time the case went to trial, there was no trace of the little girl she'd been the summer of the stabbing, and everyone made their judgments about the sullen, overweight fourteen-year-old in front of them according to who she appeared to be at that moment, not the child she had once been.

The highway is the same: the same signs, lined by the same rows of concrete wall built to shield the neighboring houses from the roar of traffic. But when her mother takes the exit and turns off onto the smaller local road, Maddie finds her heart beating fast. There's a blur of familiar stores and restaurants—Taco Bell, McDonald's, Kohl's— all right where she remembers them, but other shopping centers have sprouted in previously empty fields, and tracts of woods have been replaced by shiny new town houses. The colors seem to jump out at her, too bright.

Her stomach rumbles. Most of the day has passed in a flurry of paperwork and one last "outtake" meeting with her latest therapist. She had so many meetings the last week about how to prepare herself for "reintegrating" back into normal life, but nobody warned her that she might be suddenly overcome by the desire to make her mother stop the car and buy her a chicken chalupa.

"Can we stop at Taco Bell?"

"Steve's making us dinner," Mom says, and the Taco Bell grows small in the side mirror. The memory of thousands of past slights exactly like this one tamps down the stir of excitement she felt, just for a moment, in her stomach. The muscles in her back tighten.

They drive past the turnoff toward their old house, and Maddie feels a powerful tug, but her mother doesn't seem to notice.

Ten minutes later, they pull up in front of a small house in a cookie-cutter subdivision that didn't exist when Maddie went inside. At least all the houses in their old neighborhood were unique. This street has three distinct architectural models, distinguishable only by their different colors and landscaping. Her mother and Steve live in the smallest of the three styles, a modest two-story with an attached garage.

Her mother turns the key and pauses. "Well," she says. "Here we are."

Maddie feels slightly carsick, overwhelmed by the sights and sounds of the ride.

"Come inside," her mother chirps. "I'll show you the house."

They enter through the garage, then walk down a short corridor into the kitchen. A large man with slightly stooped shoulders is standing in front of a shining smooth countertop. Next to him on a baking tray lie three fillets of uncooked fish. Maddie's nostrils flare at the smell.

"Steve is cooking fish!" her mother says unnecessarily. "Isn't that nice? He wanted to do something special for your first night."

As a kid Maddie hated fish and still does.

"Hey there," Steve says. He holds up his hands and waves them, indicating that they are dirty. Turning to the sink, he washes them, dries them on a paper towel, and then embraces Maddie lightly. "Madeline," he says, "it's wonderful to finally meet you."

"Yeah," Maddie says. "Same to you."

"Come," her mother says. "I'll show you your room."

Her mother leads her through the dining room and a living room sparsely furnished with a leather couch, and up a staircase. "When we decorated, we didn't know when you'd be coming home. So it's still set up like a guest room, but I think you'll like it. Steve's read a lot about the power of color. Do you know about that? They must've told you about it. The psychiatrists in there? There are certain colors you're supposed to surround yourself with for positive thinking. Blue is a very positive, calming color."

That last summer, Lana had talked about painting her room black but never got around to it. A warning sign, no doubt, according to Steve's color theory.

Her mother opens the door. Maddie steps behind her into a room that's completely blue. The walls are light blue, the wall-to-wall carpet is a slightly darker shade of blue, the comforter on the bed a muted turquoise. The curtains around the windows are navy blue. The room is oppressive, and hideous.

"What about my stuff?" Maddie says. The only piece of furniture she recognizes is an old wooden dresser that used to be in Gran's room.

"Oh, we didn't get rid of anything. I mean, the furniture wasn't worth keeping. It was all mostly from thrift stores to start with; you know that. And I packed up your clothes for the Goodwill. I mean, you outgrew them. But all your other things, your books and things, they're in the basement. You can look through them whenever you want." After a pause, she adds, "Maddie, what's wrong?"

"I'm just really tired." Maddie feels an ache creep through her forehead, over her eyes.

"Of course you are. I bet you're hungry. Don't worry, the fish doesn't take long to cook."

She follows her mother back down the staircase. In the living room, Maddie pauses in front of a framed photo of Gran and her mother from many years earlier, from a time before Maddie was born.

"I wish Gran was here," Maddie says, and as soon as she says it, she hears how childish it sounds.

"Of course, honey, of course." Her mother places a single hand on her shoulder.

"I should have been at the funeral."

"Well, honey, how could you have?"

"I knew a girl at the time—she was let out for a day to attend her grandfather's funeral."

"Oh, well." Mom puts a hand to her head. "You know, she went so sudden. There was just so much to think about."

"Did you know about that rule?" Maddie asks. "Did you know they sometimes let people out for stuff like that?"

"I don't know if I knew that," her mother says carefully. "I don't know if anyone ever told us that."

When she went inside, Maddie had "anger issues." The first incident occurred on the fifth day. She was sitting in the common room, and it was finally settling in: the fact that she wasn't going anywhere, that she had lost her freedom. Still feeling that first shock of the handcuffs on her wrists, the chains that had hobbled her feet when she was transferred from the local jail. All the locked doors, all the dead-eyed stares of the other kids, sizing her up. Unbelievable that this was happening to her body, to *her*. She started trembling, and then she started screaming. The screams were loud. She thought they must have been coming from someone else, but they were hers. Then there were guards dragging her to a small concrete room, where she spent the next three days. After that, she behaved herself in juvie.

The next time was after she'd been transferred to the state hospital. A girl refused to pass her the green crayon during art therapy, so she picked up a plastic container and bashed it over the girl's head. For this, she received a week of isolation and several extra "crisis" sessions with the psychiatrist, and they upped her meds. The therapists started to ask her about her "anger," as if it were something she carried around with her, a possession, a rubber ball of suppressed rage.

On her thirteenth birthday, when she asked one of the nurses if she could be excused from the common room to use the bathroom and the nurse said no, she picked up a pen lying on the counter and plunged it into the top of the nurse's hand. She did it almost reflexively. There was a lot of screaming but only a small trickle of blood. It occurred to her much later that she was, perhaps in some vague way, reenacting the stabbing. But that time she learned her lesson. Two weeks in isolation, and they dosed her with so many extra drugs that she didn't bother to learn all their names. For a while she was in a kind of chemically induced fog, was still in that state for most of the trial. When they finally lowered her meds again, it seemed that something in her had changed. The anger was still there, but when she felt it, she was able to step outside herself, as if she could see what she was about to do and choose differently. It wasn't that she felt bad for any of the times she had acted out; she just didn't want to be punished again. So she took a breath, swallowed the anger in the moment, took it with her back to her room to scream it out into her pillow in the dark.

Now Maddie looks carefully at her mother, at the crow's-feet around her eyes and the shadow of a mustache over her top lip. She looks at her mother, and she knows she's lying to her. Maddie takes a deep breath and lets it out slowly. She counts silently to herself.

"You know," Mom says, "Gran left you something. In her will. The lawyer was supposed to send you a letter. Did you ever get it?"

"I don't think so."

"He said to go and see him when you get out. I wouldn't get your hopes up, knowing Gran. But she did have a little bit of jewelry that I never found. It might be a nice pearl necklace, something like that."

"Dinner is ready," Steve calls from the kitchen.

He has set the table with napkins and forks only. Each plate is adorned with a slab of the white fish, some sort of yellow mush, and a side of steamed broccoli.

"Couscous," her mother explains when Maddie pokes at the yellow mush with a frown. "It's really good from the box. I guess we didn't make it when you were little."

Steve clears his throat. He is sitting at the head of the table, with Maddie and her mother on either side of him. Maddie's fork is halfway to her mouth. Steve holds out his hand, and Mom takes it, giving her a quick, pleading look. She puts the fork down and allows Steve to take her limp hand in his.

"Oh Lord," Steve says, "thank you for these gifts we are about to receive from you, our Lord and savior, Jesus Christ. And tonight, we thank you especially for returning Madeline to us after a long time away. And we ask you to bless her and to surround her with your powers of forgiveness and to give her the strength she needs to atone. Amen."

Maddie knows that her mother has started attending church with Steve, but she hasn't mentioned anything about blessings over food.

She eats the couscous and the broccoli and picks at her fish, moving it around the plate. Mom and Steve pretend not to notice.

Steve eats without speaking, and when he is done, he sets down his fork and looks over at her mother. She nods.

"So," Steve says. "I think we need to establish some ground rules."

"Okay."

"As you know, we are very happy to have you here with us."

"So happy," her mother repeats.

"I don't envy the road ahead of you. No one does. You're in a unique sort of position. In terms of age, you're not a child anymore, but of course you've been kept in very controlled circumstances, in a very artificial environment. Sheltered from the world, really."

She thinks of Briony, a woman from the state hospital who contrived to slit her wrists with the melted-down end of a plastic spoon. She did such a good job on her left that she couldn't even do the right. Maddie saw her disappear down the long hallway on a gurney, the blood seeping through the bandage that one of the techs was pressing to her arm.

Pursing her lips, she thrusts out her chin. Yes, a very sheltered environment.

"Well, sheltered in some ways. But you're out in the real world now—you need to think about how you can become self-sufficient. I don't know how much thought you've given to it, but it's not easy to get a job with your kind of history."

"I finished my GED," she says and then swallows. She's surprised to hear a light tremor in her voice. "And I took classes in there. One of the teachers said I was good enough to do college courses. She said it would open up a lot of possibilities for me."

Her mother refuses to meet her glance.

"Education is a wonderful thing," Steve says. "But I think your first thoughts now need to be about how you can earn. You can live here with us for free, and that'll give you a big leg up, but I'm afraid we can't help you with school money. Maybe that's a goal you can work toward."

Maddie feels something bubbling up inside her, but she swallows it back down. She focuses on sitting perfectly still in her chair. She monitors her breathing, counting silently to herself until she can inhale normally. Steve is still talking. He is saying something about a friend of her mother's she should talk to, the manager at a nursery on the other side of town. "She's a nice woman," Steve says. "Believes in second chances. And I think it would be a good fit. There's something really healing about plants. There's something that is just really good for the soul about running your hands through the soil. Did they let you do any gardening in there?"

She shakes her head.

"That's too bad. It's really very therapeutic. And that brings us to the other part of this. And I'm sure this is something you've thought a lot about over the years. Atonement."

Maddie blinks.

"Sorry," Steve says. "Do you know that word?"

"I know what 'atonement' means." Maddie looks again toward her mother, but this time she meets her gaze.

"Now, of course, everyone has to come to it in their own way, but I know your mother has told you about our experience with the church. Faith is a consolation, but it's also a kind of road map."

"I'm not really a church kind of person."

"Well, that can change." Steve taps a finger against the table. "That can always change." He pauses, as if waiting for her to speak. "What I'm trying to say is that without that road map, you're just totally alone. You're totally alone in your conscience and in your guilt with what you've done."

"I mean," Maddie says, "I served my time." She looks down at the congealed fish on her plate, watching a streak of oil slowly spreading out in all directions. She has the sensation of no longer occupying her own body but of being an observer, floating somewhere overhead. This feeling is all that's left of the old anger, tamped down for so long it has become something else—numbness where the feelings should be.

"You weren't exactly in prison."

"It was close enough." She looks again at her mother, not understanding why she won't help her.

"You understand I'm not talking about your physical body—I'm talking about your spirit, whether you've repented on the inside."

"I was mentally ill. I believed that a supernatural power was stalking me."

Steve exchanges a glance with Mom, ever so slight, but Maddie sees it. It's a look of forbearance or disagreement or maybe even disbelief, but it passes too quickly for her to categorize it with certainty.

Steve clears his throat. "Let's try to stay on topic here. All I was trying to say, Madeline, is that I hope you'll think about coming to church with your mother and I."

Maddie nods. She blinks, and two small tears overflow and spill down her cheeks. If either of them notice, they don't say. She wipes the tears with the back of her sleeve.

When Mom starts to clear the dishes from the table, Maddie stands. "I'll clean up."

Her mother glances at Steve.

"That's so nice of you to offer, Madeline," he says.

Mom and Steve go into the living room, and she hears the TV come on. In front of the sink, she turns on the water, letting it run until it's hot. She rinses and sponges each plate before placing it carefully in the dishwasher.

At the trial, she was judged to be "not criminally responsible." This was the state of Maryland's version of "not guilty by reason of insanity." When the psychiatrists visited her in juvie, collecting evidence for the trial, all their questions were about Him—what He had promised her and Lana, whether she still saw or spoke to Him. She had sat through the expert testimony at the trial, could still remember certain phrases, the phrases that absolved her: "The prefrontal cortex, which controls complex decision-making and distinguishes between what is real and what is imaginary, remains underdeveloped in preadolescent

children" . . . "what is sometimes called 'folie à deux,' a shared delusion between two people in close contact" . . . "Careful oversight, in
the proper mental health setting, could, in this case, lead to complete
recovery."

And that's it; she's recovered. But it's easier for people to believe that
she is just evil than to extend her compassion. Even her own mother.

She's done scrubbing the forks. She picks up a glass.

The sun has set, and she can see her face looking back at her in
the black glass of the window over the sink. Her hair is a mess of curls,
barely contained by her ponytail. She looks pale. Lana told her once
that she had become afraid of mirrors, that that was where she often saw
Him. Maddie swallows. It's just her in the dark window, alone.

She has forgotten the glass she's holding in her hands. She is shocked
by its crumpling, this solid thing giving way within her grasp, a shard
lodging in her pointer finger. She freezes, waiting to hear sounds from
the living room, for them to barge in, alerted by the tinkling of broken
glass, but there's no pause in the stream of voices from the TV. Wincing,
Maddie pulls the glass out of her finger, and a pool of red forms immediately, dripping down into the sink. She runs the cut under cold water,
then presses a wad of paper towels to it. It doesn't look that deep.

With the paper towel pressed to the wound, she gingerly plucks the
remaining pieces of glass from the sink and sticks them in the garbage
can. She buries the shards beneath the bloody paper towels, which she
covers over with a fresh layer before pushing the whole mess deeper
down into the bag. The blood from the cut has slowed to a small trickle.

Her mother used to always keep Band-Aids in the kitchen. She
pokes through the cabinets but can't find any. In her search she pulls
out the silverware drawer. She's about to slide the drawer back in when
she stops. One of the spots in the silverware organizer is empty: there
are no knives in the drawer.

She looks back over at the counter. Her mother's heavy old knife
block is there, a triangle of wood standing next to the stove, but it is also

empty. She searches the whole kitchen but can't find anything sharper than a butter knife.

In the living room, Mom and Steve are intently watching a reality show about a couple buying a house. Maddie sits at the end of the sofa and pretends to be interested in the program. A real estate agent is showing the couple around three different houses, and at the end of the show the couple picks the one they want. The real estate agent is standing in the kitchen of a house somewhere in Texas talking about the backsplash. The "backsplash" seems to refer to the tiles on the wall between the counter and the cabinets, a crisscross of black and brown rectangles. Apparently this backsplash is great. The woman from the couple likes the backsplash but thinks the closets are too small; the closets in the first house were much bigger.

Mom doesn't ask about the Band-Aid on Maddie's finger, and Maddie doesn't ask her where all the kitchen knives went.

After an episode, Mom picks up a tablet. She swipes and the screen unlocks. She checks Facebook, then starts filling up an Amazon cart without purchasing any of the items.

Maddie feels a tingling sensation in her fingers. Her computer lab time at Needmore was always limited and monitored. Still, she found moments, every now and then, when no one was paying attention, to poke around, just a little bit, online. One of the girls at Needmore told her about the site, one of the anorexics who chewed every bite of her food fifty times before swallowing. The girl looked younger than her age because she was so small, especially next to Maddie. Sasha was her name. Sasha always seemed impressed by her, almost like she wanted to ask for her autograph. Maddie was puzzled, and then one day Sasha told her in a whisper during a game of Connect Four about the website.

This site was different from the typical press articles, a kind of shrine to Him. They call themselves His Followers, the fans of hers and Lana's crime. Pages of fan fiction and discussion threads, as if what they'd done wasn't reality but some sort of television show. The first time she found the site, she felt disgusted and was relieved by her own disgust because it seemed like proof that she had changed, that she was now someone who would never again do the thing that she had done then. And yet, she wanted to spend more time on the site, more time than she dared, with the computer room tech breathing down her neck. If they saw her looking, it could cost her everything; they could report it to her therapist as evidence that she was still delusional; it could be used as an argument against her early release.

She waits until Mom sets the tablet down on the coffee table.

"Is it okay if I go online?"

Mom looks a little startled. On the TV screen, a new couple is talking about their dream home. This show seems to be the same as the previous one, except that it takes place somewhere on an island in the Caribbean.

Mom glances quickly at Steve. "Sure." After picking up the tablet, Mom angles her body away to enter her passcode so that Maddie can't see it. She hands her the tablet. "We think for now that it's best if you only go online with supervision. Just to be consistent."

"Consistent?"

"It's even worse than when you were younger, Maddie. You have to be careful."

"A bunch of nutjobs and conspiracy theorists," Steve intones. "We understand that you have to have some access these days, but we're thinking it should be limited. We just don't want you to get overwhelmed—you know, to fall back into bad habits."

There was an expert witness at the trial who testified that Lana's and Maddie's screen time had been a factor in their delusion, that they had spent so much time online on fan sites, lost in their own imaginative play, that it had helped create the ideal circumstances for the development of shared psychosis. So her mother's fear probably makes a certain amount of sense. Still, she has to fight the urge to push out her lips and pout like a child.

With Mom watching, she brings up a real estate website and begins to look for studio apartments in the area. Mom stiffens next to her, but then Maddie forgets that she's even watching when she sees the cost of a month's rent. She clicks through several listings, all of them perfectly beyond her reach. Steve is right about one thing—she does need money.

At 10:00 p.m., after watching three different couples pick three different houses and pronounce themselves satisfied, every time, with their choice, Steve turns off the TV. Mom puts out a hand, and Maddie wordlessly gives her the tablet, which Mom plugs into a charger on the kitchen counter. Maddie stands up to follow Mom and Steve up the stairs but not before allowing herself one final glance at the tablet, its charge light blinking orange in the dark.

1

June 2007

Maddie dug last year's bathing suit out of the bottom drawer of her dresser. The suit was yellow, the fabric pilled on the bottom from her sitting on the rough edge of the pool. The suit looked small, and when she stepped into it, it stretched tight in the crotch. She had grown taller since last year, but worse, she'd grown wider, especially in the chest. The suit crushed her new breasts so that they spilled out the sides a little. She walked down the hall to the bathroom so she could look at herself in the large mirror over the sink. It was even worse than she had feared.

This was the sort of thing Mom would once have anticipated that now fell through the cracks, ever since Dad had moved out.

She was supposed to meet Lana in ten minutes. Maddie went back to her room and found a large T-shirt and a pair of shorts. She would just have to keep herself covered for as long as she could and then slip into the pool quickly. Maybe no one would notice.

It was a Saturday morning, but the door to Mom's room was still closed. She'd have to tell her later about needing a new suit, but that was fine. It was a money thing, which would just stress her out anyway. Gran was up as usual, sitting at the kitchen table with a cup of coffee and a crossword puzzle in front of her.

"Lana and I are going to the pool," Maddie said.

"You got any money?"

"Mom gave me some last night." Mom had given her a ten-dollar bill—pool money for the week. There were vending machines there and an ice cream truck that showed up some days and not others.

"Have a good time. Did you put on sunscreen?" Gran shouted after her, but she was already out the door.

Last summer, Maddie had spent every moment that she wasn't at camp at the pool with Lana. They played games in the water, seeing who could hold their breath the longest and teaching themselves to do flips. Maddie had even gotten pretty good at diving: not just jumping off the high board but going in headfirst, which she had always been afraid to do.

Wheeling her bike out of the garage, she blinked in the bright morning light. The air was slightly cool, and droplets of dew still glittered in the grass.

Their house was one of the oldest on their street, one of the first houses built over thirty years ago, when the old farmland was first converted to a residential subdivision, and it remained one of the smallest, a modest rancher. The house was set far back from the road so that it was almost in the woods. Already in a state of disrepair, the house had only gotten worse since Dad left. The paint was peeling off the blue siding, and half the roof was discolored, the gray shingles stained slightly green.

She hopped on her bike and pedaled quickly down the length of the driveway, soon emerging from the shade of the pines onto the unsheltered street. Lana's house stood on the corner; Maddie could still remember when it was an empty lot. When the house first went up, her father had dubbed it a "McMansion." It was two stories and had a high entryway with a large twisting staircase and chandelier and granite countertops in the kitchen. Maddie's father, who owned a used car dealership, was always making jokes about the Prescotts, saying, "I wouldn't have thought you could make that much working for the State Department" and "I guess I went into the wrong business." Of course that was before, when Dad still lived with them.

Maddie sped down the street, slowing down only once to pass a moving van, followed by two cars. In the first car sat a man and two kids, both boys. In the second car she caught a glimpse of a woman behind the wheel and a blonde girl in the passenger seat who looked about her age. Twisting her head around after she passed, she saw the van stopping in front of the Cranes' old house, which had sat empty for several months.

Lana was waiting for her in the driveway. Her bike was propped up on its kickstand, and she was drawing with chalk next to her brother, Marc, who was eight.

"There's a new family moving in down the street," Maddie announced. "With kids."

Both Prescotts stood up and walked down to the end of the driveway, where they could see the moving van parked in front of the other house but nothing else.

Lana hopped on her bike. "What about me?" Marc whined. Maddie and Lana had only been allowed to bike to the pool together without adult supervision starting last year, when they were both eleven.

"You'll just have to get older," Lana said and then stuck out her tongue.

The two of them sped out of the driveway and down the incline of the street. The pool was over a mile away, past the small park that backed to the woods, past rows of white-trimmed and redbrick colonial-style houses with neatly cut lawns. Their neighborhood was one of the wealthier ones in the area, with its community pool and playgrounds, its strict bylaws ensuring that all the houses retained their curb appeal. There were only two entrances to the warren of streets, designed to limit access, but Maddie had never had much reason to wonder who this design was meant to keep out. Too young to drive, she and Lana were confined to their residential community, the pool one of the few destinations within their reach.

Lana was wearing shorts and no cover-up over last year's red-and-white-striped bathing suit, but unlike Maddie's, her suit still fit. Lana had always been petite, and her chest was still flat. Maddie found herself yearning for the body she'd still had last summer, the trim one with straight lines instead of this new curvy one. That year, after a girl at school had made fun of her hairy legs and Maddie had come home in tears, her mother bought her an electric razor that plugged into the wall. It didn't make her legs as sleek and smooth as the women's she saw on TV, but at least they looked better from a distance. Last night, in anticipation of the pool visit, she had used it to remove the long stray black hairs that had recently appeared in her armpits. She had only to glance over at Lana leaning forward on her bike to know that her pits were still as smooth as a toddler's skin.

The last remnants of cool air were gone now, and the stagnant air was warm as it cut across her skin. When they turned their bikes into the pool parking lot, she saw there was only a single car and two other bikes chained to the rack. Inside, a middle-aged woman was swimming laps. It wasn't adult swim, but she was the only one there, other than the lifeguard. Lana promptly led them over to their favorite seats, two lounge chairs near the chain-link fence that were always in the shade, thanks to the row of pine trees behind them.

Lana stretched out on the lounger, arching her back for a moment so that she resembled her cat, Merlin, who was all black except for a white patch around his left eye.

There were already more people wandering in through the front gate. The middle-aged woman swam to the stairs and pulled herself out of the water, removing her tight cap and goggles, and as they watched, Ethan Walsh did a cannonball into the deep end. Ethan was a year ahead of them in school. Like Maddie, he'd lived in the neighborhood forever. Unlike Maddie, Ethan was popular at school. He had short blond hair, clear blue eyes, and was good at sports. That year a few girls had come up to Maddie and Lana in the cafeteria one day, asking in hushed tones if it was true they lived in the same neighborhood as Ethan Walsh, squealing when they said yes. Lana had just rolled her eyes at them. But Maddie found herself telling them that she and Ethan had carpooled together when they were in preschool.

"Was he cute back then too?" one of the girls asked.

Maddie thought about it. "Yes."

"What was that all about?" Lana asked her later, after the other girls had gone on to their table. "You don't like Ethan, do you?"

"No, of course not." That was the right answer. Lana didn't like anyone, at least not anyone real. She liked Spock and had had a crush on Harry Potter for a while, but she said that was all over now. Maddie had never liked anyone before, but now when she thought about Ethan, blood rushed to her head, and she felt her face turn red. She wondered if he remembered that they used to carpool together.

For a moment, Ethan was the only one in the pool. Although it was just the beginning of the summer, his back and shoulders were already tanned. He had probably been on vacation already with his family. They were the type who would do ski vacations in the winter and weekends at Ocean City in the summer. Even when her parents had been together, they almost never went on those kinds of vacations. As she watched, Ethan's younger brother, Andy, waded into the pool from the stairs and started splashing at him, and a few more kids trickled in through the front gate.

That year at school, Ethan had dated Amelia Lawrence for a whole month. They had walked around the halls holding hands. Maddie hated Amelia; she had been her nemesis ever since the first grade, when they got in an argument at recess over whose turn it was on the swing. Amelia had pushed her and Maddie pushed her back, but the teacher saw only Maddie's shove, so it was she who got held in the next day at recess as punishment. Since then, she and Amelia had mostly avoided one another, but in the last year, Amelia had started to pick on her. She was tricky, so her bullying never seemed like bullying but a kind of fake niceness. One time in art class, Amelia cornered her next to the sink where she was washing paintbrushes and, flanked by two of her friends, fake smiled at Maddie and asked her why she was so weird. She didn't know how to answer, so she didn't speak, just looked back and forth between the three smiling girls.

"It's even weirder when you don't say anything," said Amelia.

"I don't have anything to say."

"Maybe you could just try to be normal," Amelia said. "Have you thought about that? Just try to be less weird."

Maddie didn't tell anyone about this encounter, not even Lana, because it was the sort of thing that happened all the time at school, but only if Lana wasn't around. People found Lana intimidating. For one thing, she didn't care at all what anyone else thought and would report everything to the teachers.

Maddie had had a Facebook page for a year and a half, but she'd deleted her account that past winter, after Amelia wrote a post on her wall saying she was so ugly she should kill herself. Maddie cried a lot about it but didn't tell Mom or Gran. In the end, it was Lana, who didn't care about Facebook and had never even had an account, who told her what to do.

"You have to act like it doesn't bother you at all. Delete your profile. If they try to talk to you at school, act like you can't hear them. When they see they can't hurt you, they'll lose interest."

Lana had been right. When one of Amelia's friends asked her why she wasn't on Facebook anymore, Maddie turned away, careful to keep her face neutral. The girl looked a little deflated. After a couple of days, the others lost interest in her and started taunting another girl in the class. Maddie found that girl crying in the bathroom a few times and felt bad for her but kept her distance. Now the girls acted like Maddie didn't exist at all, as if she had erased herself when she'd erased her social media. But she and Lana decided it was better that way. They survived the hours at school and lived for the hours afterward, knowing they had each other. Now they had the whole summer before them.

"Should we go swimming?" Lana asked.

Maddie nodded. She wanted to get into the water before any more people arrived.

Lana stripped easily down to her suit. Maddie removed her shorts first so that most of her body was still covered by her large T-shirt. She hesitated, then quickly pulled the shirt off and loped toward the pool. Glancing back, she saw that Lana was watching her and frowning.

Maddie went to the stairs and quickly waded in, bending her knees so that she was submerged up to her shoulders. To her dismay, the small bulbs of flesh on her chest bobbed out from her body like miniature flotation devices. She knew her face was red. Lana took her time as she always did getting into the water, dipping first a toe and then her foot, then slowly making her way down the steps.

Now that she was in the water, Maddie realized that when she stepped out, the wet suit would cling to her, drawing even more attention to the curves of her body and her too-small suit. She should have left her towel closer to the pool edge so that she could wrap it around herself as soon as she got out.

Lana was next to her in the water. She took a deep breath, did a flip, and came up laughing and sputtering. Maddie did one, too, but it was harder than she remembered, the way that everything was just a little harder now, her body not quite as fast as it used to be. But then she did a couple more flips, blowing bubbles the whole time to keep the water out of her nose, and the more she did it, the better she got.

They swam out to the deep end of the pool, treading water and laughing. When the lifeguard blew the whistle, it was a quarter to eleven, which meant fifteen minutes of adult swim. Lana pulled herself up easily out of the water, and with a turn, she planted herself so that her feet were still dangling in the pool. Last year they had sometimes spent all of adult swim like this, talking quietly while the adults did their laps. Maddie hesitated. She didn't have time to swim back across the length of the pool, toward the chair where her towel was hanging.

She took a deep breath and pulled herself out. Water ran off her yellow suit in rivulets, forming a puddle beneath her. She got stuck for a moment as she turned herself around, and in that moment, she caught a glimpse of a single dark pubic hair, poking out of the crotch of her swimsuit. She immediately crossed her legs as she sat down, trying to pull the suit down at the same time. Her breasts were overflowing slightly out of the top, but she was afraid to adjust the suit again in case that hair tried to poke its way back out. The hairs had started to sprout a year ago, first in a small ridge around the lips of her pubis, which was not so bad. Then the hair kept growing out toward her thighs. She hadn't realized she had to worry about it sticking out of her suit. Her heart was beating fast. She wondered if Lana had seen.

Lana wasn't looking at Maddie, but Ethan was. He was sitting on the pool edge just a few feet away with Andy at his side. His eyes darted from her breasts to the rise of her hips, back and forth, again and again. Maddie felt as if there were lasers connecting Ethan's eyes to her body. When they played Mirror Universe, Maddie's character, Mariana, wanted boys to look at her like this, but now that it was happening, Maddie just wanted to be somewhere else. She wanted to evaporate from the concrete like a puddle of water, leaving her body behind forever.

Next to her, Lana gripped her arm. "Stay here," she hissed.

Lana stood and pattered away. Ethan's eyes glanced briefly in Lana's direction and then moved back to Maddie. He elbowed Andy in the chest and whispered something that Maddie couldn't hear. Both boys laughed.

Then Lana was draping her towel around Maddie's shoulders. "C'mon," she said. Maddie clutched the towel like a drowning person grasping a life preserver, pulling it down quickly to shield herself from Ethan's gaze. Lana led her back to their chairs.

"Let's go," Lana said.

Maddie held her towel around herself as she slipped on her shorts, pulling them over the wet suit. She turned her back toward the pool as she put on her shirt.

They rode for several minutes in silence. The air was so humid that their wet suits did little to cool them down, the heat of the late-morning sun reflected back to them off the black pavement. Maddie found herself swallowing, close to tears.

"I think," Lana said carefully as they turned off onto their block, "that we're too old for the pool now, don't you think?"

Maddie didn't answer, but she didn't need to. They both turned into Lana's driveway. In their friendship, Lana was the one who called the shots, and Maddie was the one who did what she was told.

Maddie's swimsuit dried under her clothes as she and Lana sat in the high swivel chairs in Lana's kitchen, eating Cheetos from the bag until the neon-orange dust was thick on their fingertips.

"Back so soon?" Mrs. Prescott asked, wandering into the kitchen. "I thought you'd be at the pool all day."

Lana shrugged. "We didn't feel like it."

Mrs. Prescott always seemed vaguely glamorous to Maddie. She was thin, her dark hair was short and stylish, and she always wore a neat line of bright-pink lipstick, even when she was just hanging around the house.

"I'm making Marc a sandwich," Mrs. Prescott said, starting to dig through the fridge. "You girls want anything?"

"We're not hungry," Lana said, scraping the Cheetos dust off the end of her fingertips with her teeth.

"You didn't just eat Cheetos for lunch, did you?"

Lana shrugged. "It was just a snack."

Mrs. Prescott threw up her shoulders as if to say *What can I do about it?* and set a jar of mayonnaise on the countertop. Maddie envied Lana for her mother's easygoing ways. Mom wasn't at home much anymore, but Maddie always had Gran breathing down her back, supervising what she was eating and when.

"There's a new family moving in down the street," Mrs. Prescott said.

"We know. We saw the truck."

"I spoke to her for a minute. Hannah Newman, the mother, seemed nice. There are three kids, including a girl your age."

Lana didn't answer.

"You could ask her to go to the pool with you one of these days. To be nice."

"We're not going to the pool anymore."

Mrs. Prescott put down the knife she'd taken out of the drawer. "What are you talking about? You girls love the pool."

"We're too old for the pool."

"I don't think you can be too old for the pool."

"We just don't like it anymore, okay?" With a jerk of her head, Lana indicated that they should leave. Maddie slipped off her chair, leaving a damp spot on the fabric.

She followed Lana into the small den off the living room, and Lana closed the door. Maddie was a little sad that they might spend the whole summer not going to the pool. She wondered if she could change Lana's mind, maybe once she had a new suit, but she also knew Lana could be stubborn about this kind of thing once she'd made up her mind.

"There's something I want to show you," Lana said, sitting down at the desk in the corner of the room and booting up the computer. Maddie scooted the folding chair next to her. In the winter they often spent hours like this playing *Snood*, but recently Lana liked going online instead, checking out Star Trek websites and YouTube.

They waited while the page loaded. It was one of those sites where people posted their own scary photos. Some of them were really amateurish: a black-and-white photo of a field with a streak across the sky that was supposed to be a ghostly manifestation but was obviously just a trick of the light. Kids dressed up in monster masks like on Halloween.

"This one," Lana said, and she clicked to enlarge the image.

Maddie leaned toward the screen. It was a black-and-white photo of the inside of a barn. A horse was standing in its stable, its eyes rolled wide toward the ceiling in terror. In the far corner of the photo, peeking around a darkened doorway, was the blurry figure of a man, the silhouette of his face just visible in the shadows.

"Creepy," Maddie whispered.

"So creepy," Lana repeated, her eyes glistening.

It was Maddie who had gotten Lana interested in scary stories. Lana had moved to the neighborhood at the beginning of fourth grade. By then, Maddie was used to doing things by herself—riding alone on the bus, sitting on the same swing at recess so no one would notice that she didn't have anyone to play with. Sometimes at lunch she sat next to a girl named Angela who'd been an outcast since second grade, when someone saw her pick her nose and then eat it.

Lana seemed a little spacey, a little different herself. Maybe that was why Maddie had sat next to her that day on the bus and took out her worn library copy of *Scary Stories to Tell in the Dark*.

"What are you reading?" Lana had asked, looking at the cover with interest.

Maddie told her the plot of the story she had just read, the one where the couple is making out in the car and they hear on the radio that a dangerous criminal has just escaped from the home for the criminally insane. When they hear a noise and the boy goes to check, he finds a hook stuck to the door of the car.

"A hook?" Lana asked.

"Yeah. Oops, I told it wrong. The criminal had only one hand. He had a hook instead of a left hand."

They talked the rest of the way home.

"What do you think?" Lana asked now, her eyes still focused on the photo of the darkened barn on the computer screen. Maddie could sense there was something else she was supposed to say, but she didn't know what it was.

"It's pretty cool. Do you want to maybe go in the backyard and play Mirror Universe?"

Lana's shoulders slumped. Maddie had let her down again. Lana was special; she was the one who understood more, who saw further.

Sometimes Maddie worried that Lana wouldn't want to be friends anymore because she so often disappointed her. But in the end, she knew Lana needed her as much as she needed Lana. They were both getting too old for pretend and had to conceal their elaborate games from the other girls at school, girls who traded makeup tips and held hands with boys in the hallways and even kissed them on the lips sometimes behind the brown brick building after hours.

"Come on, Leonora," Maddie said, leaning in and resting her head on Lana's shoulder. "Let's go outside."

2

Lana squinted in the bright afternoon sun. Maddie was standing in the grass pretending to be Mariana, who had just kissed Spock for the first time.

A few months back, Maddie had discovered some of her father's old DVDs in a box in the basement, including *Star Trek: The Original Series*. At first they had both watched it just to laugh at the old-fashioned special effects, how the punches didn't even look real. But after a couple of episodes, they'd started to get into it. Then there was an episode called "Mirror, Mirror," in which the *Enterprise* crew discovers a parallel universe where everyone is the opposite of the way they are in the real world. All the crew members are suddenly evil, and it was the best episode of the show.

Now they liked to play Mirror Universe, where they could take any fictional world they wanted and imagine they were in the Mirror Universe. They had even made up their own Mirror Universe identities. Maddie had suggested that their Mirror Universe names could be their own names spelled backward, but Lana had quickly nixed that idea (and no wonder, since her name would be "Anal," which had made Maddie laugh and laugh when she realized). In the end, they decided that their Mirror Universe names would start with the same letter as their real names, so Lana was Leonora and Maddie was Mariana. Leonora was basically a witch. She wore black robes and carried a wand. Mariana was tall and thin and wore a short leather skirt with fishnet stockings and really high heels.

Lana had liked Spock a little, too, at first, but not the way Maddie did. She could already see where this was going: a kiss today, tomorrow Mariana and Spock would be engaged, Mariana would be pregnant by the end of the week, the whole thing disintegrating into just another game of House. And that was not what the Mirror Universe was supposed to be for. The Mirror Universe was about getting away from the mundane, about imagining themselves elsewhere, somewhere where things actually happened and life had meaning.

Maddie was in many ways a very conventional person. She just wanted a nice family and friends like everyone else, and that probably made sense, given how disastrously her family had fallen apart. But that wasn't what Lana wanted.

She wanted adventure. That spring she had felt a new energy flowing through her. She couldn't shake the feeling that something momentous was coming for her, that something was finally going to *happen*. She wanted a way to break through the things she could see into that other world she sometimes sensed living and breathing beyond this one.

Lana had always had a connection to things that other people couldn't see. One of her first clear memories from when she was maybe three or four was of walking outside in their old neighborhood one day with Mommy, when a bright rainbow of colors dripped like paint from the blue sky above her head—broad streaks of red, blue, green, and purple that filled her with joy. She tried to point it out to her mother, but Mommy only gave her a funny look and told her that she had an excellent imagination.

He was different, and He came later, maybe when she was five or six. He appeared behind her one day in the mirror, a tall thin man dressed in black, his face pale and white, his deep-set eyes lost in darkness. She screamed and her mother came running, but He disappeared before she got there. Mommy assured her that whatever she had seen was only her imagination, but Lana knew better.

She saw Him maybe a handful of times after that. One day He appeared in the back seat next to her as Mommy was driving, but Mommy couldn't see Him. That was when Lana understood how alone she was, that this was a kind of personal haunting, only for her. She became withdrawn, lost interest in playing with other kids, liked to stay close to Mommy and Daddy, even though deep down she knew that even they couldn't protect her.

For a while she had tried to avoid looking in mirrors, since that was where He had first appeared. Then, at some point, He stopped visiting her. She didn't remember a single day that He stopped, just one day realizing it had been weeks since He had appeared. But He had left something behind, some marker of difference. She knew the other kids thought she was "weird." Lana didn't mind not having friends, not really, but then one day in the fourth grade, Maddie Thompson sat down next to her on the bus with a book of ghost stories, and they started talking. Lana thought that maybe she had met someone who would finally understand. But when she told Maddie about Him, she could tell she didn't really believe her.

"Maybe it was an actual guy who broke into your house?" Maddie had said, getting excited for the wrong reason.

Since then, Lana had tried again, tried to help Maddie understand the power of the supernatural forces that surrounded them. That was why she had shown Maddie that photo online this morning, the one of the face peeking into the barn. It reminded her of Him: if not the exact image itself, then the feeling that it had given her.

Lana had been thinking about Him a lot lately. Maybe it was all the horror stories that she and Maddie read, their repeated viewings of the Scream movies, the only slasher films either of them could stand. Somehow, over the last few months, she had started feeling Him again, a presence, a shadow over her shoulder, even though she hadn't seen Him, even though when she turned around, there was nothing there. She was starting to think it was possible that He had been with her always, just behind her, where she couldn't see Him.

But Maddie didn't get it, not really, and Lana was stuck playing these childish games. It was getting a little embarrassing, to be going into the seventh grade and still playing pretend. She watched now as Maddie-as-Mariana thrust out her lips to receive Spock's kiss and winced inwardly. It was all getting a little too silly.

She heaved a deep sigh, but it took Maddie a moment to stop playing and turn to look at her.

"What if, instead of the Mirror Universe, we call it the 'Dark World'?" Lana said.

Maddie frowned. "Why would we do that?"

"It's getting a little old. Playing Mirror Universe all the time."

"So what would the Dark World be?"

"It would be kind of like the Mirror Universe, but everything there is, you know, more evil."

"But that's exactly what the Mirror Universe is."

"Yeah, but in the Dark World, there's no Spock, okay? We didn't make up the Mirror Universe so that you could pretend to kiss boys."

Maddie blushed. She had the kind of pale, splotchy skin that turned red at the slightest emotion. It made everything worse. Like that morning at the pool, when Ethan was staring at her chest and Maddie turned bright red over her whole body and Lana had to get a towel just to cover her up.

"Let's just forget Spock," Lana said, warming to her new ideas about the Dark World and what they might find there. "Say in the Dark World there are monsters, like real monsters. Like vampires who kill people and suck their blood, but we're not scared of them. They're like our friends."

"I guess."

"You can have a vampire boyfriend if you want. Like in that book you're always talking about."

"*Twilight*."

"Sure."

"Can we still be Mariana and Leonora?"

"Yeah, we still have the same names. Just, like, more interesting adventures."

Maddie brightened. They spent the next half hour trying to suss out the new rules of the Dark World. In the end, the only thing they could agree on was that in the Dark World, Mariana and Leonora kept Amelia Lawrence in a cage in a damp basement and fed her only bread and water. Maddie was the one who really had a problem with Amelia, but Lana disliked all popular girls on principle, so she was fine with it. And Amelia had been truly cruel to Maddie; Lana had seen the Facebook posts where she told her friend she was so ugly she should die. Such a person could not be forgiven, was beyond redemption. As they got into the spirit of the game, it was Lana who suggested that they torture Amelia by pulling out her fingernails, and Maddie mimed walking to get the pincers, taking small mincing steps as if she were really wearing fishnet stockings and high heels.

Yes, it was silly, but it was also what sustained them. Lana could see it more and more clearly, like a horizon line they were fast approaching: the end of childhood. And she didn't want it to end, not yet.

Daddy announced that they were going to have crabs for dinner. Both girls' cheeks were flushed from the heat, and they were drinking Cokes at the counter in the kitchen.

"Maddie," Daddy said, "do you want to join us?"

Lana looked over at Maddie.

"In fact," Mommy said, wiping her hands on a dish towel, "why don't you invite your mom and grandmother over too? We can eat out on the deck."

Lana saw Maddie's face perk up at the invitation, then fall slightly when it expanded to include the rest of her family.

"I'll ask them," Maddie said.

Kat Davis

The two families used to get together every couple of months for dinner, but it hadn't been the same since Maddie's dad moved out. It was weird now that he was gone. Mommy and Daddy kept giving each other meaningful looks that meant they were all supposed to feel so sorry for Maddie and her family. Lana *did* feel sorry for Maddie, but she also felt a little bored with it all. It had been months since her dad had moved out. How long did they have to keep feeling sorry for the Thompsons; how long did they have to keep inviting her mom and grandmother over to dinner, when they all knew they'd never return the invitation?

Something had been wrong with Maddie's mom ever since Mr. Thompson moved out. They had never hung out much at her house anyway, not when Lana's house was so much nicer. But the couple of times that Lana had gone over there recently after school, it was just depressing. Maddie's grandmother spent most of the day in her bathrobe, walking around the house and sighing. Maddie said it was because she had arthritis. Gran cooked sometimes, but what she made was never very good, and whenever she used the microwave, she left the food in for way too long so that it came out all dried and hard.

Maddie's mom was working full time now as a receptionist at the pediatrician's office, so of course she was tired and grumpy when she got home, but it wasn't just that. She used to cook pretty nice dinners, especially when Lana was staying over, and she would always ask Lana questions about herself that showed she was interested in her daughter's best friend. Now Mrs. Thompson greeted her distractedly, as if she barely noticed that Lana was there. The first thing Mrs. Thompson did when she got home was pour herself a large glass of white wine. Lana understood that this was all because her husband had left her for another woman named Sharon—one of the women who worked for him at his car dealership. ("She's thirty-one," Mommy told Daddy one night at the dinner table, and she rolled her eyes.) So of course Maddie preferred to be at Lana's house, and Mommy seemed to think it was better for them to play there too.

It was nearly four o'clock when Maddie went home, saying she'd be back in an hour or so. Lana hoped that she'd change her clothes. The pool had been such a disaster. Poor Maddie, with that awful suit. Lana was relieved that her body hadn't started to change on her like that. She was dreading it more than anything. And the way that Ethan had looked at Maddie, the way he had looked at her best friend. She imagined it again now, but this time she had a pen in her hand and with a single fluid motion she stabbed the pointy end into both of Ethan's eyeballs, and they popped out and bled, and he was blinded forever.

It made her feel better to think about it. It seemed like the sort of thing Leonora would do to protect Mariana. She'd have to tell Maddie about it later.

◆　◆　◆

Maddie arrived back at the house a little before six, with Gran and her mom in tow. Daddy and Marc had already come home with two large brown paper bags, and Daddy was setting up the steamer on the back deck.

"Thanks for the invite," Maddie's mom said. Her voice sounded deep, as if she had a cold. Lana always felt sorry for Mrs. Thompson, who, next to her own mother, looked short and fat.

Mommy offered the two women something to drink, and Lana pulled Maddie by the arm out the back door, onto the deck.

"You girls want to help?" Daddy asked.

"We just wanna watch," Lana said. "Can we look?"

Daddy shrugged and pulled the staples out of the top of the large brown bag. Lana and Maddie peered over the edge. The blue crabs were squirming inside, jostling against one another, trying to get out.

"Sometimes they pull each other's legs off," Lana said.

"Gross," Maddie said.

Daddy lit the burner and placed the steaming pot on top.

"Don't get too near the flame."

"We know," Lana said, rolling her eyes.

Lana actually hated this moment, just before they went in the pot, but she came out every time to watch anyway. She felt like it was her duty, somehow, to witness it. They didn't inspire much sympathy, the crabs. It wasn't like looking at a dog or a cat, but there was still something about the way they flailed around as they went in, so desperate to stay alive. It was unspeakably cruel to kill them this way, putting them in there to slowly steam to death. For the first few minutes there was always the panicked scrabbling sound of their claws hitting against the metal, very loud at first, frantic even, then slower, then silence.

Once the pot was still, Maddie said, "Can we go back inside now?"

Mommy was sitting with Maddie's mother and grandmother at the kitchen table, each with a wineglass in front of her.

"Ready in twenty," Daddy said, pulling a beer out of the fridge.

"I'll help you get the table ready," Mrs. Thompson said, and both their mothers went about grabbing stacks of old newspaper to put down over the table as well as wooden mallets and knives and paper napkins.

"Where's Merlin?" Maddie asked.

Lana shrugged. "He's around here somewhere. Probably in the basement."

"Can we go find him?"

"You can go if you want," Lana said. She felt tired from watching the crabs squirm in the pot and wanted to eat some of the chips that Mommy had set out in a bowl on the counter.

Maddie looked disappointed, but after a moment she turned and went downstairs. Lana went over and took a handful of chips.

Maddie's grandmother was watching her from the table. Lana had never much cared for Maddie's gran. She scared her a little. She was older than any of Lana's grandparents, her face deeply lined like crumpled paper, her back twisted so she looked like a hunchback, her fingers gnarled. Maddie was always having to help her open jars. Besides, Lana had the feeling that Gran didn't like her much either.

Now she stood up a little straighter. "Would you like some?" she said in her best attempt at a polite voice, holding out the bowl toward the old woman.

"Don't give me that," Gran said. "I see you there, Lana Prescott. I see you."

Stricken, Lana put the bowl back on the counter. She turned her face away in shame, though she didn't know what she had done wrong. What was it that Gran saw that Lana couldn't?

There were shrieks of laughter from downstairs, and Lana heard Marc's voice. Still frowning, she went downstairs to join them.

The crabs, now bright red and spiced with Old Bay, were heaped in a large pile in the center of the newspaper-covered table. Across from Lana, Daddy's fingers worked efficiently, quickly snapping the front claws and pulling out the meat with his teeth. He cracked the body easily into four parts and brushed the soft gills away, pausing every now and then to use a small knife to nudge the juicy body meat out of the small recesses of the chest cavity. Daddy didn't care about the yellow-green guts that got all over his fingers, slurping them up like they were extra flavoring. Next to Daddy, Mommy worked a little more slowly, her movements a little more cautious. She knocked a mallet against her knife to break open the claws and set both down in front of Marc.

Lana sighed and pulled a stray claw out of the pile. She tried to break it at the joint the way Daddy did, but her fingers weren't strong enough, so she picked up the little knife next to her and used the mallet to cut through the hard shell. The claw was watery, and the liquid seeped out onto the newsprint. The meat inside was shriveled, stringy, and dry. Lana frowned. She had never actually liked the way the crabs tasted or the way the meal would drag on for hours, the adults talking and drinking as they cracked the shells, getting a small handful of meat from each little body before moving on to the next one.

Lana had never understood why they ate the crabmeat straight off the newspaper, which grew increasingly sodden throughout the meal, the ink rubbing off onto their fingers and onto the crabmeat itself. When she'd tried to ask Daddy about it once, he'd said that this was the way they used to do it when he was a kid.

Everyone else was on their second or third crab by the time Mommy noticed that Lana wasn't eating. "You're not going to have any?" she asked. Lana shrugged.

"Get yourself some cheese and crackers or something then."

By the time Lana came back with Triscuits and a slice of American cheese, it was getting dark. Daddy asked her to switch on the light over the porch.

Next to her, Maddie was still eating crab. She liked to empty the whole thing, until she had a little pile of meat waiting for her that she dipped into the Old Bay.

"You girls still playing Star Trek?" Daddy asked, taking a swig of his beer.

Lana frowned into her strip of American cheese. She would have liked to keep everything she and Maddie talked about a secret from their parents, but they had overheard them talking one too many times about Spock.

"We're not *playing* Star Trek," she said.

"Star Trek? Really?" Maddie's mother said. "Not the old series? The one from the sixties?"

"That's the one," Daddy said.

Mrs. Thompson shook her head. "I can't believe you girls would find that interesting. The special effects must be so outdated."

"That's what I would have thought," Daddy said.

"I think there's a lot of interest in a certain character. Spock, isn't it?" Mommy said, and she exchanged a look with Mrs. Thompson.

"Spock, really?" Mrs. Thompson's eyes widened, and all the adults shook their heads, as if sharing in some secret. Everyone except Maddie's gran, who had trouble with her hearing and probably didn't know what anyone was talking about anyway. Lana's parents and Maddie's mom laughed. Lana sank into herself, slouching down in her seat.

"We're just teasing, honey," Daddy said.

"It's not funny," Lana said. She left the rest of her cheese and crackers untouched in front of her, to make them feel bad, but they didn't seem to notice. She sneaked a glance at Maddie, who met her eyes and shrugged. She could tell Maddie didn't like being laughed at, either, but what could they do? The adults were always laughing at them.

There were crickets chirping now and moths flying in little circles around the porch light, drawn to its glow. Lana looked at Daddy's fingers, smeared with guts and Old Bay, as he reached for another beer. Mommy's knife flashed across the table as she picked up the mallet again. The longer they sat there, the longer it seemed to her that the two families were encased in the separate glow of the porch light, set apart from the dark of the woods. The faces around the table glowed. The bubble of light formed a kind of force field, encasing them in its radiance. Behind them, the woods were black and impenetrable. Under the table, Lana tapped her feet against the deck and tried not to look too often into the darkness. Sometimes she thought she could hear the creak of a tree branch or the scuttle of some swiftly moving creature. She didn't like thinking about all the life that was out there, invisible, in the seething dark.

Before bed that evening, Lana contemplated her face in the mirror that hung above her dresser. She had the same dark eyes and dark hair that she had always had. To everyone else, she looked like the same person, but recently she'd felt, sometimes, that her skin was a sort of mask that she wore. Underneath that skin was a constellation of muscle and blood vessels and bones. A skeleton was a much more solid part of a person than all the soft organs and flesh lying on top.

The main question was: Who was she? What was this "I" that had been with her since early childhood and that she still felt herself to be? Her life was an endless series of repetitions, which, she had realized with a shock the previous fall, would end one day in her death. Someday, like every living thing, she would die, and her "I" would flicker out just as it did every night when she closed her eyes and went to sleep, but with no prospect of ever waking up.

Meanwhile, her parents went about their daily lives as if they didn't know this to be true. She loved her parents, but their life choices were unfathomable to her. Of all the grand destinies they might have chosen, the two of them had chosen the most predictable, the most mundane— marriage, a house, two kids. Every night, Mommy had to cook dinner and do the dishes; every week, stacks and stacks of laundry piled atop the washing machine. Every Sunday night, Daddy made the same lame joke about hating his job but went to work the next day anyway.

Her father worked at the State Department, but Lana could never figure out what he did there. "I sit at a desk," he told her wryly, whenever she asked. "Nothing exciting."

But if that were really true, then why did he always have to take work calls in a different room? Every couple of years, Mommy said, her father had to have an updated background check for his security clearance. Lana knew what this meant because it had happened once with their neighbor two doors down. A man in a black suit with an FBI badge came to the door and sat with her mother in the dining room, asking questions about those neighbors, wanting to know if they had loud parties or whether they used drugs or came and went at strange hours of the night. Mommy seemed intimidated by the man's presence and kept offering him something to drink, which he repeatedly refused. To most of his questions, she said "I don't think so" and "I really can't say. We hardly know them."

The person Lana loved most was her little brother. Sometimes when Marc had a nightmare, he would come into her room and crawl wordlessly into bed with her. They never talked about it, but Lana always felt happy when he did this. She liked the feel of his small body curled next to hers, the knowledge that she was older and capable of protection.

The only other person in the world that Lana could stand was Maddie, and sometimes just barely. In the last year, Lana had watched Maddie's chest swell with unease, had noticed the appearance of a continual rash of small red pimples on her friend's forehead. So far her own chest was still flat, but she had noticed a new, sharper smell in her armpits and had started showering every day to try to get rid of it.

Lana sighed and turned from the mirror. She slipped out of her clothes quickly and pulled on her pajamas, not pausing to examine her body. If it was trying to change on her the way that Maddie's was, she preferred not to notice.

It was her habit to peek out the window of her room every night before pulling the curtains shut. She was always afraid that she would see something in that dark mirror, that the reflection would be not her own but the face of some crazy-eyed killer, even though that was impossible because her bedroom was on the second floor.

But tonight when she glanced out she saw a thin, tall figure, standing silent and unmoving in the backyard, near the tree line.

It was Him.

He almost resembled a tree himself, He was standing so still, so hard to see in the shadows. His face was a white glowing oval, and He was looking up, toward her window.

She yelped and jumped back, dropping the curtain. She stood for a moment staring at the covered pane, trying to work up the courage to take another look. But she decided she would not look. She turned off the light, and the glow of the night-light she still used diffused the room. Diving into bed, she pulled the covers up over her head.

He was back. Maybe she had called Him somehow, just by thinking about Him; she had thought about Him just that afternoon, while playing with Maddie in the backyard. Her heart was beating fast in her chest, and it took her a long, long time to fall asleep.

Kat Davis

II

2017

Waking up the first morning in the blue room of her mother's new house, Maddie enjoys the idleness of doing nothing, of feeling her body lying in repose upon the clean blue sheets. The clock next to the bed says it's 9:30 a.m., which is the latest she's been allowed to sleep in many years. Light filters through the blue curtains and splashes across the geometric pattern on the blue comforter. She holds up her hand in the blue-tinged light and examines the Band-Aid wrapped around the pointer finger on her right hand. A black stain, a small blot of dried blood, has seeped through the cotton.

Against her own rules, she finds herself thinking of Lana.

It's been so long since she's seen her that it's easy, now, to blame her for the way that it all happened. It was Lana who told her about Him, Lana with the plan, Lana with the knife. Lana's sickness casting a spell over her that she couldn't help but fall under. It made her weak, perhaps, but she was only a child—a victim, too, in her way.

They haven't seen each other since the day they rode together in the back of the police car to the station. They didn't speak then but only exchanged quick glances with one another, aware of the policemen eyeing them in the rearview mirror. They were not handcuffed, but it didn't occur to either of them to try to run; up until that day, they had always been the kind of girls who followed the rules.

The police officers took both their backpacks. Maddie's contained a couple of granola bars, used wrappers, an empty plastic water bottle (she didn't want to litter), a couple of pairs of underwear, an extra T-shirt, a pack of playing cards, and several photos she had taken from the family album, stowed in a plastic sandwich bag. Lana's held the same, along with the knife, which they hadn't known what to do with. It was one of Mrs. Prescott's nice kitchen knives that Lana had taken from the block that morning while Sage was in the bathroom. They had tried to wipe the blood off on the grass but hadn't been able to clean it completely. Finally, Lana had wrapped it in her extra shirt and stuck it in the bottom of her bag.

Maddie did not really understand what was happening then, didn't understand that her last moments of freedom had been spent walking with Lana along the side of the road, both of them wilting in the heat, starting to wonder if maybe they wouldn't be able to walk all the way to the Eastern Shore after all. They were already lost, trying to find their way to the highway that would take them to the Bay Bridge. It was in those last minutes that Maddie had finally started to doubt Lana's plan; she didn't doubt that He was there, in that deserted farmhouse on the other side of the Chesapeake Bay, waiting to welcome them, but she did doubt that she and Lana could walk that far in the heat. She had already eaten three of her five granola bars—and they did not even taste very good.

In the back of the squad car, she felt the relief of the air-conditioning against her face. For a moment, it occurred to her that that must be what it's like to die, to not feel anything anymore, not even cool air on your skin, and she felt something twist in her stomach, but she immediately pushed the thought away. They had done what they had to do. It seemed now that they would not get the reward they had been promised, that they would not get to be with Him, but she didn't think He would hold it against them that they had gotten caught. It was disappointing, but maybe not so bad, to think she would sleep again in her own bed after all.

She still remembers the look on the face of the woman who interrogated her in the small room at the police station, part horror, part incredulity, as Maddie tried to explain it all.

"And your actions weren't in any way influenced by anti-Semitism?"

Maddie looked blank.

"Because the Newmans are Jewish?" the cop clarified.

"Sage is Jewish? But she's blonde!"

This is what is impossible now to explain to others, to the police officers and the judges and the psychiatrists—that when Maddie was picked up from the side of the road that day, her innocence was still intact. Yes, despite the thing she had just helped Lana do. She still believed in Him as she had once believed in Santa Claus. She still believed that she would return, in some matter of time, to sleep again in her mother's house in her own bed. She knew she was in trouble but could not conceive of the depth of that trouble and, at first, could only see it in glimpses, the first glimpse coming late that evening, when, after hours, sitting in a little room answering everyone's questions about the knife and Lana and the stabbing, she finally said she wanted to see her mom, that she was ready to go home, and the police officer, the one with the bald head shining in the ugly fluorescent light, looked at her as if she had just requested that she be allowed to fly to the moon. It was only then that she had started to cry.

"Maddie?" Mom's voice, tentative from behind the closed door. "Are you coming down for breakfast?"

When Maddie sits down at the table in the kitchen ten minutes later, she's relieved to learn that Steve has already left for work; he does cybersecurity for some company Maddie has never heard of.

She pours herself a bowl of her mother's shredded wheat and adds some milk. When Mom offers her coffee, she nods, and the dark liquid poured into her cup has a thickness and an aroma completely unlike the flavored water that she used to get for herself from the machine near the nurses' station at Needmore. Her mother always used to read the newspaper at the breakfast table, but now instead of an actual paper she reads on her tablet, tapping periodically with her finger and sneaking glances at Maddie.

"Did you sleep well?" Mom asks.

"It was fine," Maddie says, though actually she woke up several times in the night, tossing and turning in the unfamiliar bed. Up through her last night at Needmore, she had faithfully taken her Seroquel a half hour before bed. It was a general policy; no one was willing to risk a mental patient waking in the middle of the night, or suffering the effects of a bad night's sleep the next day. But it meant that Maddie hadn't fallen asleep without a chemical aid in years. The night before, she had stared up at the ceiling for a long time, exhausted, but somehow not drowsy.

"I was thinking we could go to the mall, get you some new clothes. We'll need to get you something nice, for interviewing."

Maddie had imagined for herself a day of rest, a day of being truly alone, unsurveilled, in a way she has not been alone in years. At Needmore and the state hospital before that, she was kept to a strict schedule, waking up at 6:30 a.m., not returning to the empty little room where her bed was until 8:30 p.m. The in-between was filled with hours of sitting around in the common room, three trips daily downstairs to the cafeteria, an hour a day of exercise in the yard or the gym. Of course all the patients complained about having time managed for them in this way, but Maddie knew that the strict daily schedule had helped her through, each morning marked with its group meeting, photocopied packets of schoolwork, reading her book in a chair (hard plastic at the state hospital, comfortably overstuffed armchair at Needmore), puzzle time, so-called art therapy (drawing with crayons). It was possible to take time as it came hour by hour, and this turned into days, which turned into weeks, months, years.

What she's imagined for her first day of freedom, she realizes, is something like the freedom she had that last summer with Lana, each day stretching out in vast chunks of unplanned time, open for anything. What was her mother thinking, allowing that? Why leave two young girls completely on their own, to get into any trouble they could think of?

Maddie feels her head buzzing, probably from the coffee. The sunlight filtering through the windows in the kitchen seems unnaturally bright. She isn't surprised that they don't speak about last night, that Mom carefully avoids mentioning the tense conversation over dinner. Maddie is still wearing the Band-Aid over the cut on her finger, but Mom doesn't ask about that either.

On the drive to the mall, she finds herself again experiencing the same sense of disconnection she felt the day before, as if she is returning to a place she knows only from her dreams, and everything is not quite as she remembered it. But when her mother turns into the endless parking lot, Maddie knows that she really is home, for here is the endless building as long as an airport terminal, the store names announcing themselves in large, neon colors, the implicit promise that everything she needs for her happiness exists in some tangible form here, in this building divided into little boxes, each containing in its turn more and more boxes containing more and more things.

Once inside, though, it's clear that time has not actually stood still. Several of the storefronts have been boarded over. "Everything's moved to the outdoor mall," Mom explains, "or online."

In her memories, all the familiar places still look the way they did in 2007, but of course they, too, have kept pace with the outside world, changing just like the fashions on the TV screen at the hospital and in the glossy magazines, passed from patient to patient until they lost their sheen. Still, there's something shocking about the ordinary scene in front of her, the women wearing large eyeglasses as if to accentuate their nearsightedness, the young men sporting well-trimmed beards and long hair pulled back into small buns on their heads. Around the fountain where she used to throw coins as a child, people sit looking at their phones, glued to the glowing icons on their screens. She is the alien visitor here, beamed down from her spaceship orbiting the earth, observing but apart.

Mom leads Maddie to the Macy's, the only place in which time does seem to have stopped. There's a comfort in the department store, all the different sections still promising to house everything under one improbable roof. Mom walks confidently to the section of upscale women's wear, pretending not to see the red-eyed-rabbit look in Maddie's eyes. The short walk through this new world has already overwhelmed her. She's used to the same walls, the same furniture, the same routine, day after day. She isn't used to seeing so many different things and people in one place. Even this collection of everyday goods threatens to overwhelm her: athletic shoes, fall coats, women's underwear, men's sportswear.

Mom pulls some black suits off the rack, and Maddie has the disheartening feeling that her mother is dressing her for a funeral.

"Does it have to be black?"

"You can't go wrong with black. It's always good to have a black suit. They were saying so just the other day on the *Today* show."

"This is nice." Maddie reaches out and rubs the synthetic fabric of a purple jacket between her fingers.

Her mother frowns. "Not professional enough. I mean, you could probably wear that to interview at this place, but what about in a year or two? What if you want an office job? Suits are expensive."

A store employee, a matronly middle-aged woman, has appeared at Mom's elbow. "Can I help you?"

"Yes, my daughter needs a suit. A black one."

The woman squints at Maddie. "I would look in the corner over there. Where the plus sizes are." Seeing something on Maddie's face, she adds, "No offense, hon. That's where I shop myself."

Even on the hangers, it's impossible to be excited about the plus-size suits, which hang down like drapes or the sheared skins of dead animals.

In the dressing room, Maddie sweats as she tries on the different pants and jacket combinations, pulling the blazers on and off over a white blouse that the saleswoman grabbed for her from another section of the store.

"We just need to figure out your size," Mom says from the waiting area. But one size is too large, the next one down too tight. Finally they find some pants that don't hug her hips too much or dig into her stomach.

"We'll just go one size up on the blazer," Mom says. "You got busty."

At the register, her mother produces a handful of coupons that the saleswoman scans, greatly reducing the price of the suit.

They leave the Macy's with Maddie carrying the large bag. She doesn't much care for the suit, but Mom seems pleased, and she's relieved to have the ordeal over with. They're talking about the new chain restaurant that recently opened at the other end of the mall when someone says her mother's name.

At first, Maddie doesn't recognize the woman, but she instantly knows the girl at her side as an adult version of Amelia Lawrence. Another moment and she recognizes the woman, too, suddenly sees an image of Amelia's mother bent over her daughter, clipping a merit badge onto Amelia's Brownie sash sometime in early elementary school. Today, both mother and daughter have long, nicely styled blonde hair. They are wearing fitted jeans, and their faces are heavily made up. Maddie is wearing a T-shirt and one of the pairs of sweat-pants that she used to wear at Needmore. She hasn't showered since she got home, and her curly hair is pulled back in her usual loose, unruly ponytail.

Amelia's mother is smiling broadly, her eyes shining with curiosity. Amelia recognizes Maddie first. Her eyes widen, and in them is a sort of shock and paralysis.

"Wait," Amelia's mother says. "Can it be? Is it really Madeline? Wow." Her eyes now mirror her daughter's. The smile remains frozen on her face.

Maddie's mother doesn't bother to smile. "Yeah," she says, "we got her back. At last."

"Oh, how wonderful, how wonderful." Mrs. Lawrence's eyes sneak toward Maddie, but she seems unable to make eye contact. She appears to be resisting a strong urge to flee.

Mrs. Lawrence clears her throat and talks cheerfully through her forced smile. "Just doing some mother-daughter shopping? Us too. Amelia just graduated from Dartmouth, finished up her summer internship, and is applying for jobs."

"Maddie, too," her mother says, "is looking for a job."

"Right."

"What did you study at school, sweetheart?" Mom asks Amelia.

"I did law and society? It's basically prelaw." The words come out of her mouth in the assured manner of someone who is used to uttering the same sentences over and over again, but she focuses her gaze somewhere in the distance between Maddie and her mother. She would not have lasted a day in juvie, Maddie thinks. She shouldn't enjoy this, the other girl's fear—but she does.

"She has an interview with a firm next week," Amelia's mother adds. "So she can get some real-world experience for the law school application."

"Mom," Amelia says, a warning. Her eyes jerk meaningfully toward the distance.

Amelia's mother's face puckers. Still not looking Maddie in the eye, she says, "Well, it's so nice to see you, Madeline. You must be so happy to have her back."

Mom nods and makes her lips curve into the semblance of a smile. "It's God we have to thank," she says. "It's all thanks to God."

Mom doesn't speak as they walk away. Maddie tries to imagine the conversation between the Lawrence women, Amelia castigating her mother for stopping them, her mother's helpless, "Well, it didn't even occur to me. And she got so fat . . ." Mrs. Lawrence will probably wait until they're outside the mall to fish her phone out of her pocket: "You won't believe who I just ran into . . ." Amelia is probably already composing a text message to everyone she's ever known.

So much for anonymity.

Next to her, Mom must be thinking the same thing. Maddie bristles at the memory of Mrs. Lawrence's smile—full of pity and condescension before she even recognized Maddie. That must be who her mother is now, the woman whose daughter did that awful thing. Maddie tries to remember Mom mentioning any of the women she used to be friends with, from the time before. In the early years she spoke often with Lana's mother, but she hasn't mentioned her for a long time. Now she only mentions Steve and people from their church.

"You hungry?" Mom asks, her gaze directed away from Maddie, down the long corridor of the mall.

Maddie is looking at her feet. She swallows. "Not really. Maybe we should just head home."

That evening, after Mom and Steve are in bed, Maddie picks the tablet up off the counter. She tries Mom's birthday first, then her own. One more try and she'll be locked out.

She carries the tablet with her upstairs, then creeps as quietly as she can down the hall. She hesitates to turn on the overhead light in Steve's office, settling instead for the small desk lamp next to his computer. It also requires a password, and since he works in computers, she assumes Mom's tablet is her best bet. She opens a drawer in Steve's desk, and it creaks. She freezes, waiting for sounds of life from the primary bedroom.

Afraid to force the drawer further, she squeezes out some of the papers there. Finally she finds what she's looking for: a stack of paperwork with Steve's birthdate filled in at the top. When she enters the numbers into Mom's tablet, it unlocks. She can't believe her luck. Maddie tucks the papers away and closes the drawer, which emits another little squeak. Quickly turning out the light, she exits the office and carries the tablet to the guest room.

Several sentences were on the paperwork she signed on the forms the day before, specific wording about "avoiding engaging with any content online or elsewhere that pertains to the crime. This includes but is not limited to specific information relative to HIM and to sources dedicated to the occult more broadly. The undersigned will also not fraternize or otherwise engage with anyone espousing beliefs in HIM or the occult. Failure to comply with these terms may result in immediate suspension of the undersigned's participation in the early release program and return to a state facility."

What is she doing? She's going to allow herself to look online for just tonight, to read through the articles that she never got a chance to read. A brief peek and then back to a normal, grounded life. To understand the look of horror on Amelia Lawrence's face, Sasha's reluctant admiration, she needs to know what they've been saying about her all these years. She can't be punished just for that; doesn't she still have her First Amendment rights, the ones she had to read about in her American government coursework?

It's all here now in front of her, all the reports and exposés, the Reddit threads and blogs. There is a strange thrill to seeing her name in the early news reports, before the press had to start to refer to them anonymously, as they did during the trial. There's a thrill in seeing that she, a child, did something the adults had to take note of. Thrilling, of course, in a terrible way, she thinks, as if in reply to the watchful therapist who now occupies some part of her brain, a composite based on all her years of therapy that forms a kind of chorus in her head, not unlike those old cartoons in which conscience is depicted as an angel on one shoulder, a devil on the other.

It's true there's a slight elevation in her pulse, a slight breathlessness as she skims, but she feels grounded in reality. She does not have the old feeling of being watched; she does not feel that He might be looking over her shoulder. She is in a good place.

She doesn't try to find the site; it just appears a few items down on the search list. The statement at the top of the home page reads:

> Lana Prescott and Madeline Thompson first encoun-
> tered HIM in the summer of 2007. In her statement
> on August 11, 2007, Lana Prescott stated that HE
> is a supernatural being created through the force of
> HIS followers' belief, a concept that borrows from
> the Buddhist concept of Tulpas (See Tulpas below).
> HE was believed to be a supernatural presence that
> followed Prescott and Thompson (henceforth re-
> ferred to as the Founders) over the course of that
> summer. Both girls reported seeing HIM, and Lana
> could talk with HIM directly. In July of that year,
> HE informed the Founders that HE could cross into
> corporeal existence only through an act of human
> sacrifice—

Heart thudding, Maddie stops reading. She scrolls down.

> HIS FOLLOWERS is a fan site both for those in-
> terested in the original crime and for those who are
> seeking more information about HIM. We welcome
> a variety of viewpoints and opinions but request that
> posters to the site be respectful. WorshipHIM36

is the current site administrator and WILL remove posts that are deemed insensitive or inflammatory.
WELCOME FOLLOWERS

Under a tab labeled Fanfic are subheadings for Fiction, Poetry, and something called Reflections. She clicks through several of these. Most of them are imagined encounters between the writer and Him, but some of them feature her and Lana as characters. One of the top posts seems to be a lightly fictionalized version of what happened that day in the woods.

> Lana's steps pounded over the forest floor. She advanced, the knife grasped firmly in her hand—

For a minute, Maddie thinks she's going to be sick. Is this what the site admin thinks of as "respectful"?

There's also some kind of message board, but when she clicks on it, a window pops up telling her she has to be a registered member to enter. All she needs to do to register is create a username and password. It takes only a minute.

The top thread is a short exchange. WorshipHIM36 seems to be the most frequent poster.

> **WorshipHIM36:** The thing you have to understand is that HE does not exist without us. It's our belief that calls HIM to us. It's true that HE exists for now only on the spiritual plane. That's why we need more Followers.

> **InfiniteDepth666:** I'm really fascinated by the HIM mythos but u guys have no evidence I keep looking for the evidence

WorshipHIM36: See hundreds of previous posts for proof that many of us have felt HIM

BenSterling25: This site is totally whacked. Basically "HE" can be whatever you want him to? OK snowflakes.

WWJD700: "The LORD your God is in your midst,

A mighty one who will save;

HE will rejoice over you with gladness;

HE will quiet you by HIS love;

HE will exult over you with loud singing." Zephaniah 3:17

You are worshipping a false god. HE is the LORD and HE welcomes all

Sexting_for_days: i had an encounter with HIM yesterday, bringing in groceries to set on the counter and in the hallway HE was there large dark shadow shaped like a person. Now im afraid Hes in the house how do i get rid of HIM?

InfiniteDepth666: The problem is that the only ones who can answer these questions are the Founders and they're both in jail so u guys have no idea what your doing are just stuck making up things in the meantime

Nobody who understands the difference refers to the state hospital as "jail," though she supposes that for other people, people on the outside, they probably do seem like the same thing.

She notices a recent thread in the discussion board labeled "The Next Sacrifice." Maddie swallows and clicks it open. The message was posted only four hours ago but already has several responses.

> **Follower_in_the_Distance**: Greetings, Followers! I've been on the site for a long time but am just now getting up my courage to post. Thank you to WorshipHIM36 and all the other Followers who've shared their experiences here. Like you, I have felt HIS presence and read a lot about the Founders etc. I guess my main question though is why those of us who are believers don't do more to bring HIM to us. If we're really serious shouldn't we be thinking about the next sacrifice?
>
> **Legendary1453**: Ha ha. I've sometimes thought the same thing, but are we actually allowed to say that on here?
>
> **InfiniteDepth666**: OP is joking right?
>
> **BenSterling25**: If u all really believe what u say u do then OP is right on
>
> **WorshipHIM36**: I'm going to leave this thread open as a thought experiment . . . for now. But please be aware I can't allow you guys to openly plan a murder on here or we risk the site getting shut down completely.

BenSterling25: I'm confused. I thought this whole site was for people who are fans of murder. And now you're saying murder is bad?

LuminousEgo13: I'm on here because I think the original case is interesting and I do believe in the supernatural, having had my own personal experiences, but I am NOT a fan of HIM and I'd never murder anyone

Sexting_for_days: I'm going to assume OP is using this as a thought experiment. Along those lines I'd say yes if we really do believe in HIM and want to have our own personal experience with an embodied HIM then the logical thing to do is to perform our own sacrifice

Legendary1453: You're making a lot of assumptions about HIM

InfiniteDepth666: I think you either believe or you don't. If you believe, then the Founders have shown us the way and we should follow them

BenSterling25: But the Founders are locked up so they can't answer any of our questions. So we just have to speculate about it forever

Ethan_Crosby46: But isn't that the point of the internet?

WorshipHIM36: We have had this discussion before. The Founders have already told us everything we need to know

Kat Davis

Maddie takes deep breaths. At least the situation seems to be under control; at least WorshipHIM36 isn't completely delusional.

Maddie looked up the definition of "delusional" once in the old dictionary kept in the state hospital's little library, its fat spine held together with duct tape. "Delusional" meant believing in something deeply irrational, something that might defy most people's conception of reality. For a brief time, the summer that she was twelve, she believed that she and Lana were haunted by a spirit, a faceless man who lacked a corporeal body. She believed this partially because of the force of Lana's belief, which by then was so strong that it overcame Maddie's own doubts, the rational voices in her head. This was delusion.

Most of the Followers aren't actually delusional. They don't seem to really believe in Him; they're just true crime buffs having fun with it. Never mind that she and Lana are real people. Never mind the real victim.

In the discussion threads, she finds only one poster who seems to grasp this.

Re: Remember the victim

> **LuminousEgo13**: I think it's just important to remind everyone that this was a real crime, not just some story made up for our amusement. There was one real victim here, a twelve year-old girl who was stabbed eleven times. We need to remember that whenever we start to have too much fun on this site
>
> **Legendary1453**: I know what you're saying but this is true of all true crime
>
> **LuminousEgo13**: That doesn't mean we shouldn't try to be better. Notice that most victims of these crimes are inevitably female and silenced twice over.

62

Exotic_Other175: Notice that the victims that get the most attention are inevitably white girls and white women. Cases involving POC rarely get this kind of coverage or attention. Imagine this case with some inner city black folk instead of white suburbanites. Suddenly no one's surprised. Suddenly this is just some crazy shit that happens all the time to THOSE people

BenSterling25: Yeah OK whatever

LuminousEgo13: You're absolutely right, Exotic_Other175. As a white person I need to do a better job owning my bias. I see your point and will try to do better

Maddie's first roommate in juvie was a black girl named Monique who didn't speak a word to her for over two weeks. When she did finally speak one night after lights-out, she confided to Maddie that her being there was a mistake. It was true that she had stabbed the neighbor who lived across the hall in the leg with a switchblade, but he had been molesting her since she was nine. It was a form of self-defense.

Technically, it was against the rules to talk about your case, and you'd lose points if the guards heard, but Maddie was so lonely by then that she told Monique her whole story, even about Him, whispering it in the dark across the space between their beds.

"Wait," Monique said when she was done. "Are you serious?" There was a pause and then the unmistakable sound of laughter. When she could speak again, Monique said, "Girl, you're lucky you're white," and that was the last thing she ever said to Maddie.

Two weeks later, when Monique, who was fourteen, was tried as an adult, she was sentenced to fifteen years in prison. Nearly two years later, thanks to the maneuvering of their lawyers, Maddie and Lana were tried as juveniles and they pleaded "not criminally responsible," which the lawyer called a Hail Mary because it almost never worked— but for Maddie and Lana, it did. And she knew that Monique was right, that it was because they were white girls with fancy lawyers that the judge accepted their plea and she and Lana were sent to separate hospitals.

Maddie's belief in Him survived for only a few days after her arrest. At one point on the day of the stabbing, after they had been walking for hours and were tired and hot, they both called out to Him for help. Of course nothing happened. The first couple of nights in lockup, she tried to talk to Him, to make Him come to her the way that Lana said He did, but He never spoke back. On her own, Maddie felt her belief evaporating as quickly as it once had with Santa Claus—one moment she felt certain of His existence, and the next she was filled with doubt, and then a horrible new certainty pooled in the pit of her stomach.

While Maddie has been reading through past threads, Follower_ in_the_Distance has added to the original post.

> **Follower_in_the_Distance**: I appreciate all the responses, but I guess I'm just looking for something a little more concrete. If HE really exists, then don't we have to do what HE says? Or risk the consequences? You guys are treating this like some sort of joke but either HE is real or HE's not. If HE's real and HE is ordering me to do something, don't I have to do it? What happens if I don't?

Maddie takes a deep breath. Follower_in_the_Distance is in the danger zone, the territory that leads to trouble, what one of Maddie's therapists called "disorganized thinking," the slow slide that can precede a psychotic episode. She can see it, with her own experience and years of therapy behind her. She can see it, so shouldn't she do something about it? Her pulse throbbing through her fingers, she starts to type.

> **Mad_as_a_Hatter22**: Hi Follower_in_the_Distance. Maybe you are just saying this as a joke but if not I think you may need some professional help. Please seek help if you need it.

It's after midnight. It takes almost an hour for the reply to come through.

> **Follower_in_the_Distance**: Thanks Mad_as_a_ Hatter22 for your reply. I can see you mean well by it. If Jesus himself were walking among us now or any of the Biblical prophets people would think they are all psychotic. If you've never felt the presence of something beyond this world I understand the desire to say it's impossible and assume there's some psychological explanation. Maybe you need to open your own mind

> **Mad_as_a_Hatter22**: I speak from my own personal experience when I say that these kinds of thoughts can lead somewhere bad. It seems to me that you may be losing touch with reality. That's why I suggest you get help from a therapist. Trust me I know what I'm talking about

There. The username may be a little too cute, a little wink to herself, but no one on the site seems to even know that Maddie has been released. And if some judge were ever to see her posts, what would he or she see? Just Maddie counseling someone away from believing in Him, encouraging Follower_in_the_Distance to seek professional help. That's not the kind of thing you get taken back into custody for.

Maddie closes the window on the tablet. She fetches a glass of water from the kitchen and drinks it down, simple and clean. She sighs. It feels good, what she just did. She sees now that she's not in any danger of relapse. Who better than her to help Follower_in_the_Distance sort through their doubts and uncertainties—someone who has been there and won't judge them for it.

Maybe this is what she's meant to do: help the Followers see the light of reason, to use her own experience to help them see the truth.

As she climbs the stairs to the blue room, she can't help but imagine all the news articles being rewritten: **Child Murderer Atones, Takes Down Dangerous Website.** Of course it's silly, but she can't help it. Steve is annoying, but maybe he's not totally wrong with all that atonement talk. *That was the moment I realized how much power I had,* she imagines telling the interviewer of an imaginary profile piece. *I understood that I could use that power for good, to make a real difference. It was only because of everything I'd been through that I could do this.*

She's had these fantasies before. For many years, she has imagined an alternate version of events, one in which the events of that day in the woods played out differently. Sometimes she confesses what they're planning the night before to Lana's mother. Sometimes she fights Lana for the knife, takes it out of her hands, and screams for Sage to run. The newspaper headlines proclaim her a hero. At Lana's trial, Maddie is a witness, but she pleads for understanding for her friend, for leniency. It was a nice story to fall asleep to, but every morning when Maddie wakes up, she lives in the version of reality in which she made the worst choice, in which she lives her worst life.

She can't change the past, but perhaps there is still some small absolution for her, some way to make things right. Hope is a powerful drug, and dangerous for someone like her, who hasn't dared to feel it for so long. The key is to keep the fantasy clear from the reality, to see things as they are, not as she wants to believe them to be.

And that's exactly what she's doing, she assures herself as she finally drifts off to sleep: she is hopeful but not delusional; she is grounded in reality and not at all in danger of relapse; she is guilty and unloved but maybe not completely beyond redemption.

1

Maddie was on the couch watching TV after breakfast when she felt something different between her legs, something wet. Standing up, she saw that a dark-red stain had spread between her thighs, soaking through her shorts and onto the beige fabric of the couch.

"Gran!" she called. "I'm bleeding!"

She knew what it was. Her mother had warned her about it and even given her a pad to carry around in her backpack at school the previous year, just in case. But somehow she hadn't realized the blood would be so red.

Gran appeared in the doorway in her ugly floral nightgown. She took in Maddie standing in her shorts with the big red stain, and then she looked at the couch.

"Quick!" she said. "Don't just stand there. Get a rag!"

Maddie scampered into the kitchen, took a paper towel off the roll, and ran it under the water in the sink.

"*Cold* water," Gran said, coming up behind her. She turned the handle of the faucet to the cold position. "Always cold water for a bloodstain. Got to get it before it sets."

Gran seemed annoyed, and Maddie understood that this was something she was supposed to already know, that she was supposed to expect to bleed and also to know how to clean the blood away, to make it so no one else ever had to see it. It was shameful to bleed, and she had doubled the shame by bleeding on the couch.

Maddie felt Gran's eyes on her back as she patted tentatively at the red blotch on the beige cushion. Finally Gran vanished down the hall and returned with a wet washcloth. Pushing Maddie out of the way, she scrubbed with the cloth until the red from the couch had transferred to the white washcloth. Maddie pouted, placing her arms over her chest.

"Well?" Gran said. "Go get changed already!"

In her room, Maddie dug through her closet and pulled out her purple backpack. In the outer pocket, covered in a film of eraser dust, she found the pad, still wrapped in its sheet of plastic. From her dresser she removed a pair of light-blue leggings. In the bathroom, she shimmied out of the stained shorts and then out of her underwear. She hesitated, then placed them both in the sink and ran cold water over them. Stripped of its plastic package, the pad inside was clean. Maddie placed it carefully in her underwear with the adhesive strip down, although nobody had ever shown her how to do this. She pulled up the underwear, then slid into the fresh leggings. She examined herself in the mirror. She looked the same, but the pad made her feel like she was wearing a diaper, like a baby.

The first person she wanted to tell was Lana.

Back in the living room, Gran had cleaned the stain off the couch. Maddie hesitated in the doorway, thinking that Gran might say something to her, something about how now she was a woman.

"Did you soak those clothes?" Gran asked. "I gotta get them in the wash."

"They're in the bathroom. Can I go to Lana's?"

Gran squinted at her. "You feeling okay? Do you have cramps?"

Maddie shrugged, not really sure what cramps were.

"Okay, but I don't want you over there all day again."

Maddie had been spending most weekdays at Lana's, slipping out right after breakfast and not coming home until dinnertime if she could help it. Gran had never liked Lana, though Maddie didn't know why.

Just as she reached Lana's driveway, Mrs. Prescott pulled out in her car, a shining Ford Explorer. Marc was in the back, on his way to summer camp. Although Lana's mother didn't work, she was rarely home, always heading out to do some shopping or to meet friends for lunch or get her hair done. Even before Dad left and she started worrying all the time about money, Maddie's mother liked to comment on the Prescotts' expensive tastes. Even though they lived in the same neighborhood, they always had things that the Thompsons didn't, like new cars and redone kitchens. Seeing Maddie, Mrs. Prescott stopped at the mailbox and rolled down the window.

"Hi, Maddie!" she said. "Lana's inside. You girls have a good morning!"

Maddie knocked once on the front door and let herself in. She found Lana in the kitchen, seated on one of the stools at the kitchen island, her notebook open next to her. This was her purple notebook, the private one she never showed Maddie, and she shut it as soon as Maddie walked in.

"Hey," Maddie said.

"You're early."

She decided to just say it. It seemed easier. "I got my period," she said breathlessly. They were already behind most of the other girls at school, but at least before, they had been behind together.

"Huh," Lana said, and her eyes flicked beyond Maddie, to a spot somewhere behind her. Maddie had thought she would've wanted to know what it was like, but Lana only shrugged. "No offense, but it'll help toughen you up. You know what I mean."

Maddie pressed her lips together. A few weeks before, one afternoon after school when they were walking in the woods behind the playground, they had found a dead animal. Lana said it was a possum and Maddie thought it was an armadillo, but it was so decayed it was hard to tell what it had once been. Lana insisted on flipping the body over with a stick, and when Maddie saw the swarm of maggots underneath, she screamed and ran; it was just her instinct. She waited for her friend to come find her, but finally she gave up and went back to Lana, who was still standing over the dead thing and seemed lost in thought. Lana didn't say anything to Maddie, but Maddie knew she had stored the incident away in her memory in the way that she did, to be used against her later. She was using it now.

"It's not such a big deal, actually," Maddie said. "It's just a little bit of blood."

"Good," Lana said. "That's a good way to think about it. Do you want to play *Snood*?"

They played *Snood* for nearly an hour on the computer in the den. It had been nearly a week since Lana had tried to change all the rules of the Mirror Universe, and since then, whenever they'd tried to play, they just ended up fighting about it. Lana insisted on calling it the Dark World now, and she had said there would be vampires, but it quickly became obvious that she wasn't actually interested in vampires. She was interested in Him.

Lana kept introducing storylines where Leonora could see a mysterious man she referred to only as "Him." At first, Maddie didn't know what Lana was talking about. It took a little while for her to remember: that creepy story from when Lana was little, how she looked up from the mirror and saw a dark figure behind her. It had given Maddie goose bumps when Lana had told her about it the first time, but Lana was always claiming to be able to see things that weren't there. That's why they got along so well, because they both liked scary stories. But now He was taking over the Dark World, becoming the only thing Lana wanted to talk about.

When they were done playing *Snood*, Lana took Maddie up to her room. The room was deeply familiar to Maddie from the hours they had spent there, but recently Lana had begun to make changes. She had packed away her Precious Moments figurines, for one, a collection that she had carefully curated over the course of several years. Now there was a Ouija board on the dresser and the healing crystals her mother had bought for her last birthday from the new age store at the mall hanging in pride of place above her mirror.

"My dad finally said I could paint it," Lana said, motioning to the light-pink walls.

"Wow. What color you going with?"

"Black."

Maddie's eyes widened. She shook her head. "They won't let you."

"My dad said I could. My mom is all upset, but I reminded him he said I could do whatever color I wanted. He just didn't think I'd choose black."

"You really want the walls to be black?" Maddie said.

"It's not me," Lana said. "It's what He wants."

Maddie pursed her lips. "What do you mean?"

"I mean, I just think that He would like black."

"Whatever." Maddie didn't mind Lana telling scary stories about Him if she wanted, but the last few days, she had started acting like He was some sort of imaginary friend. She and Lana were really too old for imaginary friends.

Lana removed some papers from a drawer near her bed and spread out three new drawings across her pink bedspread. Two of them were self-portraits. Her mother had bought her a book on pencil drawing, and Lana was getting very good at shading. Both drawings were close-ups of her face, one in profile, the other head on. In the profile picture, Lana's head was tilted downward. Dark pencil lines crisscrossed the shadows of her neck. The head-on drawing was less realistic, designed to look like her favorite painting, Edvard Munch's *The Scream*. A large poster of it hung on the wall across from Lana's bed. In her drawing, she had her hands up to her face, and her mouth hung open like the man in *The Scream*, a dark black cave. Whorls of shadow enveloped her.

Lana was actually a very good artist, much better than Maddie. Maddie often wished she had some special talent, just one thing that she was especially good at, the way that some kids are good at math, or English, or soccer, or music, the way that Lana was good at art—but

Maddie had nothing. The most interesting thing about her was that Lana Prescott was her best friend.

"What do you think?" Lana asked.

"Wow," Maddie said, reaching for the third drawing.

It was a profile picture of a man's face. It was possible to make out the large ridge of the man's nose, the lines of his forehead, and the sharp point of his chin. The one visible eye was deep set and appeared to be closed, so the face looked strangely blank, almost blind. Maddie felt something cool creep down her spine.

"Is that Him?" she asked quietly.

Lana nodded, then carefully stacked all the drawings and put them back in the drawer.

Maddie mainly felt frustrated by this new fixation. It was unfair for Lana to create a person only she could see. It excluded her automatically, for one thing. But it was also starting to get a little creepy. It was almost like Lana was forgetting that she had made the whole thing up.

"I'm hungry," Maddie said, even though she was not that hungry and just wanted to change the subject. They wandered down to the kitchen. Although it was only ten thirty, they made themselves peanut butter and marshmallow crème sandwiches on white bread and ate them on the couch. Maddie always put on too much marshmallow so that it dripped onto her fingers, and she had to lick it off. As they ate, Lana put on her DVD of the first Scream movie. In general they were too easily scared to watch most horror films, but Lana had all three of the Scream films on DVD, and they had watched them over and over again, always in daylight, until they'd gotten used to them and they weren't so scary anymore.

Today they watched only the intro, where Drew Barrymore ends up dead in a tree, and then they decided to head out to the park. In her backpack, Lana packed two cold Coke cans, one for each of them, while Maddie made two more Fluffernutter sandwiches and put them carefully in plastic sandwich baggies. She added the sandwiches and two napkins to Lana's backpack, and they set off.

At the park, they claimed their usual spot on the roundabout. Since they had given up the pool, this had become their new spot.

Two small children were playing over in the sandbox, while their mother sat on a bench in the shade. Otherwise the playground was empty. The park was hardly used, given that most families in the neighborhood had their own backyards with their own swing sets, and most of the playground equipment was old and in need of replacing. The yellow paint on the roundabout had mostly rubbed away, leaving behind the dull color of rusting metal. Both girls sat cross legged, scorching their calves, and Lana removed the two Cokes from the backpack. Maddie was so hot she drank half of hers in one long swallow and then gave a loud belch.

"Gross," Lana said, swatting away a yellow jacket that was buzzing around her can.

Maddie glanced toward the tree line. For just a moment she thought she saw something hanging from the trees, a body rocking in the wind. She startled and blinked. It was nothing, just an afterimage left on her retinas of Drew Barrymore's character from the movie. The trees were still and empty.

"Hey, what are you guys up to?"

Sage Newman, the new girl from down the street, was standing over them, smiling. She had short blonde hair and very straight, perfect teeth. They had run into her here a few times over the last week. Lana and Maddie hadn't decided what to do with her yet.

Maddie looked to Lana, who shrugged. "Not much," she said.

"Can I sit with you guys?" Sage asked.

"If you want," Lana said.

Sage sat on the rusted roundabout. "Ow," she said when the hot metal touched her legs. Maddie and Lana looked on impassively. Maddie suspected that Sage had come to the playground hoping to run into them. There was nothing particularly likable or unlikable about Sage. Their coolness toward the other girl was just an instinctive response to her eagerness.

Maddie and Lana sat drinking their Cokes.

"Are you guys going anywhere this summer?" Sage asked.

One week out of the year, Maddie and her parents used to take a vacation, just the three of them, to a different place every year, camping or staying in cheap motels. Once they had even gone to the Grand Canyon, driving both ways. But she knew there would be no vacations this year. In the kitchen one night she had overheard her mother complaining to Gran about Dad taking Sharon on a trip to the Bahamas: "He's too strapped to pay for summer camp, but he can afford the Bahamas with her?" Before that, Maddie hadn't realized that she wasn't going to camp because they couldn't afford it. She thought maybe her mother had just forgotten to sign her up. She didn't really care, though, because Lana would be home all summer. She had refused to go to camp, and if she was home, then Maddie wanted to be home with her.

"I'm not going anywhere," Maddie said.

"We go to New Hampshire every August," Lana said, "to visit my aunt and uncle."

"What about you?" Maddie asked.

Sage brightened. "We're going to California."

"Is that where you're from?" Lana asked.

"No, we moved up from North Carolina. But my mother's sister lives out there, near San Francisco. We're going to see the giant redwoods. Do you know about them? They're these huge trees. Some of them are over a thousand years old. There's one they call the Mother of the Forest. It's over three hundred feet tall."

"Cool," Lana said. She finished her Coke, picked up her backpack, and walked over to drop the can with a clank into the metal trash barrel. She gave Maddie a look, and Maddie scrambled to her feet.

"We have to go now," Lana said. Sage looked stricken. Maddie hesitated.

"We'll see you around," she said to Sage. "Bye." Lana was already some distance ahead, and Maddie had to hurry to catch up with her. "That was mean," she said.

"Sorry if I'm not super interested in the giant redwoods."

"She seems nice."

"Maddie," Lana said, pausing to look her in the eye. "Anybody can be nice. I'm interested in people who are more than just nice."

"Right."

When they got back to Lana's house, they were so hot they lay down under the AC vents in the living room, letting the cool air dry the sweat on their bodies. They ate their second round of sandwiches. A little past noon, Mrs. Prescott came in carrying grocery bags.

"What have you girls been up to?"

"We went to the park," Lana said, "but it was too hot. Can we rent a movie?"

"We pay enough for cable," Mrs. Prescott said. "Why don't you go play in the basement?"

Maddie stood up abruptly. "I have to go to the bathroom," she said. In the guest bathroom with the nice-smelling soaps, she discovered that the pad she was wearing was covered in blood. She'd thought only a little was coming out, but the whole pad was soaked, and there were two red spots on her underwear that hadn't yet leaked through to her leggings.

"Um," she said when she got back to the living room, "I think I have to go home."

"Why?" Lana asked. "It's still early."

"Gran said she didn't want me to stay here all day."

Lana appraised her coolly. "Okay," she said. "See you tomorrow?"

"Yes," Maddie shouted over her shoulder, hurrying for the door.

2

Sage's new room had windows on two sides. Sunlight poured through the closed blinds as she lay on her stomach on her mattress, her hand between her legs. Two large cardboard boxes sat on the floor; she was supposed to be unpacking them.

She had found the nub a few months earlier. Well, not found, exactly. Of course it had always been there, a particularly tender place between her legs, nestled behind the large lips of flesh. Vulva. Disgusting: a word her mother would say.

But it had been one of her mother's books that she was reading the first time it happened, on the couch in the living room of their old house. Thomas, the extremely handsome young man from the neighboring plantation, came to call on Misty. The scene ended with Misty on her back on the divan, her skirts up around her shoulders, Thomas on top of her, his "pulsing member thrusting into the moist flower of her maidenhood." Sage had felt a stirring down there before, but now the stirring grew stronger. It became a kind of wave that carried her away. She was trying to hold still, but instead she was squirming on the couch.

"You okay?" her father had asked, glancing up from his magazine.

"Fine!" she shouted, jumping to her feet. With the book in hand, she dashed to her room and shut the door.

Since then, she had learned how to make the wave happen again, by touching the nub with her fingers. It was hard work sometimes, but the wave was always worth it. This afternoon, though, it was taking a very long time.

Maybe it was the new house, the unfamiliar room.

The three Newman siblings had been devastated by the news of the move. It was necessary, according to their parents. Unavoidable, her father's promotion an "amazing opportunity." Sage and her older brother, Henry, who was fourteen, suffered the most, while Cody, eight, seemed to still be young enough to see the whole thing as some sort of adventure instead of the disaster it so clearly was.

The worst part was being taken away from all her friends, from Charlie (short for Charlotte) and the group they had so carefully cultivated in their first year of middle school. At Charlie's birthday party that spring, Sage had had her first kiss, in a game of spin the bottle, with Lucas Morales. His lips were surprisingly sweet, like licorice, and soft, but he thrust his tongue into and out of her mouth like a dart. Nevertheless, it was an experiment she would have been open to trying again.

Instead, she was in an unfamiliar house, in a different state, and she missed everything. She missed the smells of the old house, how she could walk through the hallway at night on the way to the bathroom with her eyes closed and no lights on because she knew exactly where everything was. Now she spent the evenings chatting with Charlie online, but in only two weeks their connection seemed to have stretched thin. Charlie told her about roller-skating with the gang and their friend Lucy's new haircut, but they both knew that none of that had anything to do with Sage: she didn't live there anymore.

The nub usually responded to the most gentle of touches, but today something was wrong, and in frustration, she sped up the rhythm with which she moved her finger, but it was still not enough.

Then there was a knock on the bedroom door.

She fished her finger out of her underpants, even though she knew the door was locked.

"What?" she called.

"Can you come to the door, please?" Mom asked.

Sage sighed. She ran her hands through her hair. Her cheeks felt warm.

She cracked the door, peering out through the slit.

"What are you doing in here?" Mom asked.

She shrugged. "Unpacking."

"I ran into Mrs. Prescott at the supermarket. You know the Prescotts, from down the street? They have a daughter your age. I invited them over for dinner."

Mom looked proud of herself, but Sage met this news coolly. She hadn't told her mother that she had been trying to befriend Lana and Maddie, the two girls from down the street, making a point to be at the playground around the same time every morning when they were. So far they had been unfriendly.

Sage's mother had a sunny disposition; she saw all girls of the same age as potential friends, without any accounting for differences in personality or social status.

"What?" Mom said, evidently seeing something in her face. "I thought you wanted to make new friends."

"Those girls seem kind of strange," Sage said. "Lana and the other one."

"Well, the mother seemed perfectly nice. Anyway, they're coming over tonight at five. And they have a son who's Cody's age."

After Mom left, Sage closed and locked the door. The moment had passed for the wave. With a sigh, she started unpacking the box on the floor nearest the bed.

When the doorbell rang that evening, Sage went to the door with her mother. Henry and Cody were playing outside. Her father was fiddling with the barbecue out on the deck. He had seemed the most

put out by her mother's announcement that the Prescotts were coming
to dinner, complaining that he hadn't had time to figure out the new
grill. Dad had moved up two months before them to oversee some
major construction projects, staying in a hotel paid for by his company,
while Mom packed up and sold the house. Now that they were all back
together, Sage would have thought he'd be happier, but lately he was
always in a bad mood.

Mr. and Mrs. Prescott were a little dressed up, Mrs. Prescott in a
yellow dress, Mr. Prescott in a white shirt and dark pants like the kind
he probably wore to work. Mr. Prescott was a surprisingly short, muscular man. His wife was about his height, very thin, and had a kind of
distracted air as if she were always looking at something just beyond the
other person's head. Mr. Prescott was holding a bottle of wine.

While the adults greeted one another, Sage took quick glances at
Lana, who stood a short distance away from the rest of the family. She
was wearing black leggings and a purple shirt with a strange frill around
the collar. She avoided eye contact. Her brother, Marc, was hanging on
to Mrs. Prescott's skinny leg.

"Sage, honey, you want to show Marc where the boys are playing
outside?"

"Lana, why don't you go with?" Mrs. Prescott said.

Dutifully, Sage led Marc and Lana through the house to the back
deck. The brand-new grill was smoking, and her father was issuing a
string of curse words under his breath just as the three of them stepped
out through the sliding screen door. Sage decided to pretend that this
wasn't happening.

The yard was a flat expanse of new green grass surrounded by
woods. Henry and Cody were passing a soccer ball back and forth in
front of the goal they had dragged out of the garage.

"Go ahead," Lana said. "You like soccer." Marc looked up at his
sister with hesitation in his eyes.

"It's okay," Sage said. "They set it up for you."

Marc's eyes brightened, and he shot off to join them, leaving Lana and Sage standing next to one another a few feet from the smoking grill. Her father swore again under his breath.

"Let's go over here," Sage said, leading Lana toward a corner of the lawn where there was an old rusted glider, the kind that the adults liked to sit on. Sage sat down, and the metal hinges squealed under her.

"This isn't our swing," she said. "It was here when we moved in."

Sage's mother and the Prescotts appeared on the deck, sweating drinks in their hands. It was clear from a distance that her mother was telling them something about the yard. The three of them were looking out toward the trees. Her father had set down the spatula he'd been waving about and came over to offer Mr. Prescott his hand.

Lana continued to stand next to the glider without sitting. Sage felt oppressed by the silence.

"Um, where does your dad work?"

"At the State Department."

"Really?" She had heard her mother explaining to their relatives on the phone how strange it was to live this close to Washington, DC, with so many people working for the federal government. She told Sage that when people around here said they worked for the State Department, you never knew if they really worked for the State Department or if they were spies. But it was clear that Lana found this to be the single most boring question she could possibly have asked.

Lana scowled at the grass. She had dark shadows under her eyes, as if she hadn't been sleeping well.

"What's your astrological sign? I'm Gemini."

"Scorpio," Lana said, visibly perking up.

"I have a book about astrology. I can show it to you."

Sage led her back inside the house. She had left the astrology book in the finished room in the basement, which was one reason she had suggested it. She didn't want Lana to see her room with its light-green comforter, her teddy bear, and the single poster she had put up so far of a stretching kitten that said I'M FINE. REALLY.

The astrology book was the right choice. She let Lana page through it, and they each read aloud the description of their sign.

"What's Maddie?" Sage asked.

"Taurus," Lana said.

"Really?" Sage turned back to the Scorpio page. "It says, 'Your deepest friendship is likely to be with Taurus, but exercise caution. These two types can ascend together to the highest reaches or descend to the lowest depths.' That's weird."

"Let me see that," Lana said, snatching the book from her hand.

"What does it mean?"

"I think it means you have to be careful with someone who is too much like you."

"It says Taurus is also a good friend match for Gemini," Sage said.

"These things don't really mean anything. You know that, right? They write them in this vague way so that you can make them mean whatever you want."

"I know," Sage said. "I just think it's fun."

When she heard her mother's voice calling down the stairs that dinner was ready, Sage felt relieved.

At the table, Sage eyed the platter of meat: the hot dogs were burnt black, but when she bit into a burger it was red and cold in the center. Her mother was shooting her father glances with her eyes that even Sage didn't know how to interpret.

"I don't like the black parts," Marc whined as his mother cut one of the burnt hot dogs into pieces for him.

"Shhh," Mrs. Prescott said.

"I'm afraid I'm still getting the hang of the new grill," her father said.

"Phil, maybe you should put these burgers back on?" Sage's mother said.

"I like mine rare, but this one is still mooing," Mr. Prescott said, and the adults laughed, as if it were all very funny.

Her father picked up the platter and headed out toward the grill. They heard the heavy thud of the sliding door.

Sage tried to hide her red face behind her plate, slowly forking tiny bites of potato salad into her mouth. Her father returned a few minutes later with the platter of cooked burgers.

Next to her, Lana was eating one of the burnt hot dogs, smothered in ketchup. Marc was still frowning at the black hot dog rounds that his mother had cut for him, his hands crossed over his chest. He leaned over and whispered something into his mother's ear, and Mrs. Prescott nodded, dabbing a napkin at her lips. "Do you know where it is?" she asked.

Marc slipped off his chair and padded out of the room. Mr. Prescott asked her father how business was going, and he began to talk about construction and the differences between foundations in North Carolina and Maryland. Lana heaved a sigh.

Then her mother started to tell the story of how they'd found this house, what "a miracle" it was that it had come on the market at just the right time.

Mrs. Prescott nodded. "Such a wonderful place to raise a family," she said.

"Good schools, good people," Mr. Prescott agreed.

"And it seems very safe," Sage's mother said. "I've been letting Henry ride his bike to the pool by himself, and it seems all right."

"Oh, absolutely," Mrs. Prescott said. "How old are you?" she asked, turning to Henry.

"Fourteen," he said.

Mrs. Prescott nodded. "I've been letting Lana ride to the pool with her friend Maddie since last summer, when they were eleven."

"That's rare these days," Sage's father said. "To be able to let the kids roam like that. It's important. Gives them a sense of independence."

"Well, it's just so unusual, to find a place where you don't have to worry about crime," Mr. Prescott agreed. "I tell you, some of the neighborhoods I drive through on my way to work, it's a whole different story."

Sage's family hadn't had time to visit DC yet. Once they were more settled in, her father had promised they would do day trips into the city to see all the museums and national monuments. So far, Sage had seen only downtown Baltimore, on a day when Sage's mother said she was "losing it" and made her dad take Sage and the boys to the aquarium. On their way home, they had gotten lost trying to get back to the highway and drove for several minutes through what Sage understood to be a "bad" neighborhood where there were rows of old town houses and deserted buildings with boarded-up windows.

"There's no need to mention this to your mother," Dad said as he drove faster and faster through the empty streets. They passed a boy around Henry's age, riding a bike that was much too small for him. At the corner outside a small convenience store, two men stood drinking from bottles in paper bags. When they got home and Mom asked how the day had been, they didn't say anything about getting lost.

Now the adults were talking about commuting, and Sage had lost the thread. Marc reappeared in the doorway with a look of consternation on his face. "Mommy?" he said.

Discreetly, Mrs. Prescott put down her napkin and followed her son into the kitchen. There was the distant sound of a toilet flushing and then the approach of footsteps.

"I'm so sorry!" Mrs. Prescott gasped. "The toilet is overflowing."

Both her parents jumped up from the table. Lana didn't move, so neither did Sage. Both brothers followed the adults. She and Lana listened to the sound of muffled voices, the opening and closing of cabinets, Mr. Prescott's voice, angry and raised, followed by Mrs. Prescott's, conciliatory and almost pleading.

"I didn't flush it," Marc said loudly. "*Mom* flushed it."

Next to Sage, Lana was still as a statue. If she was embarrassed by what her brother had done, she didn't show it, but she did make a point to never look at Sage. After another minute of silence, Sage stood up and walked into the kitchen. There was water on the floor in the alcove off the kitchen leading to what her mother liked to call the "powder room," and a foul stench hung in the air. Her mother thrust a plastic basin at her, filled with a large mound of wet toilet paper and what she realized, to her horror, was a puddle of watery poop. "Take this and dump it in the other toilet down the hall." Sage opened her mouth to protest. "Just do it."

She hurried to dump out the basin like her mother had said, rinsed it once in the sink and emptied it again, and then scrubbed her hands with lots of soap. By the time she returned to the kitchen, most of the filthy water had been sopped up. Her father was putting a mound of paper towels into a trash bag, while her mother was gathering cleaning supplies.

"I am so sorry," Mrs. Prescott said again.

"These things happen," Sage's mother said. "We know how it is."

"Mommy?" said Marc. "I think I need to go again."

"Oh," Mrs. Prescott said.

"Looks like this just isn't our night," Mr. Prescott said.

"We should head home," Mrs. Prescott said.

"That's probably a good idea," Sage's mother allowed.

Mr. Prescott stuck his head into the dining room. "Honey, your brother's sick. We're going to head out."

Another minute more and the Prescotts were gone from the house, leaving everything in a state of messy stillness. Her mother was saying something to her father about the plumbing, and her father was saying that that kid had used half a roll of toilet paper at least, and wasn't he old enough to know better? Cody wouldn't have done such a thing.

Sage peeked her head into the dining room. The table was a still life of a meal half-finished, napkins thrown on the table over half-eaten burgers and mounds of untouched potato salad, forks abandoned mid-bite, half-filled wineglasses and emptied soda cups. Deserted, the set table seemed to hold a promise that hadn't been there when it was filled with actual people, the possibility of some greater conversation that hadn't taken place and never would. A single knife was balanced against the edge of Mr. Prescott's plate, twinkling in the light from the overhead chandelier.

3

The next morning, after Mommy had left to take Marc to camp, Lana sat at the counter in the kitchen, drawing in the purple notebook. She sketched the trees quickly, then she sketched Him, his tall body silhouetted against the wooded background. Later, when the police searched through her things, they would confiscate the purple notebook, and the prosecution would include this simple pencil sketch in a photocopied packet of Lana's artwork.

After she finished the drawing, she turned to another page. Sometimes it seemed that the air changed according to her moods, and her mood right now was creating a kind of orange energy beam that pulsed around her; she could see it when she rested her hand across the white page of the notebook.

She hadn't seen Him again since that night after the Thompsons had come over for dinner. Since then, she'd darted quickly into bed right after turning off the light. She kept the curtains in her room shut even during the day so there was no chance that she would see Him. Every night, she had a vague feeling of dread in the pit of her stomach, and she could feel it creeping back now. The dread wanted to take over her whole body, but she couldn't let it.

She'd thought about telling Mommy and Daddy, but then she realized there was no point; they wouldn't believe her, would try to tell her it was just a dream—and then they might tease her about it later.

Lana picked up her pencil and wrote in the purple notebook:

*NO NO NO NO NO NO NO NO NO NO NO NO NO NO NO
NO NO NO NO NO NO NO NO NO NO NO NO NO NO NO
NO NO NO NO NO NO NO NO NO NO NO NO NO NO NO
NO NO NO NO NO NO NO NO NO NO NO NO NO NO NO
NO NO NO NO NO NO NO*

*NO NO NO NO NO NO NO NO NO NO NO NO NO NO NO
NO NO NO NO NO NO NO NO*

*NO NO NO NO NO NO NO NO NO NO NO NO NO NO NO
NO NO NO NO NO NO NO NO*

*NO NO NO NO NO NO NO NO NO NO NO NO NO NO NO
NO NO NO NO NO NO NO NO*

*NO NO NO NO NO NO NO NO NO NO NO NO NO NO NO
NO NO NO NO NO NO NO NO*

*NO NO NO NO NO NO NO NO NO NO NO NO NO NO NO
NO NO NO NO NO NO NO NO*

*NO NO NO NO NO NO NO NO NO NO NO NO NO NO NO
NO NO NO NO NO NO NO NO*

She filled the entire page. Then she went back and carefully drew an *X* over each word. After she finished, she felt much better.

"You were at her house? What was it like?"

Maddie and Lana were on the swings in the park. Maddie paused from dragging her sneakers through the dust and turned to look at Lana.

"You know," Lana said. "It's the Cranes' old house."

"No, I mean, what is she like?"

"She seems okay," Lana allowed. "We talked about our zodiac signs. But we had to leave early because Marc got sick."

What had happened with Marc at the Newmans' house was so humiliating that Lana couldn't even describe it. She preferred to pretend that it hadn't happened at all.

Lana looked over toward the tree line and was quiet for several minutes. She bit her lip and felt a twinge of panic in her stomach, but nothing stirred in the woods.

"Maybe we should be nice to her—Sage."

"Yeah," Maddie said. "Why not?"

"I mean, we can play with her. But she's not going to be one of us."

"Well, yeah," Maddie said. "Because we're best friends."

Lana had been trying to prepare Maddie by introducing Him into the Dark World, reminding her of the time when she was little. She knew that Maddie was a little freaked out at the idea of Him, and that was good; she should be scared. Lana hadn't been planning to tell, not yet, but she suddenly felt the secret was too big to keep, so much bigger than her.

Lana turned and looked Maddie in the face gravely. "If I tell you something, do you promise not to tell anyone?"

"Sure," Maddie said easily.

"I'm serious."

"What is it?"

"Promise?"

The playground was empty, and the air was thick with humidity. Although it was only ten in the morning, it was already hot.

Maddie swallowed. "I promise."

"I saw Him again."

"What are you talking about?"

"I saw Him. The other night. He was standing in front of the woods behind my house."

For a moment Maddie looked blank; then she seemed to understand. She scrunched up her face, scrutinizing Lana. "Um, how do you know that it was Him? I mean, how do you know that it wasn't just some guy?"

Lana spoke more quietly. "It wasn't just some guy, Maddie. Normal people don't look like that."

Maddie was still looking carefully into Lana's face. Lana tried to keep calm; she hadn't really expected Maddie to believe her, not right away. Maddie bit her lip. "I mean, is this for real, or is it just pretend?"

Now Lana couldn't keep the exasperation from her voice. "Oh my God, Maddie. I'm not pretending. It was real. And it was terrifying, okay?"

Maddie glanced over at the woods behind the playground. "So is He here now?" she asked in a low voice.

"I don't know," Lana said, shaking her head. "I don't think so."

Maddie seemed to relax a little. "Okay, why is He back? What does He want?"

Lana didn't answer. She knew that Maddie was only playing along now.

Maddie cleared her throat. "Do you think He could be dangerous? Maybe we should tell someone? Like an adult?"

Lana looked at Maddie, her face telegraphing her disdain.

"They wouldn't believe me, Maddie. Remember? I'm the only one who can see Him. He only appears to me."

"How do you know?"

"I just know, okay? I thought you'd want to know what I'm going through because you're my best friend."

"Of course I want to know."

Lana frowned. For a moment they sat in silence. It was all wrong. Telling Maddie was supposed to make her feel less alone, but it was only making her feel worse.

"It's too hot out here," Lana said abruptly. "Let's go back to my house."

Kat Davis

III

2017

Maddie continues to use Mom's tablet after Steve and her mom are in bed, her only small act of defiance. There's been no response from her last post to Follower_in_the_Distance. The site seems to have gone quiet.

She's already in her second week of work at the Green Thumb. She was surprised to find that a job she expected to hate actually suits her. The name made her cringe when she first saw the sign from the two-lane highway, dark green on a white background, accompanied by a logo of a big green thumb. To her relief, the place itself is simple, functional. There's the small building that holds the cash register and inside tables, a few racks of seed packets, a fridge of freshly cut flowers. She spends most of her time outside, setting up the displays, dragging plants into and out of the greenhouse, putting out spades and shovels, and then locking everything up again at the end of the day.

The store doesn't open until nine, but Maddie has to arrive by seven to help set up, to drag the ten-pound bags of fertilizer out of the storage closet, water the potted plants and mist the flowers, unload the new arrivals from the truck.

The first few days her arms and shoulders ached, but her body is adjusting. It isn't so bad. She's used to her time not being her own, to following someone else's schedule, so the long hours don't bother her. The hardest days are her days off, when she's stuck in the house with nothing to do, moving restlessly between the too-blue bedroom and the claustrophobic living room. If Mom and Steve aren't around, she can go online on Mom's tablet; when they're home, she pages through a book or watches TV. Sometimes she takes walks outside, past the rows of small trimmed lawns and cookie-cutter houses, but she worries about running into the neighbors, having to explain who she is and what she's doing there.

This morning Mom drops her off as usual in the parking lot, giving her a nod. She asked the other day about driving lessons, but Mom only shrugged and said, "We'll see," which Maddie knows means that it's really up to Steve. She doesn't remember her mother ever being so deferential to her father, even when they were still married.

The other night she asked Mom about the information for the lawyer. "What lawyer?" Mom asked.

"Gran's lawyer. You said she left me something. Like some pearls or something."

It would be nice to have a keepsake, something to remember Gran by, but it would also be nice to have something to sell, a way to get some cash, if she needed it.

"Right," Mom said. "Let's just hold off on that." She waved her hands vaguely in the air.

"What? You're the one who mentioned it!"

"Honestly, Maddie, I have a lot on my mind right now. Remind me some other time, okay? I'll have to look for the information."

Maddie turned and saw that Steve was watching both of them from the kitchen table, listening attentively to the conversation, and she felt sure that he must have said something to Mom. But they couldn't keep something like that from her, could they, something that legally belongs to her?

Now Maddie raps on the glass door, and Cindy, the store manager, comes over and lets her in. Cindy is middle-aged and wears a pair of wide-rimmed red glasses. She always has a bounce in her step. Cindy greets her with a peppy, "Good morning!" the same as she does every day, as if Maddie is a customer. Maddie walks to the door labeled "Staff Only" and puts her lunch box in her cubby. She ties on the green apron with the unfortunate logo.

"I was thinking," Cindy says when she comes back. "It's time to do some rearranging. It's a cold day. Let's keep the mums and black-eyed Susans inside today. We need to start moving a lot of the others over to the greenhouse. This is almost pumpkin weather. I hope you're not allergic to hay," Cindy says with a wink.

"I don't think so." Maddie can't remember the last time she saw actual hay.

She helps Cindy move the flowers from the display outside the door, rearranging the yellow and orange mums in a cluster on some low shelves near the register. She doesn't want to admit that Steve could ever be right about anything, but there is something nice about working with plants—something, well, wholesome.

Cindy was the one who interviewed her for the job. Cindy's kids went to the pediatrician's office where her mother worked for many years, and she knew that Cindy already knew about her because she didn't ask her any questions about her education or her work experience. The day Maddie showed up, ridiculously overdressed in her black suit, Cindy asked only if she was hardworking and knew anything about plants. When Maddie said she was hardworking but knew nothing about plants, Cindy, unfazed, asked if she was willing to learn.

"I hope you appreciate what your mother has done for you," Steve said that night at dinner. "That's got to be the easiest job interview you're ever going to have, especially in your situation."

When she's done with the flowers, Maddie goes outside and fetches the hose from the side of the building, then drags it out to the parking lot to water the potted hydrangeas, which she recently learned are also called hortensias.

Cindy gave her a pamphlet about fall plants. Maddie found that she liked reading the lists. First, the straightforward litany of the vegetables: asparagus, beans, beets, broccoli, brussels sprouts, cabbage, and carrots, all arranged alphabetically to the very last item—winter squash. Then the flowers, some familiar, some exotic: celosia, chrysanthemum, eucalyptus, dahlia, lily, ornamental fruit, phlox. The last one sounded like something straight out of a Harry Potter book.

Lana would have loved such a list, Maddie thinks, and then shakes her head as if to clear it. The way Maddie has dealt with Lana for many years now is by not thinking about her at all. She puts her in a room of her mind and shuts the door. Lana was the problem, the bad influence that ruined her life.

At Needmore, there was one therapist who wanted her to talk about Lana. The others usually asked about Him, whether she still saw Him, but this one, Dr. Zacks, wanted to hear about Lana. "What was it that you liked so much about her?" she asked once, and Maddie didn't know how to answer.

"She was my best friend."

"You risked a lot for that friendship," Dr. Zacks said, and Maddie nodded. It was always better, she thought, to agree with the doctors. "Madeline, would you say you are someone with a strong sense of self, or are you more of a follower, do you think?"

"I don't know."

"What about Lana? Would you say she had a strong sense of self?"

"Yeah, I guess."

"I ask because sometimes people who don't have a strong sense of themselves find it easier to follow other people. Those other people give them something they think they are missing. Does that make sense?"

"I guess."

"So," Dr. Zacks said, smiling and spreading her hands across the table that separated them, "my goal for you is to cultivate a stronger sense of yourself. What do *you* like, what do *you* want. Does that make sense?"

Maddie nodded again. She understood what Dr. Zacks was saying, but she didn't see how, practically speaking, she could cultivate what she liked or what she wanted while in a locked ward, even one as nicely furnished as the one at Needmore. Still, it was a nice idea, and when, two months later, Dr. Zacks didn't show for their usual appointment, and her replacement, an older man whose name Maddie has already forgotten, informed her that Dr. Zacks wouldn't be returning, Maddie was surprised to feel the sharp sting of disappointment. It was always like that, though, with the therapists, the nurses, even other patients—no point in getting too attached to anyone.

She's already had two meetings with Miranda, her "supervising officer." She's required to meet her every two weeks from now on, on Thursday afternoons, at a McDonald's off the highway. Miranda always has a large plastic cup of iced coffee and a booth near the back. She has bags under her eyes and the slightly bored expression of someone who's seen it all before.

"I apologize for the unprofessional environment," she said at their first meeting. "But I share an office with two other people. And some people prefer the casual setting. You can get something to eat if you want."

"Um, no, I'm okay, thanks."

"So," Miranda said, resting a hand on the closed folder in front of her on the greasy table, and a slight animation appeared in her face. "You're quite the little celebrity."

Maddie didn't know what to say to this, so she said nothing.

"There are two things I always want to see: the first is a job—regular employment—and the second is positive integration into the community. Of course those two are related. A person needs friends; you need to join something. A volleyball team. A trivia night. It's up to you. But the research all says that these two things are important, these two things will prevent recidivism. Do you know that word?"

Maddie confirmed that she did and then told her about her job at the Green Thumb.

"Well, that's great," Miranda said. "I'm so happy to hear that. You're already ahead of the game. So then you need to think about that second part, the integration into the community. And with your situation, there's one other thing I need to see—and that's mental health. You still taking those antidepressants? And what about the therapist? It says you're supposed to contact a therapist."

"I'm planning to."

"Okay, so by next week, I need you to have contacted her. I'm going to have to give her a call to make sure you're attending your weekly sessions. You understand?"

Maddie nodded, and Miranda raised her eyes. "Yes, ma'am," Maddie added.

"So if you have those three things—the job, the integration into the community, and the mental health—I think you'll find that will smooth the transition back. You're really very lucky, you know." Miranda leaned forward and took a sip from her massive iced coffee. "You got off pretty easy, all things considered."

Maddie wishes that "mental health" was something she could simply have or not—but she's spent too long in the hospital to believe that.

After watering the plants, she unloads several pounds of fertilizer from the truck out back. Although the day started off cool, the sun has appeared, and she finds herself sweating underneath her sweatshirt and apron. From time to time, she leans over to peer inside the shop at the round clock that hangs over the register.

At 8:28 a.m., Omar's car pulls into the parking lot.

"Hey, Maddie," he calls as he hurries to the door. A few minutes later, he reappears in his Green Thumb apron, wearing a pair of gloves and holding some shears.

Omar has worked at the Green Thumb for almost three years. If Omar is working and Maddie has questions, she prefers to ask him. He knows the rules of the place, as she thinks of them, and he also knows the names of the different plants, and unlike some of the other employees, he doesn't expect her to already know these things. "Hey," he said the first day when she had to ask which flowers were the marigolds and which the mums, "I didn't know anything when I started here either."

Here are the things that Maddie has learned about Omar over the last two weeks: He is five ten, which may not be short but in his case was not quite tall enough to get him on the varsity basketball team in high school. He drives an old Ford Taurus with a scraped-up bumper but is saving to lease an Explorer. His hair is cut in a short 'fro. His body is lanky and lean. He has large hands, with long, almost delicate fingers and well-maintained nails. When he's concentrating on something very hard, his mouth forms into a frown, his lips tugging down slightly on one side.

The first time Maddie was kissed was against her will. A new admittance to the state hospital, a heavyset boy about her own age who smelled of cigarettes, grabbed her off her chair and pushed his lips up against hers before the techs could pull him off. Sometime after that, she met Jeremy. In group, Jeremy said he was there because of his "homicidal tendencies." It turned out he had attacked his uncle with a steak knife, though Maddie would later learn he hadn't landed a single blow, had never felt the knife sink in. All the other kids on the ward knew what she'd done, what she'd helped Lana do, and they tended to stay away from her, to give her space. In juvie, she'd been no one in particular, but in the state hospital she was considered one of the dangerous ones. Jeremy didn't seem to mind. He had very light-blue eyes. She felt drawn to him immediately. Soon they were making out, sitting during free time at awkward angles in the chairs in the corner of the common room that were just out of sight of the nurses' station, watching for techs out of the corners of their eyes. She was seventeen, and it lasted three weeks. Then Jeremy got out. He promised to send her letters, but she never got any. Now she is twenty-two and hasn't kissed anyone since.

She doesn't expect anything to come from her crush on Omar. It's enough, for now, to have found someone who makes her feel this way, to discover that she is still capable of normal human feeling. For now, she does her work and finds reasons to ask him questions when she can.

For now, as she stacks bags of fertilizer until the muscles in her back start to pulse warmly, she's happy enough to be outside in the open air.

By the time Mom picks her up that evening, Maddie's back is throbbing. Back at the house, she limps through the garage door and into the kitchen.

"My back hurts," she says, as if to the air. Her mother unloads a few purchases in silence from a plastic bag on the counter. Maddie waits a moment and then limps toward the staircase, up to the blue room. A couple of days ago, she grabbed a thick romance novel from one of Mom's bookshelves about a time-traveling nun, but she hasn't been able to get past the first chapter.

After a few minutes, she hears Mom's footsteps on the stairs and a soft knock on Steve's office door. There's a delay before the door opens. Her mother says something in a soft voice about dinner; they alternate nights for cooking, and tonight it's Steve's turn.

"You expect me to do everything around here!" Steve shouts. It's less the words and more the tone that upsets Maddie, the voice angry and aggrieved at the same time. She understands now that the silence that reigned in the last years of her parents' marriage was actually a sign that the relationship was already over, but at the time, that silence had allowed Maddie to believe that everything between her parents was normal. Her father, at least, had never shouted, not in such a tone.

Her mother's voice becomes softer in response. Steve's voice drops to a whisper so that she can hear only a quick back-and-forth of hushed voices. A few minutes later, the door slams shut.

Maddie allows the pages of her book to fall closed. She stares at the blue wallpaper for a moment and then slowly walks downstairs. In the kitchen, her mother is standing in front of the microwave, thawing a pound of chicken breasts.

"Everything okay?"

"Yes," Mom says. "Everything's fine."

Maddie waits.

"He's just upset," she says. "He had some calls from a reporter, asking questions about Luke."

Luke is Steve's son, the one in prison for raping a woman in an alley. They usually talk once a week, on Sunday nights, which was also the night that Maddie used to call from the state hospital. When she was younger, Mom used to come at least once a week on visiting days, but over the years, these visits had fallen off. They just didn't seem to have enough to say to fill the space of forty-five minutes in each other's presence. A brief phone call had become enough.

Maddie has spoken once with her dad since she got out. The day after she was released, she called their house phone, the only number she had. The phone rang and rang, and then Sharon picked up.

"This is Maddie."

"Hi, Maddie," Sharon said, her voice neutral. "Let me put your dad on."

A full minute later, her father picked up. "Hi, Maddie. You at your mom's?"

Dad knew all about her official release date. He was the one who had paid the bills for all the lawyers and for the last two years of her treatment at Needmore, in a program that was supposed to facilitate her reentry back into the world.

"Yeah," Maddie said. "I'm at Mom's."

In the background she could hear high-pitched screams, the sounds of her two half brothers tussling on the couch. "Knock it off!" Dad shouted.

They spoke for another couple of minutes, Maddie struggling to come up with something to say. She was waiting for Dad to invite her for a visit (they lived in Ohio now), but the invitation never came.

"Take care," Dad said before they hung up.

Dad wrote her off a long time ago, but her mother is here, in front of her, her shoulders sloped, defrosting the chicken. Maddie remembers the way that Mrs. Lawrence looked at her in the mall, with that smug sense of superiority. Perhaps she and Mom still have something in common; perhaps it's not too late for them to find their way back to each other.

"So what did the reporter want?" Maddie asks.

Mom bats a hand through the air. "There are always reporters. They're like sharks. Drawn to other people's tragedies. It's blood in the water to them. We have a policy. We don't talk to reporters."

Her mother granted a couple of interviews after the stabbing, but she came to regret them all. "They twist your words," she said once. "They pick and choose, and you come off like an asshole no matter what you say."

Maddie knows the details of Luke's case only because when her mother first met Steve, in her initial enthusiasm for the relationship, she was eager to talk. At the time, Luke was out on bail, awaiting his trial, and there was the constant drama of the back-and-forth with lawyers, the highs and lows of trial prep that Maddie knew so well from her own experience. She supposed that in those early months, Mom must have been important for Steve, a source of both practical advice and emotional support.

As in Maddie's case, the evidence against Luke was clear and particularly damning. Most rapists got off, her mother told her, practically speaking, "he said, she said" and all that. But Luke had been caught in the act, pressing the twenty-one-year-old up against the wall behind a bar. He had assaulted her on her way into, rather than out of, the bar, before she'd had a single drink. Two other men heard her screams and found her struggling, still trying to push Luke away.

The prosecution made liberal use of Luke's extensive online posts prior to the rape. He did not come off at all well in these posts, made on well-known white supremacist websites, sprinkled with misogynistic comments.

Mom told Maddie that Steve was heartbroken. "This just isn't how Luke was raised."

But the final nail in the coffin of Luke's case was that the woman he assaulted was the daughter of a well-connected former state senator, and this, as much as anything else, seemed to explain his strict sentencing.

"Why doesn't he just take a plea deal?" Maddie had asked. She was eighteen by then and knew more than her fair share about how these things worked. "Just plead guilty and get a reduced sentence."

But for some reason Luke refused to plead guilty to the crime that everyone knew he had committed, and the case went to trial. Steve drained his life savings paying the lawyer fees, and in the end, Luke got twenty-five years.

It seemed to Maddie, standing in front of the phone stuck to the wall in the state hospital, that Steve and her mother had lost some sense of proportion when it came to Luke's case. Maddie's mother seemed more and more aggrieved for Steve and his son, as if Luke were some sort of injured party.

"It's like they keep forgetting that he actually raped this girl," Maddie said to her then therapist.

"How did your mother feel about *your* case?" the therapist asked. "Did she feel like you were being treated unfairly?"

"Well, yeah. But that was different. I was just a kid."

"And you don't think that you lost sight of the real victim?"

Maddie fidgeted in her chair. "We were all victims," she said. "Because Lana and I were sick. We were confused."

"I see. Do you think Luke has any mitigating circumstances like that?"

"We were *seeing* things. Luke just hates black people and women."

"Okay," the therapist said in a tone that Maddie had come to recognize as resigned, and she made another note in her file.

At dinner that evening, Steve is sullen. He lets Mom say the prayer over the food, and they eat in silence. Maddie chews the overcooked, dried-out chicken, forcing herself to swallow. At least she seems to be losing weight.

When Steve is finished, he pushes his plate away.

"It's hard to know what to tell these people." He speaks as if he's answering a question they haven't asked. "These reporters. They want to know how bad I feel. They want to know specifically how I messed up as a father. That's what they want."

"It's between you and God," Mom says. "That's the only relationship that really matters in the end. We don't need any of these people's forgiveness. Just God's."

Steve nods and rests an arm on the table. Her mother covers his hand with hers. Feeling a familiar flutter of discontent in her stomach, Maddie looks away.

◆ ◆ ◆

Only after Mom and Steve are in bed can she relax. She'll be getting her first paycheck soon, and she already knows what she'll spend it on: her own smartphone. They can't control what she can buy with her own money; even Steve has to concede that.

There hasn't been much new activity on the site. A few new photos, a new Reflection, a not-very-promising discussion thread.

OMG this photo. You can see HIM in the background, that black smudge.

I think I saw HIM yesterday, outside my house. This creepy guy just looking at me.

Been having nightmares. Is HE haunting me?

While she's clicking through, a dialogue box pops up in the corner of the screen. Follower_in_the_Distance has sent her a direct message.

Follower_in_the_Distance: Hi. We interacted briefly a couple weeks ago on this site. You seem like someone who's pretty knowledgeable about the case and about HIM. Is it OK if I ask you a few questions?

Mad_as_a_Hatter22: Yes definitely

Follower_in_the_Distance: I'm just wondering, what's your attitude toward all this? Do you believe in HIM?

Maddie bites her lip. She doesn't want to say anything that might scare Follower_in_the_Distance away.

Mad_as_a_Hatter22: I try to keep an open mind about things but I think this is an example of some people choosing to believe in something that just isn't there

Follower_in_the_Distance: I thought so too at first. But the more I read about HIM the less sure I am

Mad_as_a_Hatter22: What specifically makes you think that HE could be real?

Follower_in_the_Distance: Well, all the people on this site. A lot of them seem to believe

Mad_as_a_Hatter22: I don't think they all believe. I think some of them just find it amusing

Follower_in_the_Distance: But some of them believe

Mad_as_a_Hatter22: Yes some of them

Follower_in_the_Distance: Can I share something private with u?

Mad_as_a_Hatter22: sure

Follower_in_the_Distance: I had an experience recently that I'm trying to make sense of. I walked out of my school at the end of the day and when I looked over I saw a man in the parking lot. I think maybe it was HIM. The man was dressed in black with a really pale face. Doesn't that sound like HIM?

Maddie feels her chest constrict. The tablet screen wavers for a moment in front of her. She takes a deep breath.

Mad_as_a_Hatter22: It's possible that the man you saw was just a normal man dressed in black. But it's kind of creepy to have someone like that lurking around a school. Maybe you should tell someone?

Follower_in_the_Distance: Idk. It didn't seem like anyone else noticed

Mad_as_a_Hatter22: If u think u r the only person seeing this then you may need professional help. I know its scary to admit but there are people who can help u. Its really important to get help before its too late.

Follower_in_the_Distance: I don't think I'm ready to do that but it means a lot to me that u seem to care. I don't really have anyone in my life right now that I can talk to about this

Mad_as_a_Hatter22: I'm glad I can be there for you.
Please feel that u can reach out to me. I have been
in a very similar place to where u r now which is why
I feel like I have something to offer u

Follower_in_the_Distance: I really appreciate that

Maddie clicks on Follower_in_the_Distance's profile. It includes a low-resolution profile pic of a teenage girl with long brown hair and round, owl-rimmed glasses. She first started posting only a month before and has no posts other than the ones Maddie has already read.

Maddie's own profile has no photo or identifying information. Follower_in_the_Distance is probably harmless, just a weird kid who spends too much time online, someone who reads too many horror novels or watches too many movies. Still, Maddie decides to keep an eye on her.

She moves to turn off the light in the blue room, and just for a moment, out of the corner of her eye, she sees something, a shadow moving toward her. Wheeling around, she finds only empty air. Stay grounded, she thinks, shaking her head. She's tired, that's all, her eyes playing tricks on her before bed. It's nothing, she thinks, flipping the switch and crawling into bed. It's nothing.

1

After dinner, Maddie used the computer in the living room. She was trying to find information about Him, but she didn't really know what she was looking for. She typed "man that only one person can see," but the websites that popped up were all about mental health and had hotline numbers to call. She typed "man that only one person can see real?" but that wasn't much better. She kept another window open so that if her mother came over to see what she was reading, she could simply click on it and it would appear that she was looking at a website about puppies. It had been very easy for her and Lana to conceal all their darker interests in this way—all the sites filled with horror stories and urban legends. Once a day, Maddie wiped her browser history, and that took care of it.

Ever since Lana's revelation the day before, Maddie had felt a kind of pressure in her chest. She didn't actually believe Lana. She was pretending again, the way they sometimes pretended about Leonora and Mariana and spent so much time pretending to be those people that they almost became them. Or she was pretending to try to make things more exciting, to trick Maddie into getting scared. Maddie was almost sure of it, though something about the way Lana had spoken about Him did seem different, which made her less sure about everything.

Did Maddie believe there were forces greater than her that existed out in the world, that there was more to this life than what she could see with her own eyes? Sometimes she suspected that Lana really did have some talent or gift that Maddie lacked, the ability to sense things that others couldn't. Lana, for instance, claimed to be able to see people's auras, that everyone was surrounded by a cloud of color that said something about them. Maddie's was purple, while Amelia Lawrence's was a sort of brown smudge. Then there were those moments Maddie experienced sometimes that maybe everyone did—a feeling like she was being watched, a sudden shiver down the spine, that moment the other day when, just for a second, she thought she'd seen a body hanging in the trees.

But these stories about Him felt different; Maddie didn't want them to be real. The more she thought about it, the more she had a gnawing feeling in her stomach, as if she'd eaten something that did not quite agree with her.

Her mother wandered into the living room, and Maddie clicked away from her web search to the puppy page. Mom had had white wine from a box with dinner and was now on her second glass. Every evening she drank wine and watched TV before staggering off to bed. Gran, who watched soaps during the day, preferred to spend her evenings reading thick romance novels in her room, the kind that always had pictures of muscled shirtless men and large-breasted women in flowing dresses on the covers.

On the TV, some detectives were trying to solve the murder of a young woman who had been found dead in her apartment. They were interviewing the girl's roommate, who was dabbing her eyes with a tissue.

"Guess what?" Mom said. "A man did it. It's always a man."

"Mom?" Maddie asked.

"Huh?"

"Do you believe there are things we can't see?"

Her mother frowned slightly into her glass. "What do you mean, honey?"

"Like, do you think that this is all there is, or is there something else, something, like, beyond this—"

Her mother put her glass down and with a fluid motion hit the button on the remote to mute the TV.

Her mother looked at her solemnly. "I believe in God," she said. "I know your dad and I didn't do a good job with that. I wanted to take you to church when you were little; I always meant to." Maddie knew that her mother used to go to church when she was a girl, back when her mother's father was still alive. But either Gran changed her mind about God or she had just never cared very much, because they stopped going after Mom's father died from a heart attack when she was still in high school. Gran seemed to have no interest in God, but every once in a while, Mom mentioned Jesus like he was one of her best friends from childhood whom she hadn't spoken to in a long time.

Now Mom shook her head. "There is a life beyond this one. I do believe that. I do believe that Jesus is waiting for us on the other side."

"Oh. But what about, like, ghosts or spirits or whatever?"

Her mother frowned again. "That stuff is outside of God, honey. That comes from people being afraid, people who haven't accepted Jesus into their hearts. Oh, isn't that the cutest puppy! What is it? A dalmatian?"

"It's a pit bull with spots."

"We should go to church sometime, you and me."

Maddie shrugged; she had never felt much about God either way. That stuff was just so much more boring than ghost stories or playing Mirror Universe with Lana.

She looked at her mother. Mom's mascara was a little smeared, which Maddie had noticed at dinner, but neither she nor Gran had pointed it out. After Dad left, Mom had started smoking. Apparently she had smoked back before Maddie was born but had quit when she got pregnant. Now she smoked outside, on their back porch. She kept an ashtray out there just for that purpose, and Maddie and Gran both pretended like they didn't notice.

Maddie cleared her throat. She kind of wanted to tell Mom about Lana, about Him, to see what an adult would say. But she was also worried, worried that her mother would think the thought that Maddie felt bad for even thinking because it felt like a betrayal—that maybe Lana really was seeing things that weren't there, that there was something wrong with her. But if that was true, Mom wouldn't let her see Lana anymore. She would lose her best friend. Maddie's throat was dry. She turned back to the computer and looked at the puppies on the screen.

After the detectives had arrested the woman's boyfriend for her murder, Mom wordlessly carried her glass into the kitchen. "I'm just going out back to get some fresh air," she said.

As she climbed into bed that night, Maddie hesitated before she turned off the light. She thought of Him, how He had appeared to Lana at night. It was a creepy story, even if Lana had made it all up. She walked into the hall and turned on the light out there; then she came back, turned out her own light, and left the door slightly ajar, so that a thin ray fell across the foot of her bed. Just in case.

2

When the bell rang, her mother was folding laundry, so Sage opened the door. There stood Lana and Maddie.

"We're going to the park. Want to come?" Lana asked.

"Who is it?" her mother shouted from upstairs.

"It's Lana and Maddie," Sage shouted back over her shoulder. "Can I go to the park?"

Her mother appeared at the top of the staircase. "Oh, hi, girls! So nice to see you. Yes, sweetheart, go ahead, have fun."

Sage found herself walking next to the two girls. She felt disoriented, her face flushed with excitement. Perhaps the other night had been some kind of test, and she had passed after all.

At the playground, the girls assumed their habitual seats on the roundabout. Lana folded her legs under her, while Maddie kicked up a cloud of dust with her worn sneakers. Sage perched next to Maddie.

"We brought you a Coke," Maddie said, fishing a can out of her backpack and handing it to Sage.

Seeing Maddie and Lana together reminded Sage of Charlie, how the two of them used to be attached at the hip. Once they had sneaked cigarettes out of Charlie's mom's purse and smoked them in the backyard when no one else was around. Sage had liked it, had liked the feel of the warm smoke filling her chest and then the slight buzzing feeling in her head, but afterward Charlie had felt sick to her stomach, and they forgot to put the pack back. When her mother found it sitting out on the deck, she put two and two together. Charlie was grounded for a week, Sage for two.

Lana and Maddie seemed like good girls to Sage, not the kind to sneak cigarettes out of purses, but that was okay—Sage knew how to adjust herself, to tone herself down if she needed to. The important thing was to have friends.

The girls sat in the heat, drinking their sodas. Lana and Maddie began to quiz her, in a gentle way, about her interests, her favorite shows and songs, even her favorite foods. When she named something familiar, the other girls would nod politely. It felt a little like an interview.

Once they'd all finished drinking their sodas, Lana stood up and dusted herself off.

"You can come to my house," she told Sage. "My mom's out."

Lana's house reminded Sage of the Prescotts themselves—a little too dressed up, trying perhaps a little too hard. Lana led them upstairs, but instead of going to her room, they turned off into what looked like her father's study. There was a large desk in the center with a computer on it. Lana exchanged a brief glance with Maddie, who gave a small nod, and Lana sat down in the swivel chair, while Maddie and Sage leaned over her shoulders.

Lana opened a web browser and carefully accessed the history menu. She clicked on one of the links. A video appeared on the screen of a naked woman with large breasts. She was on all fours on a bed, and a man was ramming into her from behind. Lana unmuted the sound, and the woman's moans filled the room. Her breasts shook and flopped around. Sage couldn't look away.

"So gross," Maddie said.

"Isn't it disgusting?" Lana asked, looking carefully at Sage.

Sage nodded. "Yeah," she said, though she had the same squirming hot feeling she'd had when she was touching herself in her room. She cleared her throat. "Have you guys ever had a boyfriend?" Lana and Maddie shook their heads. "Me neither," she said, though she thought suddenly of Lucas Morales, the licorice taste of his mouth.

Lana closed the web browser. "What should we do now?"

"Let's play hide-and-seek," Maddie said.

"You can be it," Lana said to Sage. "Turn around and cover your eyes."

Before she could argue, Maddie and Lana were already running out of the room. It had been a while since Sage had played hide-and-seek. She counted loudly, hearing the two girls whispering out in the hallway. "Here I come!" she said, exiting the office. She looked down the hallway of the Prescotts' upper floor, realizing that she was playing hide-and-seek in a house she'd never been in. She took a deep breath and started toward the bedrooms at the end, with their firmly shut doors.

3

That evening after dinner, Lana felt restless. Mommy was doing dishes, and Marc was watching a cartoon for little kids in the living room. Daddy was on the computer in the den.

She wandered up to her room, took out the purple notebook, and flopped down on the bed. The notebook was full of drawings of Him, standing at a distance, surrounded by trees. She was happy with these pictures, with the dark outline of His body, the long, almost spiderlike quality of His arms and legs, the blank oval of His face. She wanted to do more close-ups of that face, to better trace its features (or lack of features), but she was never satisfied with the result.

She picked up a pencil and started to sketch His face. She'd been far away when she saw Him in the woods, so no wonder it was hard to see Him clearly. But what bothered her as she drew was that she wasn't sure if she had simply been too far away to see the details or if His face was actually just a blank. Did He have eyes, or just a smooth indent of skin where the eyes should be? Was He missing a nose, the way Voldemort was in the Harry Potter movies? Did He have a mouth at all, or could He speak directly to a person's thoughts?

This time she drew Him with a wide-open mouth, the upper lip curled back to reveal a row of glistening white teeth. She thought it was going well, but when she was done, she sat back to look and saw that it was all wrong. The teeth were meant to be threatening, but instead He looked like He was smiling, like a grinning jack-o'-lantern on Halloween.

She took the pen and violently scribbled over the page until it was covered in black lines. Then she ripped out the paper and tore it into long strips that she deposited in the wastebasket next to her desk.

The faucet was running down the hall in the bathroom she shared with Marc; his bedtime was an hour before hers.

Lana went back downstairs. The TV was off. She went to the cupboard where they kept the snacks and drew out a strawberry Pop-Tart wrapped in shimmering foil.

"What's in these hair products? Magic?" It was Daddy's voice. Mommy came into the kitchen with Daddy behind her.

"It's a three-month supply," Mommy said.

"I can't believe we're spending as much on your hair as we're spending on speech therapy." The speech therapy was for Marc, who still spoke with a slight lisp.

Mommy shrugged, picked up a sponge, and began to scrub at the counter, even though it already looked clean. Her lips were set in a smile, but it was not her real smile. It was the smile she made when she was trying not to see something that was right in front of her.

"I make the money, and it flows out every month," Daddy said. "And we're still paying off the loan for the renovation."

"You don't have to tell me things I already know," Mommy said quietly.

"Yeah, Gina, but it seems like I do. It seems like I do."

Daddy stepped toward Mommy and tapped her suddenly on the forehead, twice, with his forefinger. This meant that he thought Mommy was stupid, but instead of arguing with him, Mommy just stood looking at him with the fake smile on her face, as if she were actually stupid.

Then Mommy turned away and acted like she was looking out the window over the sink, even though the blind was closed.

Lana was only on the third bite of her Pop-Tart. It had turned mealy and dry in her mouth. She slid off the high stool and deposited the rest of it in the trash can.

"You going to bed, honey?" Mommy asked.

Lana didn't answer. She went back up to her room and shut the door.

She tried not to think about anything as she stripped off her clothes and put on her pajamas. She tugged at the drawers of her dresser a little more roughly than she needed to. Noticing that the purple notebook was still out on her bed, she tucked it away in her desk.

She wondered if she had made a mistake, telling Maddie about Him. Maddie was her best friend, but she still disappointed Lana sometimes. She seemed to think it was all just a game. Lana didn't know how to make Maddie believe that what was happening was real, didn't know why she needed Maddie to believe with her.

Brushing her teeth, she made sure that she looked down at the sink, never in the mirror. In her room she glanced once at the blind over her window, which she kept pulled down all the time now, even during the day. She turned off the light, climbed into bed, and stared up at the ceiling, willing herself to fall asleep. Occasionally beams from the cars up the hill would trace across her ceiling, the shapes of their shadows intimate and familiar.

Her eyes were closed and she was drifting off to sleep when she heard a loud whooshing noise, a sound like a fan or a turbine, that made her jump. The noise was so loud that for a moment she could hear nothing else. The sound intensified, and it seemed to her that it contained the energy of a frightened animal caught in a cage, trying to break free. Then there was a popping sound, and for a moment the room fell silent. She was too scared to open her eyes.

Lana.

He spoke in a soft voice, masculine but surprisingly high pitched.

She didn't answer but only shut her eyes more tightly. Somehow, she knew that if she looked at His face now, it would kill her. But she also knew that something awful would happen if she did not answer.

Lana?

Yes?

I'm here. You know who I am, don't you?

I'm scared. Her voice cracked, and tears slid out from the corners of her closed eyes.

I won't hurt you. Not if you do as I say. Tell me: Do you know who I am?

She swallowed. The tears rolled down the sides of her head. She whispered into the dark: *You're Him.*

IV

2017

At night Maddie continues to message with Follower_in_the_Distance, from her new smartphone now, up in the blue room. Their conversations have become more expansive, no longer limited to things related to the site. She knows that Follower_in_the_Distance goes to high school somewhere in Pennsylvania. Maddie herself claims to live in Ohio. When asked, she says that her favorite author is Stephen King. They talk about *The Stand* and *It*, both of which Maddie read back in sixth grade. When Follower_in_the_Distance mentions some of his more recent work, Maddie lies and says that she prefers the older stuff.

But mostly they talk about Him. Follower_in_the_Distance is unhealthily obsessed. She keeps bringing up the man she saw outside her school and describing the feeling she has of being watched. Afraid of driving her away, Maddie has stopped telling her to seek professional help and shifted to listening sympathetically and trying to suggest alternative explanations for her feelings.

Maddie had hoped to use the site in some bigger way, but perhaps this is the best she can do. Perhaps it's enough to try to change one person's mind, to keep one lonely girl from making the same kind of mistake she did.

She moves through her days in a fog of fatigue from staying up too late online, reading through all the previous posts on the message boards, watching YouTube videos, trying to catch up on ten years' worth of pop culture references. All the new social media apps overwhelm her; she decides to focus, for now, on the Followers site.

It doesn't seem to matter that she's only half there at her job—most of it is just mindless manual labor. She drinks the free coffee that Cindy keeps in the break room, which always tastes a little burnt. On days when she gets home early, she falls asleep on her bed in the blue room until dinner.

Her work shifts often overlap with Omar's. Sometimes she tries to come up with reasons to talk to him, questions to ask, but when she actually approaches him, she becomes embarrassed and tongue-tied; she blushes red and has trouble looking him directly in the eye.

A girl named Gabriela manages two mornings a week when Cindy isn't there. Gabriela is around Maddie's age. She wears tightly fitted jeans under her Green Thumb apron, and her face is always nicely made up, her lashes long and thick. At the end of her shift, she checks her phone and sometimes makes quick calls, speaking rapidly in Spanish. Maddie finds her intimidating, mostly because she is beautiful and thin. She assumes she's beneath the other girl's notice, and Gabriela is aloof at first, communicating with her only about job matters until one afternoon when they're both repotting some dahlias, and Gabriela asks where she went to high school.

Maddie bites her lip. "I actually didn't go to school around here," she says. "My family moved from Ohio."

Gabriela nods. "You need to break up the roots a little more. Gently, or the transplant won't take. Is it really different here, from what you're used to?"

"Kind of different."

She's been waiting for ions, knowing they would come, perhaps hoping they would. Normal questions like this mean that her coworkers don't know about her, don't know what she did.

Gabriela starts talking, unprompted, about her high school, about people she knows—who went to college and who dropped out and who has a good job. She talks for a while about a friend of hers who got knocked up a year after they graduated and is now married with a second kid on the way.

"We were basically like best friends in high school, but now she's just home all the time with her kid. I mean, he's cute and everything, but she has no life, you know? She was going to be an accountant, but now her boyfriend—husband, I mean—works construction. And whenever I talk to her, I can just tell that she isn't even in love with him anymore. Like, she's led this whole life, and it's already kind of over at twenty-three. It's kind of sad. We still try to get together sometimes, but we have almost nothing in common anymore. I'm not saying I have the perfect life. I mean, I work all the time and barely have time for school, but at least I have some goals, you know?"

Gabriela is slowly working her way through prerequisite classes at the community college so that she can apply for the nursing program there. Maddie feels wistful at the thought. There was always a registered nurse on staff at the state hospital. The nurses were almost always nicer than the techs. Rachel was a nurse, the closest thing Maddie had ever had to a friend for the two years she worked at the state hospital, before she got married and took another job. If she had a different life, Maddie sometimes thought she would have liked to be a nurse.

She told one of the therapists at Needmore about this thought once, and the therapist asked, "What is it about nursing that appeals to you?"

"You know, helping people, I guess."

"That's interesting. I've never heard you say before that that's a priority for you."

"I mean, I think if you have to work, it's better to have a job where you're helping people than one where you're just, like, working a cash register or something."

"Do you think that this desire to nurse others has anything to do with Sage?"

"What do you mean?"

"I just find it interesting that when you think about meaningful work, you're thinking about a medical career. It seems like some part of you wants to undo the past."

"No," Maddie said, shaking her head. "It's not like that. I just always liked life sciences."

Now she asks Gabriela questions about the nursing program, the prerequisites, the tuition. Maddie does the math; she might be able to afford it in a year or so if she keeps working, but she'd have to give up on the idea of her own place. She'd have to keep living with Mom and Steve.

"So," Miranda says, taking a sip from her iced coffee, which is already nearly empty. "Have you been thinking about the things we discussed last time? The community and mental health?"

"W-well," Maddie stutters, "I've been going to church with my mom and stepdad."

This is a lie. Every Sunday, Mom asks hopefully if Maddie wants to go with her and Steve, and every Sunday, Maddie says no. She has never been able to buy into any of her mother's religious talk. This is just another story, she thinks whenever her mother tries to talk to her about God and Jesus. She once chose a story to believe in, and she believed in it very much. It made her do an awful thing. How can she ever trust herself to believe in anything again?

But why lie about going to church? A lie that Miranda can so easily verify with a single phone call? Why take that risk?

"Well, now," Miranda says, raising her brows and smiling. "Look at you. Going to church. That's wonderful, Maddie. That's just great." Miranda opens her folder and scribbles something on a sheet of paper. "You know, I'm a churchgoer myself."

Maddie, having suspected as much, nods nervously and waits for Miranda to ask about the therapist she hasn't called yet. She figures she'll tell her the truth about that, but Miranda doesn't ask, as if it's slipped her mind. After so many years of therapy, Maddie does not feel much either way about the prospect of a new therapist. Maybe she'll call this week.

Across from her, Miranda sucks the last few sips of her iced coffee until all that's left is melting ice, the gurgling noise of air through an empty straw.

Tonight when she logs on to the site, there are no posts or messages from Follower_in_the_Distance, but there is a new discussion thread that catches her eye.

RE: Insane or just guilty?

> **Legendary1453**: I've been thinking about the girls recently. Sorry, Founders, whatever. It seems like the one with the knife was legit crazy. She was a schizophrenic. But the girl that helped her is maybe just a psychopath? Like isn't that worse?

> **Ethan_Crosby46**: I've read some of the articles and watched the interrogation tapes. Lana is definitely schizophrenic. Madeline seems like maybe schizotypal or sociopathic

> **LuminousEgo13**: Is Madeline the one that stabbed her?

> **Ethan_Crosby46**: No that's Lana

> **InfiniteDepth666**: I don't know what schizotypal is. Madeline definitely seems like she could be a psychopath

LuminousEgo13: What's the difference between sociopathic and psychopathic?

Ethan_Crosby46: Nothing. They're the same

Maddie has taken several tests for psychopathy. On the first one she took only a few weeks after she was arrested, the psychiatrist admitted she had scored slightly higher than the average person. But when she took the test again several weeks later, her score was in the normal range. She has also voiced this fear to several therapists over the years. The best one told her that the visible distress with which she asked the question was itself a strong indication that she was not actually a psychopath.

Maddie hasn't posted anything other than her comments to Follower_in_the_Distance. She's been thinking about the pros and cons of contributing, but now she just wants to set the record straight.

Mad_as_a_Hatter22: Madeline's official diagnosis was that she had a psychotic episode due to a case of folie a deux. That's when two people share the same delusion. It's rare but there are other historical cases. She was never diagnosed with psychopathy

Ethan_Crosby46: I definitely read somewhere that she scored high on the psychopathy scale

Mad_as_a_Hatter22: That's different than receiving an official diagnosis

Ethan_Crosby46: How do u know? R u a psychiatrist?

Maddie sighs. It's ridiculous, to have to defend her own case to these people. She's managed to remain anonymous so far. The last thing she needs are trolls attacking her on the internet—or, even, maybe, in real life.

When she'd first signed up for the site, she waited a day or two, part of her expecting someone to break down her door and arrest her. But when no one came and Miranda didn't say anything, she figured that she had bet right—the police weren't somehow tracking her, surveilling Mom's and Steve's electronic devices; they didn't have those kinds of resources. Just look at Miranda, meeting her at the McDonald's because her office was too crowded. On the other hand, she shouldn't get too comfortable posting on the site. Maybe she should change her username, create an alternate account.

Before she can decide how to respond, another message appears on the screen.

CallandResponse26112: Madeline Thompson is an evil cunt if I could get my hands on her id stab her eleven times one time for each that she stabbed that poor little girl.

1

On the Fourth of July, Maddie rode her bike alone to the community picnic. Gran preferred to stay in and watch the fireworks on TV, and Mom was in her bedroom with the door closed.

Every year the neighborhood held festivities at the playground and picnic area behind the tennis courts. In the afternoon there was a procession of younger kids on bikes, wheels draped with red, white, and blue crepe paper and American flags taped to the handlebars. Families brought their own picnic supplies and grilled on the communal barbecues. Unlike the smaller playground near their house, this one was well maintained, with several newer-looking climbing structures and a new swing set. It was also much larger and more open and exposed, only a few large oak trees for shade in place of the denser woods behind their street. After dark, around 9:00 p.m., it was possible to see multiple rounds of fireworks from neighboring towns, though the fireworks were always far away, small and muted.

Maddie was meeting the Prescotts, who'd come by car. After the almost two-mile ride, she arrived huffing, her cheeks flushed red from the heat. Wordlessly, Lana handed her a cold Coke can from their cooler.

Mrs. Prescott was watching Marc compete in a three-legged race, and Mr. Prescott was holding an open beer in one hand, raking the charcoal on a grill with a set of tongs in the other. Maddie wanted to drink her whole soda in one go but stopped herself halfway through; the only bathroom was a single porta potty in the little parking lot, stinking of urine.

Lana was already grabbing her gently by the arm, drawing her away from the picnic table that the family had claimed. She led her away from the crowd of people gathered watching the children's games before stopping behind the large trunk of an oak tree.

"I have to tell you something," Lana said in a whispered intensity that suggested urgency.

"Yeah?"

"I saw Him again. He came into my room. He was talking to me."

Maddie glanced at Lana's face. Her eyes were sparkling with anticipation, but there was also something else there, something a little like fear. "Yeah?" she said again, uneasy.

"I know you don't believe me," Lana hissed. "I know you think I'm making it up, but I'm not, Maddie, I'm really not."

She swallowed. "I don't think you're making it up," she said carefully. She had given up that hope several days ago. Whatever Lana was seeing, she believed it was real.

"What do I have to do," Lana said, "to convince you?"

She shrugged. "I mean, I guess I believe you when you say you're seeing something. But I don't see it, so it's not real to me."

"You need to trust me."

"I trust you," she said, but she was unable to keep the doubt out of her voice.

Lana sighed, crossed her arms over her chest, and, after another moment, turned and walked away. Maddie followed her back to the picnic table, where Mr. Prescott was putting burgers on the grill, but Lana refused to make eye contact, and when she tried to talk to her, the other girl just sat, looking into the distance as if she hadn't spoken at all.

2

The Newmans arrived at the picnic early, claiming a nice spot in the shade. Cody had wanted to ride in the bike parade and had been too afraid to go by himself, so Sage's mother had insisted she go, too, although it was clear as soon as they arrived that it was only something the little kids did, that she was far too old. After that humiliation, Sage sat for a long time away from the rest of the family on a swing, dragging her feet through the dirt.

When she sulkily returned to the group, she found that Henry had brought a friend with him, a tanned, muscular boy with blond hair and striking blue eyes.

"Hi," the boy said when he saw her. She saw his eyes dart downward, taking in her body with a glance. "I'm Ethan," the boy said with a smile.

"That's my sister, Sage," Henry said dismissively, before Sage could say anything at all.

"That's a pretty name," Ethan said.

"Thanks," Sage said, blushing.

Henry suddenly seemed to notice the way that Ethan was looking at Sage. He frowned. "C'mon," he said, "let's go play volleyball." He started walking in long strides toward the volleyball net that had been set up near the parking lot. Ethan lingered for just a moment, looked at Sage, shrugged, and then followed after Henry.

Noticing Lana and Maddie sitting over at another picnic table on the other side of the playground, Sage debated whether she wanted to try to join them. They both looked a little morose, sitting and frowning, not talking.

She had hung out with them a few times now, but she was never sure whether they would receive her warmly or coolly. Just the other day they had all gone together to the small playground on their block, and in the middle of hanging out, Lana had stood up abruptly, announced that she was going home, and invited Maddie—but not Sage—to go with her. Sage had been left stunned, sitting alone on the rusting roundabout, blinking away tears. Then she walked home the long way, through the woods, following an overgrown path she had discovered that led back to a bike trail that circled eventually past the new house. She had felt sure at that moment that no one was as alone in the world as she was.

The night before, she had been on AIM with Charlie. Charlie had a boyfriend now, a kid named Nathan who went to their synagogue. He was Charlie's first boyfriend, and Sage was missing it. She'd been gone only a few weeks, and Charlie had moved on so completely that she had entered an entirely new phase of life.

Sagenewman31: have u kissed him

The_Queen_Charlotte: duh

Sagenewman31: with your tongue!?

The_Queen_Charlotte: ☺

Sagenewman31: omg! how was it

The_Queen_Charlotte: brb

But Charlie didn't come back to their chat, and Sage sat reading more about the giant redwoods instead.

She sighed. It was two weeks until the California trip. At least she had that to look forward to. School would start in late August, and maybe she'd make better friends there, real friends.

"I see Sage and Maddie over there," her mother said. "Why don't you go say hi?"

"Mom."

"What? Why wouldn't you say hi? How are you going to make friends if you don't even try?"

"Those girls are weird, Mom."

"You say you want friends, but then you just sit around moping and complaining. They've been nice to you. Go say hi."

Sage heaved a sigh and stood up, gently tugging down the ends of her short shorts. She walked slowly and deliberately across the grass toward the other girls. As she passed the volleyball net, she glanced over and saw Ethan watching her. For just a second, before she looked away, blushing again, their eyes met.

3

The picnic was ruined as soon as it began. Lana had felt bad all day. She had a kind of heaviness in her head that was not quite a headache. She had spent the morning lying down on the couch, and Mommy even gave her some Tylenol, but it didn't seem to help. Now she was stuck outside in the heat, celebrating a holiday that she hated. She hated the false cheer and the kitschy red, white, and blue decorations, and she hated that she was going to be stuck here for hours because they always stayed for hours, waiting for it to get dark and for the last spark of fireworks to fade from the night sky.

She was punishing Maddie by not speaking to her, but that was ruined once again by Sage, who appeared beside them with a smile. Maddie eagerly scooted over, and Sage sat down beside her. The two started talking. Sage asked her a couple of questions, but when Lana didn't answer, Sage simply continued talking to Maddie as if Lana weren't there. Lana fumed silently.

"We're going to go check out some of the games, watch the volleyball. Want to come?" Maddie offered.

Lana looked at her and didn't answer. Maddie shrugged and turned to Sage, and the two of them picked their way toward the volleyball net. Lana watched Maddie's sandals, noticing that the sole on her right foot was starting to come loose, flapping under her like an open mouth.

"What's the matter?" Daddy asked. "Didn't you want to go with the girls?"

Lana scowled and shrugged. Wordlessly, she stood up from the table and walked back to the oak tree where she had been talking to Maddie earlier. Her head was pulsing. She did not feel well.

She didn't realize why she was there until she felt Him, standing just behind her. She knew better than to turn around.

Why so glum? His voice was that same high-pitched whisper, hoarse and breathy.

I don't know what to do. I'm so alone.

You're not alone. Not anymore.

"Where have you been?" Mommy asked when Lana returned to the table. She blinked. She thought she had been gone for only a few minutes, but suddenly the sun was low across the river, the sky streaked purple and pink. "The burgers are cold."

Lana shrugged. "I'm not hungry." It was true; recently she hadn't had much of an appetite.

"Why aren't you with Maddie and Sage? I see them over there," Mommy said.

Lana felt confused, muddled, after her talk with Him. She couldn't think up an excuse.

"What are you waiting for?" Mommy asked. "Go ahead."

Lana walked slowly toward the group of middle schoolers who'd taken over a climbing structure at the far end of the park. She stopped several times, glancing around her.

"Hey," Maddie said when Lana approached them. Her smile seemed genuine; she seemed happy to see her.

"Hey," Lana said weakly.

"You okay?" Sage asked.

"I have a headache," Lana said carefully.

"Oh," Sage said, as if this explained everything. "Here, sit down. Do you want us to get you some water?"

"No," Lana said. She sat down between them and put her head in her hands. After a moment, Maddie and Sage began to talk over her, continuing their conversation as if she weren't there. Sage was asking Maddie a lot of questions about their school. Lana kept her head down and her eyes closed. Different colors seemed to pulse against her eyelids. She felt like He was still there, watching her, even if she couldn't see Him.

Some time passed before there was a soft rat-a-tat in the distance, like a gun being fired.

"Ooh," Sage said. "Fireworks!"

When she opened her eyes, Lana saw that the two girls had climbed up the ladder to the top of the structure and were perched there, watching the sky. It was darker now, and she allowed her gaze to wander, not toward the fireworks in the night sky but back toward the oak tree. She saw Him peeking around the trunk, His face a long pale oval watching her in the dark. She gave a small yelp and closed her eyes again. She sat listening to the fireworks, which grew gradually louder and longer, hearing the oohs and aahs of the crowd. She sat like this for a long time, until Maddie was standing next to her, saying that it was time to go home.

V

2017

Within a day, WorshipHIM36 deletes the threatening comment and posts a message saying that the offending user has been permanently blocked from the site, but by then Maddie has already memorized it: **Madeline Thompson is an evil cunt if I could get my hands on her id stab her eleven times one time for each that she stabbed that poor little girl.** It's a run-on sentence, a term from one of the English Language Arts worksheets that she always finished early at the state hospital, the ones where you had to correct the errors in the sentence, add back in the correct punctuation. Maddie always liked those exercises, liked reading back over the sentences after they had been tamed and corrected: **Madeline Thompson is an evil cunt. If I could get my hands on her, I'd stab her eleven times—one time for each that she stabbed that poor little girl.**

It becomes a kind of mantra in her head as she unwinds the hose to water the plants in the greenhouse or rearranges seed packets in the displays. Never mind that she didn't actually stab anyone.

Meanwhile, in the evenings, she continues messaging Follower_ in_the_Distance, who seems to be getting more and more paranoid.

> **Follower_in_the_Distance:** What I feel mostly right now is just this sense that HE is watching me

wherever I go. Have you ever had anything like that happen to you?

Mad_as_a_Hatter22: When I was younger there was a time I saw something that wasn't there and I had the feeling you are describing of being watched. It felt completely real at the time, but afterwards it was like waking up from a dream. You know how you do things in a dream that actually make no sense but while you're in the dream it all seems to make sense? It was like that.

Follower_in_the_Distance: I know what you're talking about but I don't think that is what is happening to me. If I tell you something, promise not to get too upset?

Mad_as_a_Hatter22: You can tell me anything. I won't judge

Follower_in_the_Distance: I've been messaging with a few other people on this site in a private group. Their advice is very different from yours

Mad_as_a_Hatter22: What do u mean? What do they say?

Follower_in_the_Distance: They're believers, like me. They found me after I started the discussion thread

Mad_as_a_Hatter22: The one about the next sacrifice?

Follower_in_the_Distance: Yes

Mad_as_a_Hatter22: Would u let me into this group?

Follower_in_the_Distance: Why? You said yourself you're not a believer. The private group is for those of us who don't want to deal with WorshipHIM36's rules. We don't need another mom telling us what to do

Mad_as_a_Hatter22: I may not be a believer like you but I am very interested in HIM. Maybe seeing what u guys have to say will change my mind

Follower_in_the_Distance: I'll have to think about it

The dot next to Follower_in_the_Distance's username blinks and disappears. She's offline.

Maddie has been sitting on the bed in the blue room, but she jumps up and starts to pace. She feels a kind of blind panic. She thought she had control over Follower_in_the_Distance, but she could be planning anything with this other group. Maddie has to get her to invite her in, so she can monitor, so she can try to talk them out of whatever they might be planning.

Her current strategy is clearly not working. She has to play along a little, work on Follower_in_the_Distance from within her own way of seeing things. She knows how to do that; isn't that what she used to do with Lana?

She composes a message for Follower_in_the_Distance and presses send. It remains a faint gray rather than black, indicating that it is unread; she's still offline. The message will be waiting for her when she returns.

Mad_as_a_Hatter22: Hi again. U just told me the truth so I'm going to do the same with u. The real reason I'm on this site is to try to find people like u, people who r true believers. I do believe in HIM. I have a long history with HIM but I've found that most people can be easily talked out of their beliefs. But u r different, u seem like a true believer and it sounds like u have managed to find some others who believe too. If u let me into the group I am sure I can help u guys out

The next morning she checks as soon as she gets up, but her message to Follower_in_the_Distance remains unread. She feels slightly panicked. And if a judge were ever to see the message she posted last night, her fake avowal of belief in Him? If it were ever traced back to her, they would lock her up and throw away the key. How can she have done something so stupid?

But she knows why: because that's where the real danger is, where she might actually make a difference. She supposes this is what they were trying to warn them about in those seminars at Needmore on responsible use of social media, how addictive these sites can be, how it's possible to feel like your real life is happening online instead of in the flesh and blood world.

And Maddie's actual life is not going so badly. She kind of looks forward to going to work, especially on days when it's just the three of them—her, Omar, and Gabriela. It's possible that Gabriela is becoming her friend, though it's hard for Maddie to tell what constitutes friendship. Gabriela talks to her a lot, but she suspects the truth may just be that Gabriela likes to talk, that she would talk to any human who happened to work beside her.

"You're a really quiet person, huh?" Gabriela asked her one morning when Maddie responded to one of Gabriela's rare questions with a noncommittal one-liner.

But Gabriela is also given to snap judgments, to blistering critiques of customers, especially those she deems "rude." She once reenacted the landscaping-obsessed housewife demanding that her underground hosing be delivered within days instead of the standard two weeks. "Bitch, I don't control the supply chain. I can't just wave my magic wand and make your hose appear."

It was one of those mornings when Cindy wasn't there and there were no customers, and the three of them were gathered around the register, drinking the crappy office coffee and chatting instead of working, a few moments of camaraderie that could occur only on Tuesday and Thursday mornings. Maddie has gotten better at dealing with her crush on Omar; she can look at him now without blushing, but she still feels awkward, directing most of her comments toward Gabriela instead. On one of these mornings, Gabriela says the three of them should go out sometime for a drink, and they exchange numbers, Maddie withdrawing her new smartphone from her pocket as if it were a precious piece of jewelry.

The Thursday after her exchange with Follower_in_the_Distance dawns overcast and cold. She and Omar spend almost an hour unloading fertilizer bags from a truck out back. Maddie is happy for the time alone with him, even though they work mostly in silence; she can't think of anything interesting to say. They finish a little before ten and, by silent agreement, go inside to take their fifteen-minute break, the one they're supposed to always take at different times, but it's become clear that Gabriela won't say anything about it to Cindy as long as they don't.

A few beads of sweat stand out on Omar's temple as they pass a display of gourds and hay bales heaped with pumpkins. He brings up a gloved hand and wipes the sweat away with his wrist.

Inside, they pour the burnt coffee from the coffee maker in the break room into three chipped mugs. Gabriela sits behind the cash register, and Omar and Maddie angle their bodies toward the parking lot so they can see in case any customers arrive. Gabriela is complaining about an assignment for her nursing program that she had to submit online, but the website crashed and she and several other students had to petition the instructor for an extension.

"If it's due at midnight and the site is down starting at eleven p.m., that's on the site, that's not on us."

Maddie nods, and Omar makes small sounds of agreement in the back of his throat.

They hear the crunch of gravel outside as a car pulls into the parking lot.

"Oh yay," Omar says in the sarcastic voice he never uses when Cindy is around, "a customer."

"It's okay," Maddie says. "I'll go."

"You sure?" Gabriela asks.

"Yeah, absolutely." Maddie smiles. She doesn't want to step outside this small circle of warmth, but she also wants to get credit for being helpful. She wants them to like her.

Maddie sets her mug down in the back room, adjusts her apron, and exits the store. She rehearses in her head what she is about to say: "Welcome to the Green Thumb. Is there anything I can help you with?"

The woman sees her first. It takes a few seconds for Maddie to recognize her. She's met her only a couple of times in real life, and in the courtroom she was always dressed very formally, her makeup done and her hair pulled back. The woman in front of her is in jeans and sneakers, her blonde hair streaked with gray.

Sage's mother is standing about ten feet away from her, her mouth open, all the color drained from her face. She has balled her hands up into fists, and her whole body is trembling. At first, Maddie thinks the other woman is afraid of her, but then she realizes that the look on her face is rage.

Their eyes meet for only a second. Maddie can't speak or move. Mrs. Newman turns and marches back to the parking lot, climbs into her SUV, slams the door shut, and squeals out of the lot.

Maddie staggers back into the store.

"That was quick," Gabriela says as the bell on the door rings. "Oh. Are you okay?"

Maddie shakes her head and, pushing through the "Staff Only" door, runs into the bathroom and kneels on the dirty tile in front of the toilet. Up come the few sips of coffee and her breakfast—a frothy mess of milk and half-digested Cheerios, stained orange with stomach acid.

Gabriela insists she take the rest of the day off, accepting Maddie's lie about a stomach bug. Maddie agrees when she can't seem to stop trembling. Mom and Steve are both at work, so she has to figure out how to download one of those ride-sharing apps that she's never used. Twenty minutes later, she's in the back seat of someone else's car, clutching her phone in her hand, still feeling queasy.

She's been waiting for a customer to recognize her, for another awkward encounter like the one at the mall. Her biggest fear was that someone would say something to Gabriela or Omar, rupturing the carefully constructed albeit thin alternative identity she's made for herself. Once, when she recognized a guy from her elementary school who was browsing seeds, she hid behind a pumpkin display. Another time she rang up some purchases for a man from the old neighborhood, but if he recognized her, he showed no sign of it.

Of course she knew that the Newmans were around, that they still live in the same house in the old neighborhood. Everyone assumed they would move after it happened, but instead it was the Prescotts and the Thompsons who left. And that was probably only fair—they were the ones who had something to be ashamed of.

Yet somehow in her mind, the Newmans became almost an abstraction, as if they existed only in the courtroom, where Mr. and Mrs. Newman had come to every hearing, glaring at her and Lana's backs, their very presence refusing to let the judge forget the reality, the gravity, of what they'd done. In Maddie's mind they had become so powerful, but in reality Mrs. Newman was just another middle-aged woman who shopped for marigolds at the Green Thumb.

When she gets home, Maddie lies down on the couch in the living room, her stomach still unsettled. She supposes it was bound to happen eventually, this encounter. Why did her mother have to stay here, in this suburb; why couldn't she have moved somewhere else?

Maddie brings up the calculator on her phone. Her mind circles with the idea of escape, the need to get away from the Green Thumb, from Steve's house and the blue room, from this stupid town where she made the worst mistake of her life. If she works for six months at the Green Thumb, she might be able to save up enough to start over somewhere new. Maybe she won't even tell Mom, just get on a bus one day and end up somewhere else, somewhere where no one will look at her and wonder if she's a psychopath. But that would mean breaking the terms of her early release, which requires that she remain a resident of the state of Maryland. Running away would be a criminal act.

She's trembling again, as if she's cold. She pulls the knitted blanket that Mom keeps draped over the back of the couch down on top of her.

She checks her phone: Follower_in_the_Distance has admitted her to the private chat.

1

When they moved, Sage's father had promised he would take her—just her, without her brothers—to Wild World, an amusement park that was about an hour's drive from the new house. They had moved at the beginning of the summer, and now it was July, and they had still not been.

Her father had been in a bad mood lately. In the evenings, he wandered through the house with his cell phone in hand, answering work texts. After dinner, everyone fled to their separate activities: Henry to his room, Cody to watch TV, her mother to the little room off the back where she liked to read her book, her father to wander through the house, mumbling to himself and responding to the texts on his phone. Sage didn't know how to respond to this slight unraveling of their family life, but she did know how to demand what had been promised: that trip to Wild World.

She brought it up one evening when her father was sitting in one of the rocking chairs in the upstairs guest room, staring at his phone. When he saw her, he jumped a little, although he hadn't closed the door.

"What's up, honey?"

"Do you remember you promised to take me to Wild World?"

He looked at her blankly for a moment, then remembered. "Oh yeah, sometime this summer, we'll go."

"I think we should go before the California trip. We could go this Saturday."

"This Saturday isn't going to work, sweetheart."

"Why not?"

"I have work stuff I have to do."

"You never had to work this much before," Sage said, pouting.

"You sound like your mother. This is a new job. I'm still establishing myself."

Histrionics had stopped working on her mother a long time ago, but her father had never been very good at discerning when her tears were real or fake. He would do anything not to see her cry. And the tears weren't totally fake. She was disappointed in her father in some way she could not name and felt genuine pity for herself, who might really never get the special trip to Wild World that had been promised.

She blinked. She could feel the tears building behind her eyes. She thrust out her bottom lip.

"Sweetheart, I said we'd go this summer."

"I don't believe you." A single tear sped down her cheek.

Her father threw up his hands. He stood up from the chair, stomped across the room, and slammed the door behind him.

Sage went to wait at the top of the stairs. A few minutes later, her father came out. He sat down next to her.

"Okay, I think I worked it out. We can go this Saturday. You can bring a friend, if you want."

That left only the delicate question of which friend to bring. Remembering the awkward dinner at their house with the Prescotts, Sage thought it might be better to ask Maddie. She and Maddie could get to know each other better if they hung out for once without Lana. But that wasn't the only consideration. A trip to Wild World was a big deal, and expensive. From this angle, she thought that it would also make more sense to ask Maddie, because money was tight in her family and she probably wouldn't get a chance to go otherwise, while Lana's whole family could afford to go anytime they wanted. This seemed like pretty sound reasoning, the sort of explanation she could offer to Lana in case her feelings were hurt—that it was not actually a personal decision, that she just felt sorry for Maddie, who wasn't even going on vacation anywhere this summer.

The next evening in front of the computer, Sage felt nervous as she typed in the invitation, then sat, waiting for the response.

> **sagenewman31:** hey do u want to come with me and my dad to wild world this sat?

> **I_love_Spock8:** yes!

> **I_love_Spock8:** OMG that sounds so fun

> **I_love_Spock8:** wait is lana coming?

> **sagenewman31:** my dad said i can only bring 1 friend

For a minute or so there was no response.

> **I_love_Spock8:** ok we can make that work

> **I_love_Spock8:** but we cant tell Lana

> **I_love_Spock8:** she gets jealous really easily

> **sagenewman31:** i dont like to lie

> **I_love_Spock8:** i cant go unless we do it this way

> **I_love_Spock8:** lana can be scary when she's jealous

Sagenewman31: ok

I_love_Spock8: yay!

I_love_Spock8: thanks for inviting me

sagenewman31: 😊

Sage sat back in her chair. This was an important step in her friendship with Maddie. And she supposed that Maddie would know the best way to handle things with Lana. Why risk hurting her feelings? There was a saying, wasn't there—*What you don't know can't hurt you.*

2

They were leaving early to make the most of the day, setting out at 8:00 a.m. to get to Wild World at 9:00, when it opened. That morning, Maddie's mother was still in bed, but Gran got up to make her eggs for breakfast and to hand her a twenty-dollar bill that she put in the pocket of her shorts.

Wild World was known for its large waterslides, and Sage had told her to wear a suit under her clothes. Luckily Maddie had a new one that Mom had bought for her one evening on the way home from work. It was ugly—bright orange, with a frill around the butt, but at least it fit. It wasn't as tight in the crotch and had a little more room in the chest, but her curves were still easily visible, her body no longer a child's body. She would still try to keep her T-shirt on as much as possible.

"I'm glad you're making new friends," Gran said, sitting across from her as Maddie shoveled the eggs into her mouth. "There's always been something a little off with the Prescott girl."

Maddie frowned. "There's nothing wrong with Lana."

"You girls watch too many horror movies. You read all those dark books." Gran had found Maddie's copy of *Twilight*, read it cover to cover, and announced that she didn't think it was appropriate reading for a girl of Maddie's age. Maddie just rolled her eyes; who was Gran to lecture her when she read all those novels with heaving bosoms on the covers?

"She's been a bad influence on you," Gran said when Maddie didn't answer.

Maddie's frown deepened, and she hunched her shoulders over the table. This was unfair. For one thing, Lana wasn't even into *Twilight*. And without Lana, Maddie wouldn't have had any friends at all, but of course Gran didn't know that.

"I know you won't listen to me," Gran said. "No one listens to me. But there's something off about that girl."

When Mr. Newman's car pulled into the driveway, Gran waved at Mr. Newman through the window as Maddie rushed out the door. Sage was sitting next to him in the front seat, but she immediately hopped out and came around to sit in the back with Maddie.

Mr. Newman greeted Maddie warmly, as if they were old friends, though it was actually the first time they had met.

"Do you want a fizzy water?" Sage asked. There was a small cooler at her feet. "We have raspberry and lime flavored."

"Uh, raspberry?"

Maddie's family didn't drink flavored water. In the seat next to her, Sage twisted the top off her lime seltzer. She was wearing some sort of white cover-up that slipped down off her shoulder. Her blonde hair glistened in the morning light.

The day before, Maddie had lied to Lana, telling her that her dad was taking her to the movies and that she'd be out all day. It was the first time that she could remember lying to Lana, or at least telling her such a big lie. Lana was so sensitive that it was hard not to tell her small lies all the time, just to soothe her feelings. For instance, Maddie often told Lana she was pretty, though she didn't think that Lana actually was. "You have really great eyes," she would say, which was true—Lana's large dark eyes were definitely her most striking feature. Maddie never did things behind Lana's back, though, not like this. Yet she had hesitated for only a moment when Sage messaged her. She'd never been to Wild World, and this might be her only chance.

Wild World was nearly an hour away. Mr. Newman turned up the volume on the radio, and Maddie watched the highway pass in a blur. When they arrived, there was already a line at the entryway, though it was just a few minutes after opening.

Mr. Newman stepped out of the car. He was wearing a T-shirt, red bathing shorts, and a loose sunhat. He was a little less heavyset than her father, but he had the same middle-aged dad look. Mr. Newman produced a bottle of sunscreen, took a large squirt in his own hand, then held it out wordlessly to Sage. Both father and daughter began to slather themselves in a thick layer of white lotion. Maddie didn't usually bother with sunscreen, but Mr. Newman kept telling her she should take some, so finally she accepted a squirt and dabbed it on her nose.

Maddie squinted in the bright sun in the unshaded area where they had to wait in line. The adult price was $45 per ticket, and it was $35 for children twelve and under.

"You're twelve, right, Maddie?" Mr. Newman asked before ordering two children's tickets.

Once they were through the front gates, the park stretched out in front of them, large and almost empty. Off in the distance loomed the skeletons of tall waterslides and roller coasters. A row of game stalls extended down one end, rows of food stalls down another. Except for a long-ago trip to Disney World when she was much younger, Maddie had never been to an amusement park before.

"If you girls want to try out the bigger slides, I'd recommend we start there," Mr. Newman said. "In another hour or two the lines for those'll be really long."

"You want to try it?" Sage asked. Maddie nodded.

The three of them walked together toward the waterslides. There was already a line formed halfway down the long, snaking staircase next to a sign that read THE TWISTER. The slide itself was a series of white tubes connected to wooden scaffolding. Looking up at the slide's underbelly, it looked ramshackle, like the only thing preventing a disaster were a few rusty nails. Maddie swallowed and looked over at Sage.

Sage didn't look concerned. Maddie followed her up the stairs, with Mr. Newman leading the way.

"I haven't been on one of these in a long time," Mr. Newman said. He smiled warmly at Maddie. She decided that she liked Mr. Newman. Sage was lucky; she had two really nice parents, the kind of parents other kids feel jealous of, and they were still together. Lana's parents were still together, but Maddie had never wished Mr. Prescott were her father. There was something bulldoggish about Lana's dad. She had once heard him yelling at Mrs. Prescott, loudly and meanly, in another room, and ever since then she had been a little scared of him.

"It looks like two to a raft, girls. Are you going to be okay going down by yourselves?"

Maddie looked at Sage. For the first time, she saw something like a glimmer of fear in her eyes. Maddie's own pulse was beating faster and faster as they climbed higher up the stairs toward the top. She had decided to stop looking down and look only at Sage and Mr. Newman. For some reason, seeing that Sage was nervous emboldened Maddie.

"We'll be fine," she said, and she nodded at Sage. This was how Lana must feel, Maddie thought, being the one to take charge.

A small trickle of water flowed from the top of the slide down into the pool far below, pushing the two-person inner tube with it. They watched the last couple disappear down a sharp twist of the slide, heard their muted screams. Sage looked very pale.

"I'll sit in the front," Maddie said, trying to sound confident. She hopped into the front hole and grasped on tightly to the little rubber knob. Once Sage was seated behind her, the attendant gave them a push, and the raft shot out and down. Maddie heard herself scream as they passed through the first big twist. Then she stopped screaming and her mouth was open in surprise. At one point the raft shot close to the edge of the slide on one of the turns, and for a moment she thought they might go over, but then they were down and around again and then they were plunging into the pool. Maddie let go of the raft when they hit the water and came up laughing. Behind her, Sage was sputtering, choking, and coughing up water. Another attendant grabbed the tube, and both girls doggy-paddled to the stairs.

"That was amazing," Maddie said. "Did you like it?"

Sage nodded solemnly.

Mr. Newman had walked back down the staircase to meet them.

"How was it?" he said.

"It was great!" Maddie said.

"You want to go again?" Mr. Newman asked.

"Yes," said Maddie.

"No," said Sage.

The girls looked at one another, both a little miffed. "Maybe Maddie and I can go down," Mr. Newman said. "Sage, would you be okay waiting down here for us?"

Sage shrugged. "Yeah, okay." She didn't look like she was happy about it, but Maddie decided to pretend she didn't notice.

Since their last turn, the line had grown. It now extended all the way down the long staircase. Maddie hesitated, realizing she was going to have to wait in line with just Mr. Newman.

"You ready, Maddie?" She nodded. They didn't say much during the slow climb to the top. When they were high enough up, Mr. Newman pointed out his car in the parking lot, and they both waved to Sage, who was a small white dot down at the bottom of the stairs, holding the bag with their towels and Mr. Newman's keys, wallet, and phone.

The ride down was not quite as exciting as the first time because it was not as much of a surprise, but Maddie could hear Mr. Newman whooping behind her as they went around the fast curves, and when they splashed into the pool, he also came up laughing, just like Maddie. He and Maddie bounded over to Sage, who looked hot and bored, her cheeks flushed.

"Should we get a snack?" Mr. Newman said.

They bought a funnel cake from one of the food trucks they had passed along the way and a large container of lemon ice, which they ate together, each slipping in a spoon. Maddie watched this casual interaction wistfully, remembering how her dad had always been a bit of a germophobe and didn't split food even with his own kid. Sage was lucky to have the father she had.

Sage said she wanted to go swimming in the large pool, which Maddie agreed to easily, since she owed her for the second ride on the Twister. Mr. Newman said he was going to sit and drink a cup of coffee, and they could go on ahead just the two of them, as long as they stuck together. Maddie glanced back once and saw Mr. Newman already bent over, texting on his phone.

At the pool, Sage stripped off her cover-up and dropped it unthinkingly on one of the lounge chairs. Maddie hesitated, then removed her shorts and her shirt. The pool had its own smaller waterslides and a row of fake lily pads floating along one side. They went down the smaller slides and then swam over to the lily pads, each flinging their chests up over the floating hunks of plastic. They bobbed in the water. Sage turned her head toward Maddie.

"You're lucky," Sage said in a low voice. "Boys are really going to like you, with that chest."

Maddie blushed. "It's a new suit."

"It looks good on you. My mom said the women in my family all have small breasts. So." She shook her head, and the little droplets of water caught in her hair pattered down onto the lily pad. Lana didn't like to talk about bodies, especially not about breasts. She had never said anything to Maddie, but Maddie knew that Lana didn't like it that she already had boobs. She could just tell.

"So," Sage asked in the same hushed tone, "did you get your period yet?"

Maddie blushed. "Yeah."

"Me too," Sage said, nodding solemnly. "Do you like anyone? At school, I mean?"

Maddie thought suddenly of Ethan Walsh, the way he had looked at her at the pool and how she had hated it but also wanted him to do it again.

"No, not really."

"There're some cute boys in the neighborhood," Sage said. "My brother Henry rides bikes with some of the ninth graders."

"There's a boy in the grade ahead of us," Maddie said. "He lives in the neighborhood. All the girls at school have crushes on him."

"Yeah? What do you think? Is he cute?"

Maddie thought about confessing that she liked Ethan, something she had never told Lana—but she decided she didn't know Sage well enough, not yet.

"He's okay," she said instead.

Maddie rolled onto her back as if she just wanted to stretch out in the sun, though really she was trying to hide the redness on her cheeks, but instead the lily pad bobbed away beneath her, and she fell back into the water with a scream. When she came up to the surface, Sage was smiling, but not meanly. Maddie splashed water into her face, and Sage shrieked and jumped back into the pool, using her hands to send a wall of water back at Maddie. They splashed for several minutes until, worn out by laughter, they both stretched out again on the lily pads, letting the midday sun dry their top halves.

It was the most fun Maddie had had all summer, and she hadn't thought about Lana or Him all day. No, Maddie thought, glancing at Sage, who was lying in the sun with her eyes closed, it was nice to not have to think or talk about Him. Today, right now, she was free.

When they finally emerged from the pool, Maddie, emboldened by Sage's compliments, didn't pull her T-shirt back over her suit. Sage put on her cover-up but let it slip low over her right shoulder. As they left the pool area, a tanned boy lying in one of the lounge chairs appraised them behind opaque sunglasses, his head turning to watch them go.

"Bye, girls," he said. Sage and Maddie giggled all the way back to the picnic table where they'd left Mr. Newman.

But when they got there, Mr. Newman was gone. Maddie turned and spotted him in the distance. He was standing in the shade near one of the smaller roller coasters, talking into his phone and pacing. He looked serious, scowling as he spoke. He must have felt Maddie's eyes on him because he looked up, wiped his face clean, said one last thing into the flip phone, and abruptly closed it.

"Where is he?" Sage asked.

"He's coming over here," Maddie said.

"Did you girls have fun at the pool?"

"It was the best," Sage said.

"Ready for lunch?"

Again Mr. Newman produced his wallet to pay for Maddie's lunch—a hamburger, french fries, and a Diet Coke. Maddie had never had Diet Coke before, but Sage ordered one, so she decided to give it a try.

The rest of the afternoon disappeared into a blur of rides—none of them too far off the ground, to accommodate Sage's fear of heights. They were supposed to be home in time for dinner, but it was suddenly five o'clock, and Mr. Newman had promised they'd have a chance to visit some of the game stalls before they left. He handed Sage a ten-dollar bill and went off to get another coffee. Maddie and Sage spent the money quickly at a stall where you had to shoot water from a gun to knock over some ducks. Maddie proved to be pretty good at this, and she won a prize—a small stuffed giraffe. Sage was disappointed when they ran out of money and she hadn't won anything—which was when Maddie remembered the twenty dollars in her pocket. Then they played a little on a Skee-Ball machine and at another stall where you had to throw balls into a high-up tub, which neither one of them was very good at. By the time they were out of money, the shadows were getting long on the ground. They found Mr. Newman sitting on a bench near the exit, again looking at his phone in displeasure.

If the day had ended there, things might have gone differently. As it was, this was the last real day of Maddie's childhood, though of course she didn't know it. In some other timeline, this is the day that begins Maddie's close friendship with Sage. Maybe she draws closer to Sage and drifts away from Lana. There it is: another life. All Maddie has to do is not walk through the exit.

But they did walk through the Wild World gates, back out into the near-empty parking lot. They started walking toward Mr. Newman's car, but they hadn't gotten very far before a woman appeared suddenly at their side.

"What are you doing here?" Mr. Newman said.

"Hi, girls," the woman said, smiling. She was wearing a low-cut pink shirt and white shorts, and her curly hair was pulled back from her face.

"Come with me," Mr. Newman said, and he grabbed the woman by her elbow, pulling her out of earshot.

"Who is that?" Maddie asked.

"I don't know," Sage said.

Maddie felt sick to her stomach. She and Sage watched as Mr. Newman and the unknown woman exchanged a few words. Mr. Newman's face was red, and a single vein stood out on his forehead as he gestured at the woman.

Once, not long before Maddie's dad had moved out, a woman had called the house asking for him. Maddie didn't recognize the voice. "Is this Maddie?" the woman had asked with a smile in her voice, as if she knew all about her, this woman she had never met. Later, of course, she realized that it was Sharon. Maddie glanced uneasily at Sage, who was watching her father and the woman with a small frown.

Maddie turned her back to Mr. Newman and the woman, turned a little away from Sage, and cast her gaze out over the vast, rapidly emptying parking lot of Wild World. The descending sun glinted off the roofs of the few cars still parked in the distance. A tall billboard near the entrance cast long shadows over the pavement, and it was there, in the shade, that she saw Him.

A single man, standing completely still, watching them; He appeared to be wearing a long, dark coat, and it was this detail—a long coat in the middle of a hot day in July—that made Maddie's breath catch in her throat, made her sure it was Him. Because of the distance and the shadows, she couldn't see the man's face clearly, but she knew: it was Him. A deep shock of cold shot through her, from her feet up to her head.

"What's wrong?" Sage asked.

Maddie tried to speak but couldn't. She shook her head.

"C'mon, girls," Mr. Newman said, appearing at their side. Maddie jumped.

Mr. Newman was walking briskly toward the parking lot.

"Dad, who was that?" Sage asked, hurrying to catch up to him.

Maddie looked back toward the billboard. There was nothing there now, nothing that even looked like Him or his shadow.

On the ride home, Maddie and Sage sat silently in the back seat. Maddie could still feel her heart pounding in her ears. Was it possible that Lana had been right this whole time—that there was something out there, something stalking them? She had to talk to Lana, to find out what it meant.

"You girls hungry? Should I stop at McDonald's?" Mr. Newman asked when he got off the highway. Sage shrugged and didn't answer.

It was getting dark by the time the car pulled up in front of Maddie's house. The curtain in the front picture window moved, and a sliver of Gran's face appeared.

Maddie remembered to say thank you to Mr. Newman. When she said goodbye, Sage nodded at her. "See ya," she said.

Maddie stepped out into the gathering darkness, a chorus of crickets whirring. From the small part of Gran's face she'd seen in the window, she thought she was going to get yelled at for being late, for not asking Mr. Newman to call on his cell.

"You're burnt," Gran said as soon as she stepped inside.

Maddie had put her T-shirt back on over her suit, but her cheeks and forehead were bright red, and later, when she went to get undressed, she'd find that the skin on her shoulders and her back was burnt badly enough that over the next few days, it would peel and flake. It would only just have healed by the time Sage and her family got back from California.

A heavy exhaustion fell over her body, and her head ached a little. She didn't bother to shower before she laid her sweaty sunburned body between the sheets. She lay in the dark for a minute or two, then reached over to turn on the small lamp on the bedside table. She hadn't been afraid of the dark in years, but now the shadows on the wall seemed to hold the possibility of a threat, the threat of Him. When she finally fell asleep, the gentle glow from the lamp was still shining on her face.

3

That Saturday Lana was up early. She was often up early on weekends. She liked being the first one awake in the house, enjoying the freedom to take whatever she wanted from the fridge, watch whatever she wanted on TV, browse the internet without one of her parents trying to see what she was looking at. Padding down the second floor hallway in her pajamas, she paused to look out the circular window that faced their street. As she watched, a car turned into Maddie's driveway, and Maddie emerged almost instantly from the front door. Sage got out of the passenger seat of the car, walked around, and got in the back next to Maddie. The car backed out of the long driveway. Through the glass, Lana could hear birds chirping.

◆ ◆ ◆

She had been lying on her bed for some time before she felt a hush in the air of her room and knew He had come to sit down next to her on the bed.

Why so sad?

Maddie has betrayed me.

That's a serious charge.

She lied to me. She told me she was hanging out with her dad so she could go off somewhere with Sage.

You sound angry.

I am.

I wish I could help.

What do I need to do?

You know.

No, I don't.

You've known for some time. You're just afraid to do it.

It's wrong.

The world you live in is wrong. The people you live with are wrong.

No.

Everyone you know is blind. Only you can see. There's a price for seeing things you're not supposed to see.

There must be some other way.

It's the only way. You know what I'm telling you is true. It takes blood to bind us together, to let me cross over.

Lana's eyes were closed, but she could feel Him next to her in the early-morning light, could feel Him reach out with his heavy hand and rest it on her shoulder. It was warm, as warm as a real, human hand.

In social studies that year, they had done a quarter on ancient civilizations. According to the textbook, human sacrifice was not unheard of among some of these societies. In southern parts of Mexico, for instance, archaeologists had found pits filled with human bones, often the bones of young children. Many of these bones showed signs of serious injury or illness.

"Well," Mr. Lopez had said, fixing them with a look through his thick glasses, "you have to understand, these people weren't living the way we live now. They didn't always have enough to eat. And in their worldview, a sacrifice could help their whole family; it could make the rains come or ensure a good crop. So, from that perspective, imagine you have a child who is sick or ailing. Maybe you think you'll sacrifice that one to save the rest of your children, the rest of your family."

Lana understood Mr. Lopez to be saying that a sacrifice was meant to hurt, that it didn't mean anything if you weren't giving up something important.

◆ ◆ ◆

Lana didn't hear anything from Maddie Saturday night or most of Sunday. Only that evening did Maddie finally message her, asking how her weekend had been. Lana answered vaguely and immediately typed a reply.

> **SacredPresence13:** how was your day with your dad?

> **I_love_Spock8:** good! see u in the morning. ur house?

> **SacredPresence13:** sounds good

That night Lana stayed up a long time, waiting for Him, but He didn't appear. She thought it meant that she was supposed to already know what to do.

The next morning, after her mother left to take Marc to camp, she stood in the kitchen. Her mother had a large butcher's block with several sharp knives, and Lana pulled out one and then another, trying to see how each felt in her hand. The largest one was too large—she would have needed both hands to wield it, and she'd have no way to hide it. If the knife was too small or too dull, it might not do the trick. She was a small person, had never been that physically strong. Maddie was actually an inch taller than her. The only advantage she had was surprise. The knife had to go in clean on her first try.

Lana hadn't eaten breakfast that morning. She couldn't even swallow her milk. Now as she laid the knives out on the counter, she felt her fingers trembling. She didn't think she could do it. What if she was just not physically capable of it?

She heard the front door open and close. "Lana?"

There was no time to put away the knives. They were all splayed out on the white countertop. Lana turned around, as if trying to hide them from view with her body.

"Hey," Maddie said.

"Hey." Lana's voice was creaky, a little too high.

"What are you up to?" Maddie's eyes traveled to the counter.

"Nothing. My mom was trying to sharpen the knives, but she didn't get to finish."

"Oh. My mom would never just leave them out on the counter like that."

"Well, you know my mom."

Maddie's face was a deep pink, and the skin on her nose was flaking. Wherever she had been on Saturday, she'd gotten a sunburn. Lana made herself see again the car pulling into the driveway, Sage scurrying around, her shirt slipping down over one shoulder. The two of them, heads bent, as the car pulled away. Lana swallowed, trying to will back her rage.

"So what did you do with your dad? On Saturday?" Her voice had an edge to it now.

Maddie looked stricken. She spoke quickly. "Okay, there's something I have to tell you. But promise you won't be too mad at me?"

"Okay."

"I went to Wild World with Sage on Saturday. I know I shouldn't have, and I'm sorry I lied to you."

Lana was too genuinely surprised at the admission to remember to act surprised.

"She invited me, and I really wanted to go," Maddie continued, to fill Lana's silence. "You know, because I'd never been."

"So," Lana said slowly, "why are you telling me?" Her legs and arms felt trembly. She moved to climb into one of the high swivel chairs at the counter so she could sit down.

"Because something happened while I was there. Something really important, and you're the only person I can tell. At the end of the day, on our way back to the car, in the parking lot, I saw Him." Maddie dropped her voice.

Lana's throat was dry. "*You* saw Him?"

"He was, like, standing next to this billboard in the shadows, staring at me. I know it was Him."

"You saw Him," Lana repeated. The tightness in her chest was unraveling.

"Yeah. I guess I did. I mean, I don't know what else it could have been."

Lana swallowed. Her body felt weak with relief.

Even the day before, Lana might have thought she'd feel jealous to have to share Him with anyone, even Maddie, but she didn't feel that now. It was such a relief, to know that it wasn't just her, that she wasn't actually going crazy. Because it had crossed her mind, once or twice, that if some other girl she knew told her she could see and hear things that other people said weren't there, she would have thought that girl was crazy. But Lana wasn't crazy; she was right. She had thought she had to do it alone, and now here was a friend, her best friend, ready to join her. He had chosen them both.

She scooted off the stool. "We have a lot to talk about," she said to Maddie. "I'm just going to put these knives away. My mom really shouldn't have left them out."

VI

2017

There are five members in the private chat, including Follower_in_the_ Distance. They all seem to take the existence of HIM as a given and are arguing among themselves only on the particulars of how best to help HIM cross over. User89274 is the official organizer of the group, and the most committed. The members spiral in and out of the same conversation, debating the pros and cons of different approaches.

> **User89274:** It's actually very simple. We choose a sacrifice. Once the sacrifice is made, HE manifests HIMSELF to us

> **Fungible_Tokens57:** Yeah cause that worked so well the last time

> **User89274:** We all know why it didn't work then

> **PraiseSatan69:** so we do it and we do it right

> **Follower_in_the_Distance:** But how do we decide? Don't we have to wait for HIM to tell us?

User89274: We've all seen HIM. What more evidence do we need?

Fungible_Tokens57: HE spoke to the Prescott girl. That's how she chose the target. Shouldn't we wait till HE speaks to one of us?

User89274: Prescott was a visionary. She was specially chosen to convey HIS message to us. Remember, the other girl never spoke to HIM, only saw HIM. We've been shown the way. We need to take the initiative here

Follower_in_the_Distance: What about the idea I had? Where we find someone—a criminal maybe—someone who deserves to die?

User89274: When HE did choose HE chose a totally innocent 12 year-old girl

PraiseSatan69: I agree. No criminals. It has to be an innocent

Follower_in_the_Distance: Wait I'm not killing a kid

Fungible_Tokens57: But you'll kill a grown-up just fine? It's OK as long as they're over 18?

They are stalled on the target, but not on the method: slitting the sacrifice's throat with a knife.

PraiseSatan69: It will be bloody but actually pretty humane. No one comes back from that.

Maddie has barely eaten anything since she ran into Mrs. Newman at the Green Thumb. She hasn't been able to keep anything down. Now her stomach does somersaults while she composes a private message to WorshipHIM36.

> **Mad_as_a_Hatter22**: Hi. I am a member of the website and wanted to alert you to a private group that has been formed by Follower_in_the_Distance. The group is devoted to what they call "the next sacrifice" and are actively planning a murder. I don't know where they live or their real names but I'm hoping you can help me find out so we can alert the police. Obviously this violates the terms of agreement that all the members sign and is a real threat to actual human life. Please respond quickly as this is extremely urgent!

Six hours later, after Mom and Steve are in bed, she receives WorshipHIM36's reply.

> **WorshipHIM36**: Dear Mad_as_a_Hatter22. Thank you so much for reaching out. Unfortunately, private group chats are not covered under the user agreement. There's little I can do about private posts so if you have a concern I suggest you take it up with the members of the group or withdraw from that group. Thanks again for reaching out. Have a nice day!

What is she supposed to do now? Maybe this has been WorshipHIM36's game all along, allowing would-be murder groups to form in the private chats while keeping them off the public discussion thread. Or maybe WorshipHIM36 is just lost deep down in a delusional hole, their disorganized cognition making sense only to them.

She could go to the police, but then she'd have to explain what she's been doing on the website to begin with; she'd be admitting to violating the terms of her early release. But wouldn't coming forward make up for that, wouldn't that be a way to prove that she is truly well? It's the sort of thing that would work in a movie but probably not in real life. No, they wouldn't believe her; they would send her back. And she can't risk that.

◆ ◆ ◆

That Saturday night, when Mom and Steve are at their weekly Bible study, the phone rings. They still have an old-fashioned phone with an actual answering machine, and Maddie can hear the prerecorded voice: "An inmate from a Maryland correctional facility is trying to contact you . . ."

Maddie accepts the call. "Hello?"

"Hello?" A moment of silence. She can hear Luke breathing into the phone. "Oh. Is this Maddie?"

"Yeah. Your dad's out. At Bible study."

"Oh, okay. I guess I got the nights mixed up. How are you doing? You adjusting and all that?"

Another moment of silence. Maddie finds that she can close her eyes and see where Luke is, or some version of where he is. The functional, run-down building. The hard, cold walls and hard, cold floors. The solidity of the telephone receiver against the wall. The constant buzz of fluorescent lights. The loneliness, the boredom. How you might want to stay on an awkward phone call with a stranger just to avoid returning to your cell.

"I'm doing okay," she says and finds herself telling him, for no good reason, about running into Mrs. Newman at the Green Thumb.

"That's rough," he says, in a way that sounds definitive. Maddie remembers how easily he was caught, how poorly planned the rape was, and she thinks that Luke can't be very smart.

"So," the voice on the other end of the phone says, "I guess we're like brother and sister now."

For some reason, this completely disarms her. She has thought of Luke only as her stepfather's son, as if she couldn't follow the implication through to the end. She's found some of his old posts online, horrible screeds about the superiority of the white race under threat due to "the dilution of its purity." I'm not like you, she thinks. I'm nothing like you. She so badly wants to believe it. But who's to say she isn't just as bad?

"Well, I mean, technically, you're my stepbrother." Her tone is suddenly harsh, uninviting.

"Okay, Maddie." She imagines him shrugging on the end of the phone, a slight flex of his head, someone used to shrugging off the judgments of others. "Tell my dad I'll try him again tomorrow. You take care."

The phone clicks, and he's gone. Maddie sits for a moment holding the receiver in her hand before she sets it back in its cradle.

It's been three days since she ran into Mrs. Newman, but she can't quite settle back into work. She finds herself glancing toward the parking lot often, half expecting to see Sage's mother there again, accompanied this time by Mr. Newman. Every time she hears the crunch of tires over the gravel parking lot, she cringes.

On Tuesday around lunchtime, she is watering the flowers in the greenhouse when an SUV pulls into the lot. She jerks her head, checking, but when she sees a young man in a suit get out, she relaxes, concentrating on unwinding the hose so she can move down the next row. After a time, she feels the hair stand up on the back of her neck, that old feeling of being watched. With a lurch, she braces herself, and she knows suddenly that she has been expecting this always, to find Him waiting for her again.

But when she turns stiffly, she finds only the customer in the suit standing in the doorway of the greenhouse with his hands on his hips, watching her. He is tall, with broad shoulders. There's something defensive in the posture, even threatening, but still she looks at him blankly for a few seconds before she understands. Something around the eyes, the mouth, is familiar.

Boys change so much in becoming men.

Her voice is a squawk, an animal cry. "Henry?"

He nods. Both his hands are now bunched into fists at his sides, and she realizes that he is blocking the only exit. She drops the hose, and the water continues spurting out over the gravel.

She takes a deep breath and waits. She wonders if he has a weapon or is planning to use his fists, but then something appears to snap in him and he relaxes, just a little.

"What are you doing here?" she croaks.

"I could ask you the same thing."

"I work here."

"So I hear. I wanted to see it for myself."

He looks around at the greenhouse, but there's nothing to see, only rows of plants. The hose shifts at Maddie's feet, and the water begins to soak through her right sneaker. She doesn't move.

Henry shakes his head, as if in disgust.

"So obviously you won't be seeing my mom around here again."

Maddie struggles to find her voice. "It was an accident. I'm not supposed to have contact with any of you—"

"Exactly. I just want to make sure we're all on the same page. You don't come anywhere near any of my family. Is that clear?"

"Yeah, I wouldn't—"

"I'm a lawyer. I mean, I'm about to finish law school. You come anywhere near any member of my family, you'll find yourself back in state custody so fast your head will spin. I have my eye on you. Do you understand?"

She nods. Henry looks at her, and his nostrils flare. He shakes his head again, as if she has given him some new cause for contempt, and turns to go.

"Wait. Henry. I just want to say—"

"Don't. Don't do that." His voice cuts through the air. Everything else he said has been a little canned, rehearsed perhaps, and this is his first genuine utterance, a refusal to even entertain the possibility of her apology. It silences her completely.

He walks back to the SUV. She waits until the car pulls out of the lot. Her right shoe is completely soaked through. With shaking hands, she bends down and picks up the hose.

The next couple of days are quiet at work and on the site, but when she comes in Thursday morning, Cindy says she needs to speak with her. She leads Maddie inside the building, through the "Staff Only" door, and into Cindy's tiny windowless office. When Cindy asks her to have a seat, she knows that she's being fired.

"I'm sorry about this," Cindy says, "and I want you to know it's nothing that you did. I mean, you've done a fine job here. It's the owner. He recently learned about your—well, situation—and he just thinks it's not a good fit. You know, he doesn't like the optics."

"Optics?" What are the optics of Maddie carrying pumpkins, Maddie trying to make some money, Maddie shoveling shit, Maddie trying to survive? She inhales and exhales, tries to focus on staying still, on not doing anything stupid, like throwing something or crying.

She swallows. "I didn't do anything wrong." It comes out like a childish whine.

"You can finish out the day. I'll mail you your check."

Maddie glides back through the store and out to the back, where Omar is unloading more pumpkins. He nods at her and then, seeing something on her face, asks, "Everything okay?"

Maddie shrugs. She swallows again. "I just got fired."

"What? Why?"

Gabriela, who has been helping Omar with the pumpkins, comes over. "What's happening?"

"Maddie just got fired."

"Fired? *Cindy* fired you? Why'd she do that?"

"Um, I guess I'd rather not say." Maddie wishes that they couldn't see the tears in her eyes, wishes that the tears weren't there.

Gabriela looks like she's about to hug her, but Maddie flinches, and Gabriela's hand drops.

She moves through the rest of the day as if the air has turned thick around her. There's no one left to try to impress anymore.

Mom picks her up at five, as usual. When she asks her how her day was, Maddie doesn't say anything. She waits until they're turning down the street to the subdivision before she says, "I got fired."

Her mother doesn't speak but heaves a deep sigh. Only when the car has pulled into the garage does she turn to look at Maddie.

"What did you do now?"

"I didn't do anything! I ran into Mrs. Newman last week at the nursery. Then today Cindy said I couldn't work there anymore. She said the owner doesn't like the optics."

"You ran into Hannah Newman? Why didn't you say anything?"

Maddie shrugs. She doesn't want to tell Mom about Henry's visit, his threat. She glances down toward her feet, at the sneakers that she always wears for work. There are streaks of dark soil on her right shoe from when she repotted some marigolds that afternoon.

"I did the best I could," Maddie says plaintively. She wants Mom to reaffirm this, to tell her it wasn't her fault, but Mom doesn't say anything, just drums her fingers slowly against the steering wheel.

"Well, that's just great. What are we going to tell Steve?"

"That's what you're thinking about?"

"It was a miracle Cindy was willing to hire you. That was a good job that you just threw away."

"I told you, I didn't do anything wrong."

"Well, we both know that's not true."

Maddie reaches up and wipes an errant tear off her face. "What do you want from me? I'm doing my best. I can't undo the past."

"No, I guess not."

Maddie feels the anger rise in her chest. "Where were you, anyway? That summer? You were there. You could have done something."

"I had my own stuff to deal with, Maddie. I was going through a very difficult divorce."

"But you were still my mom. You were still supposed to be there, to take care of me."

"I was there."

"No, you weren't. Not really."

"So I guess it's all my fault then, huh? Is that what they taught you in there? To blame it all on your mother?"

"You know, some people are compassionate toward the mentally ill? Instead of just locking them up and throwing away the key?"

"Oh, is that what you think happened here? You think we threw away the key? That's why your father spent all that money on those lawyers? That's why we got you out, ten years early?"

"I got myself out because I didn't need to be there anymore. The doctors had been saying it for years."

"Is that what you think?" Mom's voice grows quiet and taut, the way it does when she's about to reveal a secret. "You know, the psychiatrists were never sure about you. They never really agreed on a diagnosis, on what it was, on what—" Mom swallows. "They were never sure whether you really believed in Him at all, not the way that Lana did. They weren't sure whether you were actually delusional or just—"

"Of course I believed in Him! That's why I helped her. I got sucked in, Mom. Why else would I have done something like that? What, you think I'm just evil?"

The question, which was supposed to be rhetorical, hangs in the air. Maddie finds she can't speak.

Her mother pauses and reaches a hand to open the door. She clears her throat. "You were just so secretive," she says in a quiet voice, not looking at Maddie. "I can't be held responsible for what you did." She pauses, and then shakes her head as if to clear it. "No, I can't be held responsible."

She waits until Mom is inside the house and the garage door is shut. Then she hurls herself at the dashboard, punching hard with both her hands until her knuckles sting. Her right hand leaves a small smear of blood on the dash that she rubs away with the sleeve of her sweatshirt. She wants to scream, but she manages to push that down so that she emits only a few strangled sobs instead. When she tries to open the door, a sharp pain cracks through her right wrist. She cradles that arm gingerly and uses her left instead.

All the therapists and psychiatrists asking her to reflect on what she'd done, Mom and Steve insisting on atonement. Her mother has had ten years to ask herself the same questions, and that's the best she can come up with, that she can't be held responsible for the actions of her own child? Mom gave up on her a long time ago. She knew it before, has always felt it at some level, but she has never admitted it to herself so clearly. They had never been close, but after what Maddie did, it was like Mom just shut part of herself off, walled herself away from her. She gave everything she had left to Steve.

Inside the house, Maddie slips off her dirty sneakers and walks briskly toward the stairs. In the blue room, she lies down on the bed, still in her work clothes.

Lately she's been having nightmares, the kind that she hasn't had in years, not since they moved her to the hospital and she started taking the Seroquel. In the dream it is always the moment just before, and somehow this is the worst part, knowing everything that's coming and being unable to stop it. Yet it happens differently in the dream than it did in real life. The three of them are walking through the woods. Sage is in front, followed by Lana. Maddie walks behind Lana, suffused with dread. Somehow she knows exactly what is going to happen but is powerless to stop it. Lana reaches a hand beneath her coat to bring out the knife, but Maddie always wakes at that moment.

Now she rolls over onto her stomach, grabs her phone, and brings up the Follower website. She checks, but there are no new messages on the private chat. She wants to say something, but she doesn't know what. After the run-in with Henry, she's even more frightened of revealing too much about herself on the site. She doesn't even want to think about what Henry would do if he found out. He could get her sent right back to the hospital, or maybe even real prison this time. But someone has to keep an eye on the private chat, make sure things don't go too far.

The rest of the night, she flips between checking the Followers site and looking halfheartedly at job listings. Things were going so well, but it took so little for everything to fall apart. She doesn't bother to go to sleep, since she doesn't have to get up for work in the morning. She eventually drifts off to sleep with the light on and her phone in her hand.

1

It was sometime in the middle of July that Maddie's mother told her that her father was engaged to Sharon, his girlfriend. Apparently, this meant that she would have to meet Sharon, because they wanted her to be a bridesmaid in their wedding, a wedding that Maddie, in the end, would never attend.

For that first meeting, which would turn out to be the only meeting, they took Maddie for pizza at the place where Dad often took her, an order-at-the-counter place where the tables were always greasy and you could pull as many thin napkins as you wanted out of the dispenser on the table.

Sharon had blonde hair that looked like it was probably dyed because it was a little too light for her skin tone. She was not particularly thin or particularly pretty. But she was young, at least ten years younger than Maddie's mother. Where her mother had crow's-feet and little lines around her mouth, Sharon had only smooth skin. While Mom's skin was covered in freckles and sunspots, Sharon's skin was unblemished. Maddie had a sudden vision of Sharon standing next to one of the polished cars in Dad's lot, turning toward him with a smile on her face.

She and Dad always got pepperoni on their pizza, but because Sharon was a vegetarian, they had to order plain cheese. While they waited for the pizza, Sharon tried too hard to engage Maddie in conversation, asking her questions about school and what her favorite subject was.

"Math," Maddie said, even though math was her least favorite subject. She didn't want Sharon to know anything real about her.

When the pizza arrived, Maddie noticed that her father served Sharon first, placing a large slice on her paper plate. He smiled at her, and she smiled at him.

Since he had moved out, Maddie had gotten used to her father being a certain way at their weekend meetups. At times, it was as if he was trying too hard, making too many jokes, giving in to Maddie too often where before he would have said no. But now, with Sharon, he was different. He had a goofy look on his face and was always turning to look at her, as if making sure she was still there. It was like her father thought that he was a character in some romantic comedy, but he was forty-three, and it was just gross.

"So, Maddie, I hear you're a Harry Potter fan," Sharon said. She took one of the flimsy napkins and blotted it daintily against her lips between bites.

"Not really," Maddie said, shrugging. "I mean, I've read all the books. It was something I was really into when I was, like, ten."

"But you're still excited about the movie, right?" Dad asked.

"I guess. I mean, the movies are never as good as the books, obviously, but it's interesting to see what they do with them."

The truth was that she and Lana always got excited about the Harry Potter movies. They were supposed to have seen this one together, but Maddie had told Lana she was going to see it with her dad. Then Sharon invited herself along.

"You know, I've never read the books?" Sharon said. "I've been thinking maybe I should."

Maddie blinked at her. "I never really got why adults would want to read kids' books," she said.

Sharon's face reddened a little, and Maddie felt a smug sense of satisfaction.

◆ ◆ ◆

By the time they were sitting in the movie theater and the lights had dimmed, Sharon had stopped trying to make conversation with Maddie. Dad had let her get a large popcorn, and although she was full from the pizza, she ate the whole tub anyway, stuffing handfuls into her mouth. She had liked the book of *Harry Potter and the Order of the Phoenix*, but it wasn't her favorite. Now as she watched Harry and his friends forming an army to fight against Voldemort, she thought about Him. In the drawings Lana liked to show her, He looked a lot like Voldemort. But He was also different. In the pictures, sometimes He didn't even have eyes. His face was awful because it was blank: smooth and white as a balloon.

Maddie looked over at her father's and Sharon's faces, lit in the light from the screen. Suddenly she felt as if she were looking at it all from a great distance. She glanced back at the darkened crowd of heads in the theater, the shaft of light from the projector in the back wall and the motes of dust suspended there. Suddenly she was far away from everything, from the movie, from Dad and Sharon, from her own body. She realized He must be there somewhere, behind her in the crowd. What else could explain this feeling?

Her heart throbbed in her ears. She spent the rest of the movie with her body taut, waiting. She was afraid to look behind her.

"What's wrong?" her father asked as they left the theater. Usually Maddie was chatty after a movie, but now her expression was glum and she was silent.

"It was just a really sad ending," she said, swallowing.

"I didn't know the story was that dark," Sharon said.

◆ ◆ ◆

That night Maddie messaged Lana.

I_love_Spock8: omg i hate her so much

SacredPresence13: is she pretty

I_love_Spock8: not at all

I_love_Spock8: and shes stupid

I_love_Spock8: im ready to run away

I_love_Spock8: like rn

SacredPresence13: we need to meet irl

SacredPresence13: tomorrow in the clearing

The clearing was in the woods, behind the playground, where a fallen tree had made a log that was perfect for sitting on. The teenagers came at night to drink and smoke there. Empty beer bottles and cigarette butts littered the ground atop the pine needles, but during the day, Lana and Maddie could be alone. They sat next to one another on the log. Sage was in California.

They had both agreed that the sudden appearance of Him in their lives could not be accidental, that His presence must presage some great act, some monumental change. Lana had decided that the three of them should run away together, somewhere where they wouldn't be found.

Once, the summer before fifth grade, before Dad moved out, Mom and Dad had driven Maddie and Lana to the Eastern Shore. They had crossed the Bay Bridge and taken a ferry to arrive at a small town with a bunch of pretty old colonial houses, antique shops, and an old-fashioned candy store. Maddie had loved it there, even though Lana kept hissing in her ear about how all the pretty old mansions they passed used to be plantation houses where two hundred years ago people would have kept slaves that they treated horribly, and Maddie just wanted Lana to stop making her think about all that so she could enjoy the day.

Still, the small idyllic town and the miles of farmland they passed had left an impression on them of crossing into another world. It was still mostly country over there, miles and miles of empty space. They used to daydream sometimes about finding a deserted farmhouse and moving in there. They would be close to home but just far enough away where no one would think to look for them. They had started to talk about taking Him there. The three of them would live together. They'd have a better chance of being left alone because He was a grown-up. They didn't know, yet, if He would have any sort of magical powers, but just being a grown man might be enough.

"Wouldn't it be funny if when we get to the house, He's like 'Hey, girls, call me Fred'?" Maddie said once, laughing.

Lana frowned, her eyes narrowing. "This is nothing to joke about, Maddie."

"Right," Maddie said, wiping the smile from her face. "Right. Sorry."

Now Lana was telling her about her most recent conversation with Him. He had agreed to move in with them, to the house on the Eastern Shore.

"He said we'll each have our own room, with a large canopy bed," Lana added. "He's ready to join us there, but there's one last thing He needs us to do. It's sort of like a test."

"What test?"

Maddie saw Lana draw a breath. "The thing is, He needs a blood sacrifice."

Once, a couple of years before, Maddie and Lana had tried to take a blood oath to cement their friendship. Lana had smuggled a small kitchen knife out of her house, and they had come to this same spot in the woods, but when they were supposed to cut their fingers on the blade, neither one of them could do it.

"We'll do the blood oath," Maddie said, nodding. "We'll do it right this time."

Lana pursed her lips. "That's not enough. Not this time." Lana took another breath. "It has to be a person. He says we have to sacrifice a person. If we want to be with Him forever. A life for a life."

Maddie couldn't speak. Her mouth hung open.

"Don't think I haven't tried to talk Him out of it, Maddie. I have. It's the only way."

"We can't," Maddie croaked. Her thoughts whirled. She and Lana were both just over five feet tall. Maddie remembered the time she had pushed Amelia Lawrence in kindergarten; that was her only act of physical violence against another person that she could remember. She and Lana sometimes pretended to be violent, but that was different; it was only pretend.

"Don't be selfish about this, Maddie."

"Selfish? What are you talking about? We're not killing anyone."

"I've tried to talk Him out of it, Maddie. You have no idea how hard I've tried. But it's the only way. It takes a blood sacrifice. The blood will make Him real, make Him corporeal, let Him cross over fully into this world."

"Well, maybe we don't want that then. If that's what it takes, maybe we're better off without Him."

Lana blinked. Her eyes looked glassy, and she stared off for a moment into the distance. She leaned toward Maddie and spoke quietly. "He scares me too, Maddie, but it's too late. He's here with us, right now."

Maddie froze. Lana's gaze was aimed behind her back, toward the woods. "You can see Him right now?" she whispered.

Lana nodded, her eyes fixed on the distance. "He's there," she said, and she nodded with her head, as if afraid to point. Maddie swallowed. She was scared to look. She squeezed her eyes shut.

Lana hissed into her ear, "We have to do what He says. It's only going to get worse if we don't. He'll keep appearing to us, keep following us. Things will be better once He's crossed over. Not as scary. That's what He told me. He'll actually be able to help us then, once He has a body. He'll be our friend."

Maddie let out her breath, which she hadn't realized she'd been holding. She opened her eyes and looked at Lana. "What if we get caught?"

"If we plan it right, we won't get caught. We'll run away with Him, just like we've talked about."

Maddie shook her head. "I can't. I just can't do it. There must be another way." She would remember this later, how good she felt when she said this, how morally certain, how everything, for a brief moment, was so clear.

Lana went on as if she hadn't heard her. "It can't be just anyone. It has to be someone special, someone we value. That's what makes it a sacrifice."

Lana turned away from the woods and looked directly into Maddie's eyes. Maddie still didn't dare look at the place where Lana had been looking, the place where He was. She wondered if He was still there, but before she could ask, Lana continued: "I had to fight Him so hard, Maddie. To convince Him."

"Convince Him of what?"

Lana paused. "To leave our families out of it."

For a minute, Maddie heard only a shushing sound in her ears. Her vision blinked off, and when it returned, Lana was looking at her with the same concentrated, almost sorrowful look. Maddie couldn't speak.

"It could have been your gran," Lana said. "It could have been Marc." A tear ran down her cheek, but she continued talking as if she hadn't noticed it. "But I convinced Him. I told Him it could be some-one else, someone less important. It could be a friend. We lose one friend and gain another. Do you see?" There was a new resolve in Lana's voice, and her eyes were fixed on Maddie's.

Maddie's mind moved slowly, at a glacial pace. They sat in silence for at least a minute before she understood. "Sage?" she whispered.

Lana nodded. "It's not Sage's fault. I mean, she's a nice enough girl and everything. But she's not one of us."

It was hard for Maddie to speak. "I can't."

"If you're really my best friend, you'll do this for me."

This was a phrase that always in the past would have been met with Maddie's compliance, but somehow it was the exact wrong thing to say at that moment, as if Lana could bully her into doing something she didn't want to do, something this big. The energy shifted; suddenly Maddie was no longer under Lana's spell.

"No," Maddie said, shaking her head. "No." She stood up and, turning, started walking away.

"Maddie!" Lana called after her, her voice high: "Mariana!"

For once Maddie didn't look back. As she walked, she kept her eyes on the ground in front of her. She was afraid of looking up now and seeing Him in that spot that Lana had marked, afraid He might jump out at her from behind the trees. She was trying very hard to convince herself that she hadn't seen Him after all that day at Wild World. That it had been something else, just an ordinary man. A stranger wearing a coat in the middle of July. Maybe a homeless person. If He was real, then she might have to kill someone, but if He was just Lana's imaginary friend, then everything would be okay, then it all was just pretend.

When she got home, she found Gran sitting on the couch in the living room, watching her soaps. "Back so soon?"

Maddie didn't answer. She shrugged out of her sneakers and crawled over next to Gran on the couch.

"What?" Gran said. "You fight with Lana?"

Maddie considered for a moment telling Gran the truth, but then she saw it was impossible, that it was too late, that it would sound too crazy. Gran would call the police, and they would come and take Lana away, and Maddie didn't want that. Somehow, she knew that Lana wouldn't do it without her, that she needed her.

She sat silently with her head resting on Gran's shoulder and watched the small people moving about on the television screen, trying to catch up with the story. Someone's evil twin was pretending to be her. Someone the characters all thought was dead was not. Maddie sat that way until the credits rolled and another show came on. These characters had different names, but they all seemed to be following the same script.

2

That morning as they drove up into the mountains, Sage gazed out the window at a landscape obscured by fog, but by the time they arrived, sunlight was streaming through the mist, dispelling the haze. The forest was everything Sage had hoped for. The trees were wider than their rented minivan, stretching so far up into the sky that she was reminded of the trip they'd taken two years before to New York City, looking up and up to see where the skyscrapers ended. Even Henry pocketed his iPod and took out his earbuds, gazing around with his lips slightly parted.

"Wow," he said.

Her mother was in charge of the maps. She had stowed several road atlases in the car, in case the GPS went fritzy, and was now examining a large detailed foldout map. "I think we want to head this way," she said, gesturing toward one of the paths in the red soil. Sage took Cody's hand, and they started walking.

The trip so far had been mixed. Aunt Kate's house in Sacramento was a small, modern box with a tiny fenced yard near the freeway. There were only two bedrooms—Aunt Kate slept in one, Mom and Dad in the other, while the three kids were sharing the small finished basement, where there was a lumpy pullout couch for Sage and Cody and a sleeping bag on the floor for Henry.

Before the trip, looking on a map, Sage had thought that Sacramento was close to San Francisco, but this was not really the case. "That's a separate trip," her father told her. Apparently hotels in San Francisco were expensive, too expensive on top of the "fortune" they'd already spent on plane tickets. They should be happy, Dad insisted, with this day trip to Big Basin. Meanwhile, they had explored the sights around Sacramento: the zoo, a historic park where the buildings still looked the way they did during the gold rush, and an old fort. The rest of the time they sat around Aunt Kate's house, Mom and Aunt Kate talking, Dad buried in a book, Henry gazing into space while music blared from his earbuds, Cody kicking a ball around in Aunt Kate's small yard, Sage paging through the worn copy of *Twilight* that Maddie had lent her and that she had already finished on the plane.

Aunt Kate had a desktop computer that they were allowed to take turns on, but between Henry wanting to message friends and Cody wanting to play games, she didn't get much time there. Two days before, she had finally been able to get on AIM after dinner. She thought that maybe she could message Charlie, whom she hadn't heard from in over a week, but it was Maddie who messaged her as soon as she signed on.

I_love_Spock8: hi!

I_love_Spock8: how's Cali

sagenewman31: hi!

sagenewman31: its ok. Kinda boring tbh

I_love_Spock8: seen the redwoods yet

sagenewman31: we go the day after tomorrow

I_love_Spock8: have fun

I_love_Spock8: excited for when u get back

Sage had worried a little when she left for California for ten days that Maddie and Lana would quickly forget her, that they would shrink back into their comfortable pairing, the delicate trio they had worked so hard to establish in the last couple of weeks coming easily unraveled. But Maddie had contacted her, was "excited" for her return.

It helped buoy her mood the day before on the long ride from Sacramento, stuck in the minivan with her family. Henry was moody, and Cody wouldn't sit still and kept kicking the back of her seat while the GPS rerouted them yet again. "Recalculating," it said whenever Dad missed a turn, and he'd sigh, and their estimated time of arrival would be pushed back by another few minutes.

"This is a great opportunity," Mom said, "to see a whole new part of the country." Sage and Henry exchanged looks, rolling their eyes at Mom's cloying optimism.

Now they walked through the woods in a kind of hushed awe. Mom started snapping photos with an old-fashioned camera with a large zoom lens. Cody had gotten his own digital camera, his first, especially for the trip, and was stopping every two feet to take another picture. Dad didn't own a camera, and Henry had pointedly left his behind at Aunt Kate's, saying that you couldn't really take pictures of something and truly experience it at the same time. Sage's digital camera was around her neck, and she paused every once in a while to carefully frame a shot.

Supposedly, the giant trees they were walking through were between eight hundred and fifteen hundred years old. Sage had never seen anything that old in her entire life. Even people usually only lived for eighty years, a tenth of the life of one of these trees. Sage had always been drawn to the idea of old things. She had a vague idea that some primordial truth was lurking in the shadows of the old forest; even some kind of magic, she thought, seemed possible here. Recently Sage had started to think that maybe, when she grew up, she would become a park ranger. She thought it would be a job that would suit her because she loved nature and didn't seem to mind being alone too much.

They walked for some time down a fenced-off path that opened finally into a clearing.

"I'm going exploring," Henry said.

"Don't go too far off," Mom said. "It's an actual forest. You could get lost."

"I want to go too!" Cody screamed.

Mom hurried after Cody, not trusting Henry to watch out for him. Suddenly, Sage and her father were alone for the first time in days.

Ever since Wild World, Sage had mostly avoided her father. After they dropped Maddie off that night, Dad had paused for a time in the Thompsons' driveway as if he wanted to say something, but in the end he didn't say anything, and they drove down the block to their house in silence. Sage said nothing to her mother about the strange woman from the parking lot. But the more she said nothing about the woman, the more it seemed she had nothing at all to say to her father. She didn't understand what she'd seen, but she knew instinctively it was something she was not supposed to see, that it was something wrong.

Now she turned away from him, setting off in the opposite direction from everyone else. Glancing behind her, she saw that he was following behind her at a distance.

"Leave me alone."

"Your mother's right," he said. "You could get lost."

"Maybe I want to get lost," Sage said, thrusting out her lips; she didn't really mean it.

"If you want to be on your own, you should stick to the path," her father said. Sage kept walking.

When she was a small girl, she had loved the story of Little Red Riding Hood. She never got sick of it, even dressing up for Halloween in a red hood three years in a row. She didn't know what it was about that story that made it so irresistible. There was the girl alone in the woods and the wolf, of course, and the repetition about the ears, the eyes, the teeth. There was the impossibility, as she understood even at the time, of either the grandmother or the girl being swallowed whole and somehow still being alive when the woodsman came to cut them out. And how random it all was—what if the woodsman had not happened to walk by at just the right time, with his handy axe?

As she thought about the old story, she sped up, trying to walk in a straight line but inevitably curving, stepping around the circumference of a giant tree. Red mulch and branches snapped under her feet. Up in the trees, she heard the sound of birdsong, the rustle of a squirrel, all the creatures that she must have been scaring with her noise scurrying away. She stopped, panting, and looked around. She should probably turn back. But when she turned around, it didn't seem that the landscape behind her was any more familiar than the one she had just turned away from. She easily retraced her steps back around the tree, back to a place where there were two younger, smaller trees—but after that, it all looked the same.

Her stomach dipped. She cleared her throat. "Dad?" she said, and then called louder, "Dad!"

She wanted to keep walking. She felt a frantic energy fueling her limbs, but she made herself stop. If you're lost in the woods, you're supposed to stay where you are, and let other people find you. She knew this, though she didn't remember how she knew this. She took some deep breaths. She had only been walking for a few minutes. She simply couldn't be that far from the path.

And then, in the distance, she heard it, her father's voice, shouting her name.

"Sage!"

"I'm here! Dad!"

The sound grew closer, and suddenly her father was in front of her.

"I told you not to wander off."

"I know," Sage said. Relief surged through her. "I wasn't lost."

She watched the worry on her father's face turn to annoyance, then relief.

"Stay close," he said, and Sage allowed her father to put his arm around her, drawing her in to his chest.

3

"You're not wearing that to the beach?"

Mommy frowned at Lana, who'd just pulled on one of Mom's old long woolen black coats over her bathing suit.

"It'll keep the sun off," Lana said.

"You'll be hot," Daddy said. "Get in the car."

Mommy threw her arms up as Lana climbed in. Marc, who had always been small for his age, still needed a booster and was already strapped in. He had on a blue T-shirt and swim trunks covered with dinosaurs.

Lana liked the feel of her bare arms and legs against the rough wool. It felt as if the coat were holding her like a cocoon. This way, she wouldn't have to worry about people looking at her body the way that Ethan Walsh had looked at Maddie at the pool.

They'd left early to try to avoid traffic, but there was always traffic on the way to Ocean City on a Saturday in the summer. After kicking his legs for a long time against the passenger seat while Mommy told him to stop, Marc fell asleep, his neck bent at an awkward angle so that Lana could see only the dark-brown hair on top of his head. Lana looked out the window, watching the passing cars.

It had been two days since she'd spoken with Maddie in the clearing. It had hurt, watching Maddie walk away like that. They rarely fought, and when they did, one of them always messaged the other to apologize, usually within a few hours. But Maddie hadn't apologized yet.

She needs time, He'd said the night before, hovering over Lana's bed in the dark. *It took you some time too. To accept it.*

He was telling her to be patient, so she would try.

Daddy was shifting in the front seat, tapping his fingers against the wheel. Their lane hadn't moved in a long time. Daddy nosed the car out, trying to get over, and a car coming up behind them blew on its horn. Daddy slammed on the brakes and said a curse word. Mommy gasped. In the seat next to her, Marc stirred but didn't wake.

"Assholes!" Daddy said. Mommy sat stiffly in the passenger seat. The air-conditioning was on, and in her bathing suit and unfastened coat, Lana felt the temperature was just right.

By the time they got to the beach and found one of the last available parking spots in the public lot, Marc had woken up and was complaining that he needed to pee. Mommy dragged him off to one of the public restrooms, while Lana waited with Daddy next to a pile of their stuff.

"You really going to keep that on all day?" Daddy asked.

"I like it," Lana said. Though she supposed that if she wanted to go swimming, she'd have to take it off.

When Mommy and Marc came back, Mommy carried the bag with the towels and the sunscreen, Lana carried the mesh bag with the beach toys, Daddy carried the two folding chairs for him and Mommy, and they all walked down the boardwalk, passing food stalls smelling of french fries and pretzels, a burger shop, and a small arcade.

"What's that?" Marc asked, pointing to a poster with a photograph showing a long corridor of neon-lit reflective arches, announcing in big red letters: WORLD OF WONDERFUL: FEATURING THE AMAZING MIRROR MAZE!

"It's a mirror maze," said Mommy.

"I want to go," Marc said.

"Maybe later," Daddy murmured, trying to push past Marc, who had stopped in front of the poster, his mouth open.

"No, I really want to go!"

"Let's do some beach time first," Mommy said. "Then maybe we can come back in the afternoon."

"Promise?" Marc asked.

Mommy sighed, and Lana was sure that both her parents had been hoping Marc would forget about the mirror maze over the course of the afternoon, a possibility that was now remote; he took promises very seriously.

"Promise?" Marc repeated.

"Okay," Mommy said. "Later this afternoon."

After they'd passed by the largest throngs of people on the beach, Daddy turned off and led them down to the water. The hot sand seeped into Lana's sandals, and she paused to slip them off. Daddy set up the folding chairs, while Mommy spread out two towels for her and Marc.

Almost immediately, Marc ran off toward the water, and Mommy ran behind him, shouting to him not to go too far in. Daddy pulled his T-shirt over his head, revealing the pale skin of his chest and stomach and a thick rug of dark hair. Sighing, he sank into the beach chair. Lana sat down on her towel with her legs crossed, the long coat brushing the sand behind her. Now that the sun was beating down on her, it was already hot inside the coat.

Marc was wading into the ocean, the water up to his waist. Behind him, Mommy was dipping her toes in and shouting something. That year at school, Marc's teacher had insisted he be tested for learning disabilities. Marc had always done things at his own pace. He had been slow to speak, and for a long time Mommy and Lana were the only people who could understand him when he did. After several years of speech therapy, he still spoke with a kind of lisp that made him sound younger than he was. The teacher thought he might be dyslexic but reported that the test results were "borderline." One evening when they thought Lana had already gone to bed and she went to find them, she stopped outside her parents' room and heard them talking about Marc. Daddy sounded angry, Mommy resigned.

"Why can't they just lay off?" Daddy said. "Why do they have to keep finding ways to make the kid feel bad about himself?"

"It's their job to notice these things," Mommy said. "That's what they're supposed to do."

Marc was the only thing that really worried Lana about running away with Him. For a couple of years, when they'd overlapped at the elementary school, she had at least been able to watch out for her brother. There was a boy a grade ahead of Marc at their bus stop who used to make fun of him, copying the way he said words like "spaghetti" and "list." Lana gave the boy a couple of chances. The first time she said, "Please don't talk to my brother that way." The second time she said, "If you keep doing that, I'll tell our parents." And the third time he did it, she told Mommy and Daddy about it that afternoon, and Mommy called over to the boy's house in the evening, and Daddy snatched the receiver from Mommy's hand and said some stern things into the phone that made Lana feel vindicated, and after that the boy never showed up to their bus stop again but walked two blocks over to the other nearest stop instead. Daddy had a temper and yelled a lot at other people, sometimes even at Mommy, but he never yelled at Lana.

But now they were already at separate schools, and there was only so much Lana could do for Marc. Still, she would miss him. She tried not to think too much about how he might miss her.

"Don't you want to go in the water, sweetie?" Daddy asked. "C'mon, I'll walk with you."

Reluctantly, she got up. She kept her coat on. Daddy padded ahead of her, running with a whoop into an oncoming wave. Lana stood on the wet sand and let the water lick her toes. A little girl in a pink swimsuit was giving her a funny look. It was nice to feel the water against her feet, and Lana took a couple of steps into the ocean, until she was immersed to her ankles. The water on her feet was cooling, even as sweat slid down her bare back under the hot black wool. She decided she didn't need to go any farther. She stood, watching her family's heads in the distance bobbing in the water as the waves carried them up and down.

◆　◆　◆

For lunch, Daddy went and bought them hot dogs and french fries from Nathan's. Marc refused to eat the bun, and Mommy had to go fetch a little plastic knife so she could cut the hot dog up for him.

When they were done with lunch, Marc reminded Mommy and Daddy that they had promised to take him to the mirror maze.

"I didn't know they still had those things," Daddy said. "We used to call it a 'fun house.'"

"Can we go now?"

Mommy and Daddy looked at one another.

"Lana?" Mommy said. "How about you take Marc through the maze."

"I don't want to," Lana said. She was very hot beneath the black coat, and it occurred to her that the maze would be inside and maybe air-conditioned, but still, she hadn't liked the look of it on the poster.

"Couldn't you do this one thing for your brother?" Daddy said in the tone of voice that he used when Lana was not being a good big sister. This time she frowned. It was obvious that her parents wanted her to take Marc because neither of them wanted to go themselves.

Beneath the coat, Lana's bare arms and legs were sleek with sweat.

"Okay," she said with a sigh.

Daddy handed Lana some cash, which she put inside the pocket of the big coat.

"You remember where it was?" Daddy asked.

"Don't talk to any strangers," Mommy said.

"Mom," Lana said, thrusting out her lips in a pout. "C'mon." She motioned to Marc to follow her.

They walked back along the crowded boardwalk. Several people blinked at the sight of Lana in the black coat, but she pretended not to notice.

Lana pushed some cash through a small window and was handed two paper tickets, like at an old-fashioned movie theater.

"Go ahead," she told Marc. "This was your idea."

They opened a door, and a bored-looking teenager with acne took their tickets. They were standing in front of a long solid black wall. The teenager reached out and pressed a button, and part of the wall slid back slowly, revealing an entrance to what looked like a long hall of mirrors. "Straight ahead," he chirped.

Marc bounded inside and Lana followed.

From outside it had looked like one long hallway, but now they seemed to be standing in a honeycomb of small diamonds, surrounded by mirrors and arches that were blinking alternately in patterns of red and blue. Behind them the door started to retract back into the mirror. Lana had a sudden feeling of misgiving as the last sliver of door disappeared into the wall. When it closed, it, too, became a mirrored surface so that suddenly they were in a room of infinite reflections. Lana saw herself, looking wild eyed in the dark coat, while beside her, Marc was looking around carefully, but he also seemed hesitant to step forward. This image of the two of them, wide eyed and unsure, was reflected back to them over and over again, the image growing smaller as they gazed down the hallway of mirrors.

"This is so cool," Marc said softly.

Lana turned and knocked her hands against the mirrored panel they had just entered through.

"What are you doing?" Marc asked.

"This was a bad idea," Lana said. "Let us out!"

"But we're supposed to go through the maze. That's the whole point!"

There was no way to open the door from the inside. By the time Lana turned around, Marc had darted ahead into the maze. Lana tried to follow him, but when she stepped forward, she ran into her own reflection.

"Where are you?" she called.

"Right here." She could see Marc only a few steps away from her, but when she tried to get to him, she ran into another wall.

"Which way?"

Suddenly Marc took another step, and all his reflections disappeared. "Marc? Where did you go?"

"I'm right here. Can't you see me? I can see you."

"You disappeared."

Now in the blinking lights, it looked to Lana as if she were the only person in the maze. Her reflection blinked back at her all down the long mirrored corridor that she now knew was not a corridor but just an effect of the mirrors. Beneath her coat, her bare skin felt freezing in the overly air-conditioned space. She saw herself swallow, and the length of other Lanas swallowed, too, all down the line. In her black coat with her pale skin and dark hair, it occurred to her suddenly that she was dressed like Him, that she looked like Him.

Lana.

She shut her eyes and shook her head. "No," she whispered. "Not here."

She could feel Him behind her, and she was afraid to open her eyes and see His infinite reflection in the mirrors.

"Lana?" It was a different voice, Marc's voice, quieter now. "Lana, I'm scared."

Lana? Open your eyes.

She shook her head, and a tear squeezed from her shut eyes and rolled down her cheek.

"Lana! I want to get out!"

Look, Lana. Look at yourself. Look at me.

"Lana!" She could hear Marc crying. To find him, she'd have to open her eyes; she'd have to look at Him. But if she saw Him like this, here, then something would change; it would mean something, though she did not know what, some point of no return. She took a deep, shaky breath and began to weep silently.

Lana, open your eyes.

"Lana!"

She had no choice. Marc was her little brother, and it was her job to save him.

She opened her eyes. Where she should have been standing, she saw Him, his long, thin body, his dark coat, his pale blank white face, in front of her and reflected back and forth, growing ever smaller, infinitely and infinitely smaller. There was a crash in her head as if someone had just hit a gong or a drum, and she leaped toward the sound of Marc's voice, hitting her forehead hard on the glass. She spun around and took another step, and He followed her in the mirror. Then she took another step, and then she could see Marc again, and she used everything she had to look only at the image of Marc, not at Him. After she bumped into another mirror, she took one more step, and Marc was beside her in real life. He threw himself at her and put his arms around her waist.

"I want to go home," he whined.

With Him behind her in the mirror and Marc around her waist, Lana plowed through into the next compartment. Suddenly there was a black curtain. She waved her hand through what looked like open space and found it was open, an exit.

They emerged back into the same room they had entered through only a few minutes before. The same teenager with the pimples looked up. Lana was standing in the black coat with tears streaming down her face, Marc latched on to her, his head buried in her side.

"Oh yeah, sorry," the teenager said, shrugging. "That happens sometimes."

Outside, Lana and Marc leaned against the brick wall of the storefront, catching their breath.

Lana's eyes were closed again, and she was breathing carefully, in and out. It wasn't so bad, she told herself. Nothing so bad had happened.

"Do we have to tell Mommy and Daddy?" Marc asked.

She shook her head and turned to tell him that they could pretend that this hadn't happened, that they hadn't gotten scared in the mirror maze, but when she opened her eyes, she knew instantly that something was wrong. The throng of people walking down the boardwalk were faceless—or rather, where their faces should have been, there were only patches of color, as if someone had smeared wet paint. Again she heard that horrible sound in her head, like a gong being struck with a mallet. Before she could stop herself, she turned and saw that Marc's face, too, was gone; where his face should have been was just a pale smudge, the features wiped clean. This was it, what the mirror, what He had taken from her.

"Are you okay?" the Marc-shaped smudge asked. "C'mon, I want to go for one more swim."

A family passed them, a mother, father, and two little girls—she could tell from the way they were dressed, but their faces were just a blur of flesh. A young woman passed, wearing a floral-patterned dress. A group of teenage boys, shirtless, their bathing suits still dripping. A man selling cotton candy on sticks. All of them with their features blurred like smashed lumps of clay.

Lana cast her eyes toward the ground. Very clearly, she could see both of their feet in their sandals, their toes brushed with sand.

"I'm fine," she said, and she forced the foot to move forward.

VII

2017

Two days after being fired, Maddie finds papers left for her on the counter, presumably from Steve, two articles printed from the internet. The first is called "Resumé Basics" and the second "Top Ten Most Common Job Interview Questions." She glances at them, tosses them back onto the counter, and makes herself a cup of coffee. It's almost noon, and she has the house to herself for another few hours before Steve and her mother get home from work.

She checks the private group, but there are still no new posts. She reads back over the recent posts and WorshipHIM36's reply to her message and feels again a small well of panic in the pit of her stomach. At least the group hasn't set any specifics—no time, no location, no specific victim. If they do, she is thinking that maybe she could send an anonymous tip to the nearest police station, warning them when and where to find the group.

She hesitates a moment and then pulls out the drawer in the kitchen where her mother keeps some of her loose papers. Underneath a stack of tax returns, she finds her mother's old brown address book, the one she used to rely on before all her contacts went digital. Maddie sits on the couch with the TV on, flipping through the yellowed pages of the book with its cracked faux-leather cover. Finally she comes across an entry for Robert Kaplan. In parentheses next to the name, Mom has written "Dorothy's estate."

She locates the lawyer's email address online and composes a message. The lawyer responds first thing the next morning, and she makes an appointment to see him at his office. He signs his message "Bob."

That evening, Steve hands her an application for a job at Wendy's.

"They're just down the street," he chirps. He hasn't said anything to her directly about her losing the job at the Green Thumb. At dinner, he tells her there are lots of résumé templates online that she should look up.

Maddie nods, chews her meat, and leaves the table as soon as she can. She puts all the papers on the small, unused desk in the corner of the blue room. Whenever she looks at them, her stomach sinks. This is her future: slinging burgers at a fast-food place—until the boss finds out about her, and they fire her again.

Two days later, after Mom and Steve have left for work, she takes the bus across town. She has to transfer twice and then walk almost a mile on the side of the road past a supermarket and several small outlet shopping centers. The building is an old brick colonial that has been converted into offices. Even though she's on time, she still has to wait forty-five minutes in the cramped waiting room. A radiator hisses quietly in the corner.

When Bob emerges from his office at last, he seems to be trying to shoo out a very pregnant woman who's crying and holding a crumpled tissue near her face. "We'll be in touch," he tells her as she heads for the door. "Right," he says, turning toward Maddie. "Ms. Thompson?"

He motions her into his office, an undersize room that barely has space for a large desk and chairs on either side. The desk is heaped with folders. Bob himself is a middle-aged man with a mustache. He is wearing a tie, but the tie has a small yellow stain on it, maybe mustard.

Bob begins to open drawers in the desk, as if looking for something. "It's here somewhere," he says. "Right. Here we are."

He removes a crinkled Burger King bag to make space on the desk and places a small box and a stack of papers in front of him.

"I'm so glad you got in touch. We've been holding on to these for a while. So," he says, running a thick hand down the page in front of him, "'Dorothy Halloway bequeaths to Madeline Thompson this'"—he motions to the box—"'pearl necklace and the sum total of her savings account,' which came to $3,811.36 at the time of her death and, minus legal fees, is $2,636.15. So if you could sign here and here to show receipt."

He pushes a paper across the desk to her, pushing piles of paper out of the way.

"She left me money?" Maddie says, trying to suppress a smile.

"She left you all her money," he says. "I mean, obviously there wasn't much of it. She really only had social security at the end."

Maddie stares at him.

"I am going to need you to sign this to show receipt of the items," Bob repeats.

Maddie picks up the pen and forces her hand to move across the page.

Bob clears his throat. He brings a hand up and tugs at his nose. "She was a sweet gal," he says, "your grandmother." Maddie widens her eyes, skeptical. "Well, 'formidable' may be a better word. She was worried about you. She said she wanted you to have something when you got out, something to start over with." He pushes the small box and the check across the desk to her. "Good luck."

Maddie puts a hand on top of the items and stands up. She hesitates. Then she starts to cry.

Bob sighs and reaches for the box of tissues that he keeps on his desk.

"Yes," he says. "Well, yes."

Gran went suddenly one night, not long after the trial, of a heart attack. Mom never said it was her fault—that the stress of what she and Lana had done, of having her only grandchild locked away for the next twenty years, had contributed to Gran's death. She didn't have to.

Maddie blows her nose and, trying to keep her voice steady, asks, "Did she say anything else about me?"

"She wasn't a very talkative person in general."

"But why did she leave me her stuff?"

Bob looks at her with pity in his eyes and shrugs. "Well, you were her only grandchild. I'm sure she loved you."

Maddie nods. She takes one more tissue from the box and blows her nose. "Thank you," she says, picking up the items from the desk. She stumbles through the waiting room and out the door, blinking in the pale autumn sun.

On the bus ride home, she clutches the small jewelry box and the check in her hand. She could easily make a run for it with that amount of money. It's enough for a fresh start. She's used to roughing it; she could work at a diner or a fast-food joint anywhere in the country, clean people's houses maybe, get paid in cash. Somewhere where the cost of living is cheaper. Change her name, figure out how to get by without a real social security number. People do it. She imagines her quiet little life, an apartment of her own. If she gets lonely, she'll adopt a dog or a cat. She could take herself to the bank right now, then to the Greyhound station. She could do it today.

When she gets off the bus, she deposits the check at an ATM. Of course she won't be able to withdraw the money until the check has processed. She waits a long time for the next bus, the one that takes her to the stop nearest Mom and Steve's neighborhood, and walks slowly back to the house.

At home, she checks the group chat and discovers there's been a flurry of posts over the last couple of hours.

Follower_in_the_Distance: I think it's time to nail down specifics. I propose that we meet at the original location, in the woods where the girls made their first attempt. It may be a trek for some of us, but I

know I am more than willing to drive down from PA
for something this big

User89274: Totally agree on location, but we still
need a sacrifice

Fungible_Tokens57: So a little kidnapping and murder? Ouch, guys

PraiseSatan69: OK so which one of us is going to
suggest an actual target?

Reading the exchange, Maddie shivers. Of course there is no Him,
but when she reads the Followers' posts, she can't help but feel that He
is somehow nearby. Maybe He exists after all, she thinks, just not in the
way that she and Lana thought.

Maddie checks the site obsessively the rest of the afternoon, but
that last essential question remains unanswered.

1

For her day at the pool with Maddie, Sage wore the new green cover-up that her mother had bought for her on one of their excursions to the mall near Aunt Kate's house in California. It was made of a sheer fabric through which the outline of her body was clearly visible. She had stood in front of the full-length mirror in Mom and Dad's room for some time that morning examining her reflection before she left the house.

Maddie was wearing the same orange swimsuit she had worn on their trip to Wild World, the one with the funny ruffle on her bottom that looked like it was for a younger girl. It was a little incongruous on Maddie, with her large chest and hips, but Sage could tell that Maddie already felt self-conscious about her body, so Sage said only encouraging things, to try to make her feel better.

When they first arrived, Sage stripped off the green cover-up, applied sunscreen until her skin shone (she had used one of her mother's razors to shave her legs that morning so they were smooth and glossy), and stretched out on one of the long reclining chairs.

"Do you want to go in the water?" Maddie asked.

"I wouldn't mind sunbathing for a bit," Sage said.

"Oh," Maddie said. She hesitated, then lay down on a lounger next to Sage.

"That's Ethan, right?" Sage asked. She jerked her head toward the other side of the pool, where a tanned boy about their age was dunking a younger boy's head into the water while the boy shrieked. This continued for several seconds until the lifeguard blew her whistle at them and shouted something. Ethan let go of the boy, gave the guard a puzzled look of feigned innocence, and swam off.

"Yeah," Maddie said. "Ethan Walsh." Sage noticed that Maddie blushed when she said his name.

"He's older, right?"

"A year ahead."

"He's cute. Is he popular?"

Maddie shrugged. "I mean, I guess so."

Ethan's body sliced cleanly through the water, moving toward the deep end. "He's a good swimmer. Is he on the swim team?"

Maddie shrugged and didn't answer. Sage decided to change the subject.

"So did you and Lana have a fight?"

"Kinda."

She was surprised when she realized it was just going to be her and Maddie at the pool, without Lana. Maddie had made such a fuss about hiding their trip to Wild World from Lana, and now she was openly hanging out with just Sage, in front of everyone.

"Do you want to talk about it?"

"Not really. She's just been acting a little strange recently."

"She's really intense," Sage said. "Why did she call you by that other name that one time?"

"It's just a game we play sometimes. Pretending we're other people. I mean, we're kind of getting too old for it, I guess."

Sage nodded. She was trying to think of something else to say about Lana when she heard a shout and something wet smacked her in the face. Sage reeled her head back, her nose and forehead smarting.

"Oh my God. Are you okay?" Maddie was standing over her, looking concerned. In her hands she was holding a large blow-up beach ball.

"Hey, sorry! Sorry!"

Ethan Walsh was now standing over them. Water dripped from his brown shoulders and blue swim trunks. Sage's annoyance disappeared.

"Sorry," Ethan said again. "My brother Andy has really bad aim. Sage, isn't it?"

Sage nodded and brought a hand up to her nose. She was worried that it was red and that Ethan would think that was how her face usually looked.

"She's moved into the Cranes' old house," Maddie said. It sounded like she had a frog in her throat, and she was blushing bright red again.

"You sure you're okay?" Ethan asked, looking only at Sage. "I can get some ice from the lifeguard if you need it."

"We're okay," Maddie said before Sage could answer.

"Okay," Ethan said. "See you girls around." He smiled, and the smile lit up his whole face. He turned and pattered back toward the pool.

"Why did you say that?" Sage asked.

"Say what?"

"If a boy asks if he can do something for you, you should let him," Sage said. "Is my face red?"

"It's not too bad. You really want to hang out with Ethan Walsh?"

Sage shrugged. "Why not? He seems nice."

"He's not nice," Maddie said. "He's popular."

"Being popular doesn't mean you can't be nice. Popular kids are just the ones with good social skills."

Maddie frowned and looked down into her lap. It occurred to Sage that she and Maddie would probably not be friends anymore once school started, and she was fine with that. Once she was back at school, she'd be able to find her people again, not just be stuck with the weird girls who happened to live on her street.

Turning her head, Sage scanned the pool. She quickly found Ethan, wading in the shallow end. He caught her gaze and held it, just for a moment. When it happened again a few minutes later, he gave her a small smile. He swam a few laps across the pool, and this time when he looked over and found her still watching, he shrugged his shoulders, whispered something to the people he was with, and crossed to the stairs. She thought maybe he was going to come back to talk to her, but instead he shot a glance over his shoulder and walked toward the small building where the bathrooms were. He looked back up at her once and raised his eyes; when he saw that she was still watching, he turned and, instead of entering the pool house, walked around the back.

"I have to go to the bathroom," Sage said. "I'll be right back."

Her heart was beating in her ears as she walked toward the pool house. She thought she understood what he wanted her to do, but what if she was wrong? What if that was just where the kids went to smoke, and she'd have to pretend to be lost on her way to the bathroom?

When she turned the corner, he was there. "Hey!" he said. "Okay. So you're here." She stepped toward him, out of sight of everyone else. Ethan seemed suddenly shy. He blushed. "Do you want to, like, kiss or whatever?"

Sage swallowed. She stepped closer, until she was standing in front of Ethan. It turned out that they were the exact same height. He was wet and smelled of chlorine, while she was completely dry. Hesitantly, he brought his lips close to hers. At first, he kissed her with his lips closed, but then he slowly pushed them open with his tongue. But instead of his tongue darting in and out like Lucas Morales's, he searched until he found hers and their tongues moved back and forth in each other's mouths as if they were dancing. He put a damp hand lightly on her shoulder, and Sage stepped a little closer.

For several minutes the world dropped away and there was just this strange dance of tongues. Ethan moved his hands so they were clasped around the back of her head, as if holding her in place. She then felt his hands move gently back to her shoulders, where they rested for a few moments before they started to exert a slow pressure. He pulled his mouth away from hers, and she felt herself being pressed down, toward the unkempt patch of grass littered with cigarette butts. She wasn't sure what was happening until her knees were in the grass and Ethan was taking his penis out of his swimsuit. It was large, the skin taut, so different from Cody's little tail dangling between his legs on the way to the bathroom.

She and Charlie had prepared for this moment, practicing on bananas stolen from the kitchen counter, but she had not expected it to happen so suddenly. She hesitated only a moment, and then his dick was in her mouth. It surprised her, how hard it was, how it tasted like chlorine.

2

Maddie waited ten minutes before she went to check on Sage. In the dim bathroom whose concrete floors were always covered in a cold inch of water, she found no one, not even when she bent down to check for feet in the stalls. Exiting the bathroom, she looked all around the pool, but still didn't see her. She even walked back out to the parking lot, thinking that maybe Sage had left without her, but her bike was still there.

She checked the bathroom again, and then, because there was nowhere else to look, she walked around to check the little grassy spot behind the bathroom where the teenagers sometimes went to smoke.

Ethan was leaning against the wall, with his swimsuit down around his ankles, and Sage was kneeling in front of him. The skin that should have been covered by Ethan's swimsuit was shockingly pale. His penis was standing straight out in Sage's hand, and she was running her tongue over it. They were so involved in what they were doing that neither of them noticed her.

She turned and ran, then retrieved her bag from next to the chairs. The lifeguard blew the whistle at her. "No running around the pool!" Maddie slowed her pace just a little and then speed-walked out the entrance to her bike. It took her a few fumbling seconds to undo the bike lock, and then she swung her leg over and took off, pedaling as fast as she could.

Her heart thumped as she worked the pedals, pushing her way up the slight incline back toward their street. Tears formed in the corners of her eyes.

How could she have been so stupid, to think that Sage could be her new best friend? Nobody will ever love you, she thought as the hot air brushed against her face. No one will ever love you. Except Lana.

She had started to think everything might be okay. It had been days since she'd told Lana in the woods that she wouldn't help her, and she hadn't seen Him once, not even at night, when she slept with her head under the pillow, clamped down tight over her eyes and her ears.

Was Sage Ethan's new girlfriend now? Would she have to see the two of them holding hands in the halls when school started again in a couple of weeks? She couldn't do it, couldn't go back there for another year, couldn't suffer the humiliation of watching Sage leave her behind, Sage holding Ethan's hand, Sage kissing Ethan, kissing his—

What a filthy slut Sage had turned out to be.

You're so ugly you should kill yourself, Amelia Lawrence had written on Maddie's Facebook wall.

But Maddie wasn't going to do that. She would never do that. If she had to choose, she would choose herself, every time. If she had to choose between Sage and herself, she would choose herself. If she had to choose between Sage and Lana, she would choose Lana. But choosing Lana also meant choosing Him. Lana would insist. But then, Maddie thought as she crested up the hill toward their street, what did she really have to lose? Did she want to keep living with Mom and Gran in their sad little house, to hear Sharon talk about wedding planning, to go back to middle school in the fall so the other girls could tell her again how she didn't deserve to live? Or did she want to run away with Lana and Him, to that house on the Eastern Shore? If she did what Lana asked, maybe she could finally be free.

3

Lana had spent most of that morning filling more pages in the purple notebook. She drew several pictures of the farmhouse they would live in with Him, once Maddie changed her mind. It was a two-story wooden colonial with blue shutters and a wraparound porch, surrounded by fields of gently waving long grass. In the evenings, they would sit out on that porch, the three of them, Lana, Maddie, and Him, listening to the crickets chirping, marveling at their own daring, enjoying the peace of having escaped from the rest of the world. Somehow no one would ever find them there. Maddie was always asking if He would have magic powers, and Lana didn't know, but she felt sure that once He had crossed over, they would be protected somehow from everything, that His protection would be like a magic blanket nestled around them, keeping them safe. The drawings helped calm her.

Ever since the mirror maze, she'd needed to feel calm. She had waited, hoping that people's faces would go back to normal, but they had not. She had started to avoid looking at faces, looked always at the ground or at the space right next to the person's head, so as not to see that horrible smear in place of facial features, everything that made someone unique just smudged away.

The doorbell didn't startle her, but when she saw Maddie's face, distorted through the thick window glass, she prepared herself as she opened the door. Instead, to her surprise, Maddie's face looked normal, except that she was clearly near tears, her hair a mess, the orange bands of her swimsuit visible near the neck of her T-shirt. Instead of inviting her in, Lana slipped out the door and wordlessly led Maddie around to the back deck.

Lana sat down in one of the chairs around the table, and Maddie perched across from her. Maddie seemed to be waiting for Lana to ask what was wrong, but Maddie was the one who had walked out on her, and it was not Lana's job to make her feel better about it.

"So?" Lana said finally, the single syllable an invitation for Maddie to speak. Maddie told her, haltingly, about her latest betrayal. Sage again, at the pool. Lana rolled her eyes, but when Maddie came to the end of the story, Lana leaned forward in her seat, her eyes widening. Maddie could barely get out the words.

Lana gasped. "She did what? That's disgusting."

Lana had guessed a long time ago that Maddie had some sort of crush on Ethan, hence the tears, though she'd never understood why Maddie was trying to guard it like some sort of secret.

"So now you know," Lana said. "She's not one of us. She's not really your friend."

Maddie nodded and wiped a long line of snot against the back of her bare arm. "Do you forgive me?"

Lana looked at her carefully. "I don't know. You haven't really said you're sorry."

"I'm sorry," Maddie said. "For trying to be friends with her behind your back."

Lana nodded. "But what about the other part of it? The sacrifice?"

Maddie breathed out slowly. "I mean, she's not really the person I thought she was."

"Maddie," Lana said, speaking slowly as if to a young child. "This isn't about whether Sage is a good person or not. It's about Him. But if this makes it easier for you, then I guess that's okay."

"I just—are you sure we have to do it?"

"I'm sure. You know. You saw Him yourself."

Maddie nodded. "I mean, I'm pretty sure it was Him. I don't know what else it could have been."

Lana leaned back in her chair and heaved a sigh. "I thought I could trust you. I've told you everything. I thought you were my best friend."

"I am your best friend."

"No, you're not! You wanted Sage to be your new best friend, but now that she's turned out to be a big slut, you come crawling back to me. And I've told you exactly what we need to do to get away, to be best friends forever, and you won't even do it."

"We'd be best friends forever?"

"Yeah, that's the whole point. We'll be together, just the two of us, and He'll be there protecting us. We won't have to go back to school ever again. You won't have to go to your dad and Sharon's wedding. We won't need other people. There won't be any grown-ups. It'll be just the three of us in the house. There won't be any boys to fight over or anything stupid like that."

"But He'll be there."

"Well, yeah."

"What if we get caught?"

"We won't. I already have a plan. We take off for the Eastern Shore right after, and nobody will know where we went. And once we do it, He'll be there, to help us."

"I just, I don't know if I can do it."

"That's why we have to help each other."

Maddie wiped her eyes again. She inhaled deeply, trying to clear the snot out of her nose, and Lana could tell that she was getting through to her.

"I've been drawing pictures," Lana said, "of what the house will look like. Where we'll live with Him. Do you want to see?"

Maddie nodded, and Lana stood up to lead them back inside. She suddenly felt very peaceful, felt sure that she could manage Maddie and all her doubts and fears. Though she couldn't see or hear Him at that moment, she knew He was there with them, that He was watching over her, helping her every little bit along the way.

4

She didn't look any different, but she did feel different—older, more mature.

But for some reason at dinner that night, Sage couldn't stop herself from giggling. She was annoying, even to herself. She kept kicking Cody's ankles under the table until he whined, "Sage, stop!" She did it again, and Mom told her to cut it out in her angriest voice. Sage shrugged.

After dinner she went online. There was a green dot next to Charlie's name indicating she was online, and Sage messaged her right away, but Charlie didn't answer. Sage sat in front of the computer for a half hour, looking at that dot and waiting for Charlie.

While she was waiting, Maddie's name appeared.

Sagenewman31: Hey what happened

I_love_Spock8: What happened to u? i looked everywhere

Sage heaved out a sigh of relief. Maddie didn't know.

Sagenewman31: Weird. i was in the bathroom. When i came out u were gone

I_love_Spock8: its ok. Sorry we missed each other

I_love_Spock8: Hey do u want to come to a sleepover at lanas house this Fri

Sagenewman31: I thought u guys were in a fight

I_love_Spock8: we made up

I_love_Spock8: u should come

I_love_Spock8: it will be lots of fun

By bedtime, Sage had knots in her stomach. When she followed Ethan behind the pool house, she'd thought they were going to kiss. She hadn't meant for it to go that far, not with some boy she barely knew. What if he told his friends? What if she arrived at school that fall with a reputation, as one of *those* girls? She still had a couple of weeks of summer to get through, time to wait to find out if Ethan would tell anyone. Maybe she should try to find him, try to talk to him? What if he didn't want to see her again? What if he did?

She remembered Maddie's invitation, to the sleepover at Lana's. Even though she didn't have much in common with them, she should probably go anyway. Depending on how things went, Maddie and Lana could end up being her only friends. They were probably pretty disconnected from the neighborhood gossip, but still, they might have heard something. If things went really well, maybe she'd even tell them about Ethan, though it probably wasn't a good idea. She remembered the video Lana had made them watch, the porn on her dad's computer, how the girls had called it gross. No, she thought, Lana and Maddie weren't ready for that sort of thing. They weren't as grown up as she was. Still, she always enjoyed a good sleepover.

5

Maddie did it. She'd invited Sage to the party, just like Lana had told her to. It was easier, letting Lana be in charge again. Sometimes you had to make a choice, between two people, two potential friends. If she thought about it like something that had already happened, a decision already made, then it didn't feel so bad; then it was just something that had already happened, out of her control.

The lamp was on, but even so she was hiding her head under her comforter, just in case. Sometimes she heard small noises in the house, creaks and groans that almost resolved themselves into human speech. It was possible that it was Him, that He was there now, watching her. Lana would say that He was always there. But Maddie didn't want Him to speak to her, to appear to her the way that He did to Lana. If she did what Lana had said, then it would all be over. If she did what Lana wanted, then she wouldn't have to be afraid anymore, afraid of Him or the future. She and Lana would be protected somehow. Safe. They would both be safe.

VIII

2017

It's Saturday night, and Maddie is sitting in front of a blank résumé template in Steve's office. It's been three days since PraiseSatan69 posed the question on the site, and no one has answered. She checks it multiple times a day. It's possible that the group still won't follow through after all, that it's all talk. But what will she do if it isn't? Her best plan is still an anonymous call to the police made from a phone booth somewhere, if she can find one.

She picks up her phone and checks the site. No new responses.

Turning back to the monitor, she types her name at the top of the document: Madeline Thompson.

The first step, filling in her name, should be the easiest, but it's the biggest problem. People don't remember her and Lana's names as much as they remember their crime. Even on the Followers site, people seem to barely know their names, and hers especially is an afterthought—there's Lana and that other girl. Still, it seems impossible to put her name in large letters at the top of a piece of paper asking someone to hire her. Certainly there are enough people around here who still remember, for whom the name will sound familiar, familiar enough that they might search for her online—and there it all is.

She sighs. The room smells like Steve—a combination of aftershave and something else, something sweet. It was Steve who offered to let her use his computer, after he'd asked her about her résumé for the umpteenth time. It's the first time he's allowed her into his office, and perhaps it's a sign that their trust in her has grown, or at least that they no longer fear her as much as they once did. A set of dull knives has found its way back into the cutlery drawer in the kitchen, and sometimes a single, small paring knife has been left on the counter when she does the washing up.

The space beneath her name, after the phone number and address, is also empty, though it would be easy enough to fill in. She doesn't have the name of the local high school to put under the Education heading, only her GED, which will invite an explanation. She took some additional enrichment courses at Needmore, but if she lists them, she will also have to put down the name of the hospital, and there it will be at the top of her résumé: Needmore Mental Health Center. Under Job History, she has only the four weeks she worked at the Green Thumb. Cindy said she could list her as a reference, but anyone will inevitably ask why she worked there for such a short period of time, and what can she say, other than the truth?

Her phone pings suddenly on the desk, and she startles.

How about that drink? R u free now?

Gabriela has sent a message to her and another number that must be Omar's. Maddie stares at the text. She'd forgotten about Gabriela's offer. A few seconds later, the phone buzzes again, and the other number responds: I'm in! Where?

Clarion, Gabriela responds.

Maddie knows the place, a trendy-looking bar that she's passed a few times on the way to the mall with Mom.

She hesitates. She should just sit tight, work on her résumé, and keep checking the private chat, just in case. But the site has been silent for days. And this could be her last chance to see Omar.

She starts typing, deleting several times before she presses send.

I'd love to but I don't have a car

A longer pause, then another buzz, another text from Gabriela: No prob. I'll pick u up. Whats ur address?

Maddie takes a deep breath. A couple of weeks ago, when she was feeling good about the Green Thumb and her first job, she had Mom take her to Target, where she'd bought a couple of what she hoped were cute tops. She was pleased to see that, between the exercise at work and the bland cooking at the house, she'd already gone down a size since she'd gotten out. Now she selects the better fitted of the two shirts, a yellow button-down with short sleeves. She pairs it with jeans and her dirty sneakers, wishing she'd thought to buy a nicer pair of shoes. Over the top of the yellow blouse, she puts on her green army sweatshirt. She'd like to put on some makeup, but she doesn't own any, and she doesn't actually know how to put on makeup anyway. She'll have to go as she is.

She waits by the window, peeking out at the driveway. When she sees a car pull in, she walks down the stairs. Mom and Steve are watching a movie on TV.

"I'm going out," Maddie says. "A friend is picking me up."

Mom sits up, her mouth open in surprise. "But—where are you going? When will you be back?"

"A couple hours," Maddie says, and she walks out the door before Mom can say anything else.

Outside, the air is brisk. Maddie opens the passenger-side door of what looks like a new Toyota Corolla.

"Hi," she says, sitting down. "Thanks for the ride."

"Hey. Yeah, I forgot you don't have a car."

In the moment before Maddie shuts the door and the dome light flickers off, she catches a glimpse of Gabriela, wearing a sparkly top, tight black pants, black leather boots. Her makeup, as always, is immaculate. Her fingers, resting against the steering wheel, boast freshly manicured nails. Maddie clears her throat and draws her sweatshirt over her yellow blouse, which she now sees is cheap casual wear and not a going-out top at all.

Gabriela backs the car out. "Is this your parents' house?"

"Yeah. Well, my mom and stepfather's. Is this your car? It's nice."

"Took me two years of working at the Green Thumb and at Mike's to save up for this."

"What's Mike's?"

"It's the restaurant I work at. I'm a server."

Gabriela is a fast driver, speeding down the quiet residential street. She slows down at a stop sign and then lunges out onto the main thoroughfare.

"Is it hard to get a restaurant job?"

"Depends on whether or not you have experience. But that's the problem with anything. You gotta break in. I started as a hostess, and I worked my way up."

"Right."

"If you're interested in a server job, I would try to get a hostess or kitchen job. The money's not as good, but you get your foot in the door, and if you can impress them, you can move up."

"That makes sense."

"I live over that way," Gabriela says, motioning with her hand at the turnoff toward Maddie's old neighborhood. She swallows.

"Have you lived there long?"

"No, just a couple years."

The old neighborhood is much closer than she realized to Mom and Steve's house. Her mother only managed to move a few miles away. Maddie would have moved farther, to give herself a wider margin between her past and present. But maybe it's foolish to think that leaving the past behind could be as simple as changing your physical location.

She feels a twinge of guilt and slips her phone out of her pocket. She checks the Followers site: no new posts.

Gabriela is looking straight ahead at the road. By the time she pulls into the parking lot of the shopping center, the silence has stretched on long enough to become uncomfortable.

"Thanks so much for the ride," Maddie repeats as she climbs out of the car.

"Uh-huh."

Gabriela's heels click on the pavement as they approach the bar. Music is blasting from inside, and people spill out from the doorway and onto the sidewalk. A line for entering stretches down the sidewalk in the other direction.

"Oh, I am not in the mood for this tonight," Gabriela says, slipping her phone out of her bag and starting to text. "I just really hate when it gets this crowded. We won't be able to hear each other, you know?"

A second later her phone rings, and Gabriela brings it swiftly to her ear. "Yeah," she says into the phone. "Well, we're out front now and it's crazy. There's a really long line. Yeah, I did, but I've never tried to come here on a Saturday. What? Where's that? Yeah, we can try it, I guess."

She hangs up and looks at Maddie. "C'mon, we're going to try a place down the road that Omar knows." Maddie follows meekly.

Gabriela drives half a mile down the road, then turns off into a tiny lot. There's a small square-shaped building and a single lamp lighting the parking lot.

"Huh, well, we'll see about this," she says.

Inside, a bar runs the length of the far wall, with a couple of men seated there. There are four small tables, all of them empty except for the one in the far corner, where Omar is waiting for them. The floor is sticky under Maddie's sneakers.

"Hey!" Omar says.

"This is a nice place you picked out," Gabriela says.

Omar shrugs. "You were the one who wanted to be able to hear yourself think."

"Yeah, fair enough." Gabriela takes off her coat, revealing the low cut of her sparkling top, and drapes it over the back of her chair.

Maddie, who is pretty sure she has already sweated through the armpits of the yellow shirt, keeps her sweatshirt on as she sits down.

"Hi, Maddie," Omar says.

"Hi!" Maddie beams at him, blushing. Omar is dressed the same way he dresses for work at the Green Thumb, in a T-shirt and jeans, but he's taken his sweatshirt off. One thin muscular arm rests on the table next to a beer; the other hangs at his side. He smiles back.

"Let's get drinks," Gabriela says to Maddie.

They approach the bar together, and Gabriela motions for Maddie to order.

"Um, what are you having?"

"Vodka tonic," Gabriela tells the bartender. He's an older white man with a bald head and a thin, hungry-looking face.

"I'll have that too," Maddie says.

"See some ID?" the bartender says.

Gabriela reaches into her handbag, and Maddie slips her new learner's permit out of her back pocket, the one that she spent her whole day off waiting for at the DMV two weeks ago, when she still had a job. The bartender glances at Gabriela's license and hands it back quickly. He takes longer with Maddie's, his eyes flickering back and forth between her and her picture.

"Madeline Thompson," he says. "You're old to only have a learner's, aren't you?"

Maddie stammers to reply.

"How is that your business?" Gabriela snaps. "You getting us our drinks or what?"

After they pay, they troop back to the table.

"The bartender's kind of a creep," Gabriela says, settling into her chair. "He was giving Maddie a hard time about only having her learner's permit."

Omar shrugged. "Hey, I've never actually been here before, okay? I'd just seen it from the road. We don't have to stay."

Gabriela takes a sip of her drink. "Not bad," she says. "A lot cheaper than Clarion."

"You girls with your fancy cocktails," Omar says.

"Nothing fancy," Gabriela says. "Just vodka tonics."

Maddie has never drunk alcohol before. She takes a sip of the vodka tonic and struggles not to gag. Once she swallows, she rather likes the smooth burn of it down her throat. Her stomach hasn't been right ever since she ran into Mrs. Newman at the Green Thumb, and the only thing she's eaten all day is a handful of Cheerios. She takes another sip.

A large mirror hangs behind the bar, and for a moment Maddie gets a glimpse of the three of them, seated at the table. She sees herself, heavyset, her back slumped, in her wrinkled jeans and ratty sweatshirt, and then she sees Gabriela, literally sparkling next to her. She takes another sip of the vodka.

"How have you managed to get away with just a learner's?" Omar asks Maddie. "Most kids around here get their license on their sixteenth birthday. I know I did."

"Well," Maddie says. "Um, I guess I just have anxiety, like a phobia?" The lie slips out easily.

"A driving phobia?" Omar asks.

"I didn't know that was a thing," Gabriela says. "I mean, I guess people can be anxious about whatever, so."

"Yeah, it's just taken me a while to get over it," Maddie says. "I've even seen a psychiatrist." She glances at Omar.

"Yeah, okay, well, it's good to get help."

"What's the treatment for that?" Gabriela asks.

"Um." Maddie's head feels foggy, not unlike how it used to feel when the Seroquel kicked in.

"You don't have to answer—I was just curious."

Maddie wonders whether this is how Lana felt when she was being interrogated by the police, when she told them those lies. Maddie heard the tapes in court, Lana's voice, dreamy and high pitched, answering the officer's questions. "Whose idea was it to hurt Sage?"

"Maddie's, I think."

"Why did she want to hurt Sage?"

"There was this man, this man that Maddie knew? He doesn't have a name. We just call him Him. He told her we had to kill Sage."

"And who got the knife?"

"Maddie."

In her interrogation, Maddie had told the truth. She told the police about Him, about how Lana spoke to Him and how Maddie didn't believe in Him until that day at Wild World.

In the end, everyone saw through Lana's lies. All the physical evidence was against her: the knife was from her house, her prints were all over it, the blood was all over her clothes. But that didn't do much to make Maddie feel better; it didn't diminish the gut punch of betrayal that day in the courtroom, when she realized she'd never really known Lana at all.

Ultimately, though, Lana's betrayal just made it easier, over the course of the intervening years, to blame it all on her, to tell herself that Lana was the one who was calling the shots, that Maddie had been helpless in the face of Lana's will, in the face of her illness. She had thought of herself for a long time as a passive pawn on Lana's chessboard, but of course that had never been true. She had always herself been a creature of want, a desperate open mouth clamoring for more, more, more. She had always known, deep down, what she was doing. Lana wouldn't have been able to do it without her; she was sure of that. She needed her encouragement, her partnership, her witness. Yes, Maddie had believed in Him. Yes, she had been afraid. But she still knew it was wrong. Both she and Lana knew it was wrong, and they did it anyway.

"The treatment for anxiety," she says now, her tongue thick in her mouth, "is exposure therapy. Like, they make you imagine driving the car, and then you sit behind the wheel for a while without driving.

That kind of thing." She's making it up, but she thinks it sounds pretty good.

Over at the bar, the bartender is bent in conversation with the two men seated at the end, and they turn and glance at their table. Omar notices it too.

"I hope we aren't going to have any trouble here," he says.

"What?" Gabriela, whose back is to the bar, turns to look. "Why?"

"We're getting some looks from the old guys at the bar," Omar says, dropping his voice.

Gabriela glances over her shoulder again.

"You're being paranoid," she says.

"Sure, tell the black man he's being paranoid."

"Our money is as good as anyone else's," Gabriela says.

"You really know how to work that fiery Latina thing, huh?"

Gabriela's lips turn up in a smile, and a look passes between the two of them, as if they have some special secret. Maddie understands suddenly that she is only here to give Gabriela a chance to have drinks with Omar. Something in her chest swells and bursts.

The edges of the world seem softer, almost aglow. Her heart is pounding the way it does after she wakes up from a nightmare, but nothing so bad has happened. Only that Omar likes Gabriela, not her. Of course she didn't expect anything to actually come out of her stupid little crush. She brings her glass up to her lips, but it is empty. Watery ice cubes, vaguely medicinal, clink against her lips.

The feeling in her chest is familiar. She remembers it suddenly: one day that summer, at the pool with Sage and Ethan. The two of them, behind the pool house. Ethan's pale, naked skin where his swimsuit should have been.

When was that? When did that happen? Certainly that was earlier in the summer, not just before the stabbing. That was not the same day she biked to Lana's, the day she allowed Lana to convince her. Because if it was—

No, she was afraid of Him, that was why she had agreed. Not because she saw Sage with Ethan Walsh. Still, she remembered what a shock it was. Later, in the hospital, the other girls would talk about blow jobs like they were completely normal, but Maddie had been young for her age; sexuality still felt threatening to her, so foreign, so *adult*. No, she didn't decide to go along with Lana because of a stupid crush on Ethan Walsh. She hadn't done what she did over a boy, because if she had—

Gabriela is laughing next to her at something Omar's just said. "I'm going to the bathroom," Maddie says, and she stands up. The world spins slightly off its axis.

The bathroom is off an alcove in the back, a single occupancy. She locks the door and looks at her face in the mirror. Resting her fingers against her cheeks, she notices that her skin feels slightly numb.

She is struggling for breath. I'm not going to cry, she thinks. *Why do you always cry? No one will ever love you,* she says silently to her reflection.

I was a little girl, she thinks, and she splashes water on her face. I didn't understand what I was doing, didn't understand that death was permanent.

Of course you knew that, another voice says. *That was the whole point, wasn't it?* Her body trembles, and a single tear squeezes out of the corner of her eye. Her own ghostly face looks back at her in the dimly lit mirror.

Who are you? What kind of person are you?

She wets a paper towel and wipes at her face, which has turned splotchy and red. Maybe she should tell Gabriela and Omar she's feeling sick and needs to go home, or would that make everything worse? Maybe the polite thing to do is sit there and let them do their flirty thing while she sips a glass of water. That might be best.

She'll go back out, she decides, and have another drink.

When she exits, one of the men from the bar is lingering in the alcove, she assumes waiting for the bathroom. But when she moves to return to the table, he steps in front of her.

"You're Madeline Thompson," he says. His breath is alcoholic. His face is round and sweating. He's large, taller than Maddie, and about as wide. "You stabbed that girl in the woods."

Maddie's brain is working in slow motion from the vodka. The bartender, who saw her ID. Fuck, she thinks.

"They let you out of prison?" the man asks. "When they let you out?" He steps toward her, and she steps back, the open door of the bathroom looming.

"I w-wasn't in prison," she stammers, her voice barely above a whisper. "I was in a mental health center."

"Mental health center?" The man laughs. "Ain't no treatment for evil, am I right?"

Maddie tries to take a step forward, to push past him, but he blocks her, readjusts his weight. He's breathing heavily. She expected this years ago in juvie or in the state hospital. Now here it is at last, in this dark little bar: her real punishment.

"Hey, leave her alone!" It's Gabriela. She's trying to push the man away.

"Get away from them," Omar says, coming up behind Gabriela.

The man wavers, and Maddie pushes past him. Gabriela and Omar follow close behind her. Gabriela grabs her coat off the back of her chair, and the three of them walk quickly toward the door, practically running out into the parking lot.

"Shit," Omar says. "You okay to drive?"

"We're okay," Gabriela says. "You get out of here too."

"Yeah, I am," he says, hopping into his car.

"C'mon!" Gabriela says, motioning to Maddie. Gabriela has already turned the car on and is ready to back out by the time Maddie manages to get herself in the passenger seat. The car shoots out of the lot. Maddie looks toward the front door of the bar, but no one is there.

"Oh my God, that was crazy," Gabriela says.

"Yeah."

"You okay? That guy was so creepy."

"I think he was just really drunk."

"Drunk and rapey," Gabriela says. "Hey, you sure you're okay?"

"Uh-huh." With a single hand, Maddie wipes away tears from both of her eyes. Her legs are trembling.

She's still trying to understand what happened. The man was in front of her. She was finally going to get what she deserved. Then Gabriela and Omar saved her. A mistake: they don't know who she really is.

"When I saw that guy get up from the bar and you weren't back yet, I just had a bad feeling. You know, after what Omar said," Gabriela says, eager to replay the event, to make sense of it.

Maddie nods. Omar thought the men from the bar were racists who didn't like their little mixed group. What else could he think, when he has no idea who she really is, no idea how dangerous Madeline Thompson can be?

Ten minutes later, they pull up in front of Mom and Steve's house. "I'm so sorry," Gabriela says. "That's not how I meant for the evening to go."

Maddie has managed to stop her legs from bouncing up and down, but her hands still feel shaky.

"No, that's okay," she says, her voice surprisingly steady. "It's not your fault."

As she approaches the front door, she notices the lights are dim and the TV is off in the living room, and she thinks that she's been lucky, that they're both already in bed. But when she opens the door, she finds Steve, sitting in his armchair next to a single lamp, one of his large tomes about military history open on his lap. Seeing her, he shuts the book and places it carefully on the side table.

"You weren't out long," he says, looking her over.

Maddie shrugs.

"You out at a bar?"

"Yeah."

Steve sighs and taps his fingers on his knee. "This is disappointing, Madeline. I think I've made it clear how I feel about drinking. I won't have it in this house."

"I'm not drinking in this house."

"Well, I won't have drunkenness in this house either."

"You didn't mention it in your ground rules."

"I thought it went without saying."

"I'm twenty-two. I'm a grown-up, and you can't tell me what to do."

"You're a grown-up living in my house. And yes, I know, I'm not your father either. But your real father isn't here, is he?"

Maddie blinks. They both know it's a low blow.

"I'm going to bed."

"This is your one warning. If you want to live in this house—"

"I don't want to live in this house," Maddie says, and she climbs the stairs.

As soon as she closes the door, she sinks to the floor and takes out her phone. She reads over the most recent exchange again, over the final question.

> **PraiseSatan69:** OK so which one of us is going to suggest an actual target?

It seems suddenly very clear, what she needs to do. She starts to type.

> **Mad_as_a_Hatter22:** Hi, I haven't posted here before. Thank you to Follower_in_the_Distance for admitting me to this group. I am a twenty-two-year-old

female and I believe that I would make a suitable sacrifice. I would be happy to die for the cause of allowing HIM to cross over. Let me know the day and time you are planning and I will be there

After she posts, Maddie sits still. Her stomach feels calm for the first time in several days. She closes her eyes and breathes.

1

The day of the sleepover, Lana was filled with a sense of calm purpose. Mommy told her that she had to help clean the house, and she didn't complain because it was important to do nothing that might make her parents angry and prevent the party from taking place, and also because it was going to be her last day with them.

It wasn't easy to kill another human being. On that point, all the websites agreed. People's survival instincts kick in; there's a rush of adrenaline that shouldn't be underestimated. One website pointed out that it was easier to kill someone in their sleep. That's why Lana had decided on the slumber party. After all, the person was motionless, they couldn't fight, and they wouldn't see it coming. Also, Lana felt, it would be more humane. If they were fast enough, Sage wouldn't need to suffer at all.

Early that morning, Lana had crept downstairs in her pajamas to say goodbye to Daddy. By the time he got home from work that evening, Maddie and Sage would probably already be there, and she wanted to say a proper goodbye. Daddy was dressed for work, fastening his tie in the mirror next to the front door, his briefcase next to his feet.

"You're up early, bean sprout."

Lana shrugged. She hadn't gone out of the house much in the last week or so, to avoid seeing everyone's messed-up faces. Even now,

Daddy's face was just a smudge; she had to force herself to remember what he had looked like before.

"Is something wrong?" Daddy asked.

"No, I just came to say goodbye," Lana said. She wrapped her arms around Daddy's chest and breathed in the smell of the detergent from his shirt, mixed with soap and shaving cream.

"Bye, sweetie," Daddy said. She could hear the confusion in his voice.

She ate breakfast with Mommy and Marc, avoiding looking into their faces. As soon as Mommy left to drive Marc to camp, she got to work cleaning up the mess in the basement. She packed Marc's toys away in their bins and carried a stack of plastic cups up and put them in the sink. She dragged the old vacuum out of the downstairs closet and ran it over the thin, fraying carpet, using all her weight to do so. Then she brought down the Ouija board from her room and her sleeping bag, which had been a Christmas gift five years before and had a picture on it of Princess Leia wielding a blaster.

After this, she went upstairs and played several rounds of *Snood* on the computer while on AIM with Maddie. That afternoon Mommy drove her as promised to the local Blockbuster, where Lana picked out the DVDs that she and Maddie had agreed on. These included the second Harry Potter movie and *Fantasia*, which Maddie had suggested because every time she'd watched it at sleepovers in elementary school, girls always seemed to fall asleep.

Back at home, Lana locked herself in her room. She carefully placed a change of clothes in her backpack, along with two granola bars and a bottle of water she'd taken from the pantry that morning while Mommy was out; she added a stack of photos she'd removed from the family album several nights before, after everyone had gone to bed. She took a copy of last year's Christmas card photo, the one of them posed nicely in front of the cabin up in New Hampshire. She also took one photo of Mommy holding her as a baby and another photo of her and Marc playing in the backyard when they were little. Picking out these three photos had taken her hours, but now she wrapped them quickly in a ziplock bag and placed them in the outer pocket of the backpack.

Once all the tasks were done, she realized she was starting to feel a little nervous, a little like the way she used to feel when she was younger and trying to fall asleep the night before Christmas, knowing when she woke up the next morning that all the presents would be so nicely arranged under the tree. The next time she woke up, she would be with Him. He'd been quiet the last week, the way He always was when He was waiting for something.

Around three thirty, the doorbell rang. Maddie stood on the front steps with her backpack and sleeping bag, although they had agreed the party wouldn't start until five. Lana took a quick look at her face and found that she could still see Maddie's eyes and mouth. Her skin was pale. Lana motioned for her to follow her downstairs. On the way they passed Mommy, who was sitting on a stool at the kitchen counter, paging through a magazine. She greeted Maddie warmly, glancing at the clock on the microwave.

"I've set everything up," Lana said, once they were downstairs with the door closed. "You're sure she doesn't suspect anything?"

"I talked to her yesterday, and she was totally excited," Maddie said. She swallowed and looked pale again. "I'm not going to back out," she said, taking a breath. "I'm ready."

Maddie stuck out her hands, and Lana grabbed them. They both squealed and spun each other around until they were so dizzy they collapsed laughing on one of the beanbag chairs in front of the downstairs TV. Lana plugged her iPod into the portable speakers and blasted Gwen Stefani's "Hollaback Girl," and they both danced around the room, and Maddie tried to twerk her butt the way that Gwen did in the music video, which actually just made Lana notice that Maddie was starting to put on weight around her middle, not that she was going to say anything.

By the time the doorbell rang again upstairs, they had both worked themselves into a dancing frenzy and collapsed again on the gray carpet.

Lana remembered that she'd forgotten to empty out the cat's litter box, and the sharp, acrid smell of cat piss hit her nostrils as she rolled over onto her stomach.

"Where's Merlin?" Maddie asked, probably because she had noticed the same smell.

Lana shrugged. "He's around somewhere," she said, leaning forward onto her knees and pulling herself up to standing. She and Maddie padded up the stairs to find that Mommy had already opened the door for Sage, who strolled in with her sleeping bag tucked under one arm.

◆ ◆ ◆

Later, everyone would ask for details. What did they do minute by minute that night at the sleepover? Already by the next evening, the details would be dim for Lana. "It was just a sleepover," she said, shrugging in the windowless little room where the police put her. "We did normal things."

◆ ◆ ◆

Sage, it turned out, liked to eat her pizza backward, starting with the crust and working her way forward to the last triangle bite, which Lana and Maddie thought was hilarious.

"I'm saving the best bite for last," Sage said, but she laughed and didn't seem offended.

They were eating the pizza on paper plates, alone in the dining room, while Mommy, Daddy, and Marc ate in the kitchen. Mommy had even let them have Coke with dinner, which Lana was almost never allowed to do.

After dinner, they retreated to the basement, where there was more dancing.

It was Sage who noticed the Ouija board and said she'd never played. Lana turned grave.

"You don't play it," she said. "It's not a game. It's for communing with the spirit world."

"So you believe in it?"

"Do you have a question you want to ask?"

Although they were having a good time, Lana was distracted throughout the evening by Sage's face, or rather, by trying not to look too hard at Sage's face. She was pretty sure that if she did, it would be horribly blurred, and so as not to see it, she aimed her gaze just past Sage's right ear, or over her blonde head. Occasionally she had the sense of seeing one part of Sage's face, as if in isolation—her lips pulling into a smile or a laugh, her blue eyes blinking—but Lana always looked away quickly, trying not to give the face time to break down and blur.

"I can think of a question," Sage said, and Lana opened the Ouija board box, glad to have somewhere else to direct her gaze.

The three of them sat on the carpet on the floor, forming a triangle around the board. Although it had been Lana's most exciting birthday present, she and Maddie had actually only used the board a couple of times. The first time, they'd sat for a while with their fingers on the indicator before they finally gave up. The second time, they'd spoken to a ghost who used to live in the house, but Lana was fairly sure that Maddie had been moving the indicator, even though she swore she wasn't. After that, she'd started talking to Him, and she didn't need to use the board, though the truth was that she was afraid to. But she wasn't going to admit that to Sage, or even to Maddie.

"Okay, so what's your question?"

"Um," Sage said, and before she looked away, Lana noticed that she was biting her lip the way she did when she was thinking. "Are we going to die?"

"We're all going to die," Maddie said, rolling her eyes. "Everyone dies eventually."

"Is there something more specific you want to ask it?" Lana said. "Maybe you should ask it when *you're* going to die."

She saw Maddie swallow. She tried to talk to Maddie telepathically, to tell her not to worry, but she couldn't tell if Maddie had gotten the message.

Sage gave an uncomfortable laugh. "Okay. When am I going to die?"

They sat for a moment in silence, with each of their pointer fingers touching the plastic indicator. Then, Lana felt a gentle tug, and the indicator began to move.

"Are you moving it?" Sage squealed, looking at Lana.

"Maddie, stop it!" Lana said.

"I'm not doing it!" Maddie shouted.

The indicator came to rest with its clear little window over the letter *T.*

Stop it, Lana said again, in her mind, to Maddie.

The indicator tugged again under their fingers, gliding smoothly to the letter *O.*

Maddie's mouth dropped open.

Lana closed her eyes. This time she spoke to Him. *Please, stop.*

When the indicator tugged again under her fingers, she waited for it to find the *N,* but instead it stopped at *M.* She looked over at Maddie, who frowned, looking just as puzzled as Lana.

"T-O-M," Sage said. "What's that? Tom?"

The indicator moved again. It stopped at *O.* Lana was thinking it through, figuring it out. As the indicator slid toward the end of the alphabet, seeking the *R,* Maddie pulled her fingers away. Sage startled and gave a small shout.

Lana was miffed. It was obviously Him they had been speaking with—that was the only explanation—and it wasn't up to them to sever the connection. It was like Maddie still didn't understand how to serve Him.

"What do you think it was trying to say?" Sage asked.

"We'll never know now," Lana said, looking meaningfully at Maddie.

Maddie was silent. She shrugged and retreated into herself in the way she did when she was upset about something. Lana hated when she did this, as if she was cutting herself off from the world, from Lana.

Maddie cleared her throat. "Maybe we should watch a movie?" she said.

They popped in *Harry Potter and the Chamber of Secrets*, but it took Lana a little while to get into it. She was still thinking about the Ouija board. It should have said "tonight" but seemed to be spelling out "tomorrow" instead. Was it some kind of message from Him? Lana glanced at the digital clock on the DVD player. It was already 9:15 p.m. If they waited until Sage was asleep, if it was after midnight, then it would technically be tomorrow. She felt relieved to have figured it out, and then she was able to turn her attention to the movie.

When the credits rolled, the three of them crept upstairs to the kitchen and made popcorn in the microwave. They left the first bag in too long, and it came out charred and smoking a little. But the second bag they did just right and carried it back down to the basement. They took turns changing into their pajamas in the downstairs bathroom. Lana noticed that Sage's pajama top had a picture of Winnie-the-Pooh on it. They turned the lights off in the half of the basement where the TV was, leaving the lights on near the bathroom and Mommy's exercise machine, and popped in *Fantasia*. After they'd eaten the popcorn, they all settled into their sleeping bags.

Lana's favorite part of this movie had always been the bit with the Sorcerer's Apprentice, but that came early, and then it was all dancing hippos and fairies and flowers. Sage grew still in her sleeping bag, but Lana decided to wait, just to be sure. She waited until the clock on the DVD player said it was 12:34 a.m., and then she glanced over at Maddie. Maddie had fallen asleep on top of her sleeping bag.

Lana shook her shoulder. "Hey," she hissed in her ear.

Maddie woke with a start. "What?" she said, then looked at Lana and seemed to remember.

Silently they crept over to where Sage was, her legs in the sleeping bag with the top half of the blanket thrown back. She was lying on her side, her light hair spread out across one of the pillows she'd taken from the couch. Her lips were slightly parted, and her skin was smooth and almost glowing in the dim light. Her Winnie-the-Pooh shirt had slid up, revealing a sliver of her bare back, and Lana could just make out the pattern of tiny flowers near the top band of her underwear, peeking out from under her pajama bottoms.

"Should we do it?" Maddie asked, under her breath.

According to the plan, they were supposed to sneak up to the kitchen now and get the knife. Then they would take their backpacks and flee into the night. Lana thought about how warm her sleeping bag was and how peaceful Sage looked.

"Let's give her one more morning," she said.

Maddie stumbled back to her sleeping bag, climbed in, and seemed to fall asleep immediately.

Lana went to use the bathroom. She closed the door behind her and moved to turn on the light, but before she could, she saw Him behind her. He loomed above her in the mirror, a long, dark shape rising up behind her shoulder. His smooth, featureless face was unreadable. She was too scared to turn around.

You didn't do it. He spoke in the same high-pitched lilting whisper that He always did.

I'm sorry. I couldn't. She was just lying there like a baby.

So do it tomorrow.

I will.

She swallowed and reached out to turn on the light. In the mirror, her face was pale and there were purple crescents under her eyes. She took a couple of breaths and was surprised to find that tears were rolling down her cheeks. She dried them and blew her nose on some toilet paper.

She was afraid she wasn't going to be able to sleep, but almost as soon as she climbed into her sleeping bag, a yawning blankness rose up to meet her.

2

When Maddie woke up, her head felt heavy. Sunlight was shining through the two window wells on either end of the basement. Lana was awake, seated on the couch, and paging through a Goosebumps book with a library sticker on its spine, squinting in the low light. When she saw Maddie sitting up, she closed the book as if she was about to say something, but then Sage rolled over in her sleeping bag and opened her eyes.

The three of them trooped upstairs in their pajamas and found Mrs. Prescott at the stove, making pancakes, Mr. Prescott sipping his coffee at the kitchen table, and Marc in the living room watching cartoons.

"How late were you girls up last night?" Mrs. Prescott asked.

Lana shrugged. "Midnight," she said.

"We fell asleep watching *Fantasia*," Maddie added.

"I didn't know kids still watched that," Mr. Prescott said, not taking his eyes off the newspaper he was reading.

"They do," Mrs. Prescott said.

When the pancakes were ready, Lana, Maddie, and Sage ate them at the kitchen island. Marc joined them from the other room, and Lana let him sit for a while on her lap as he ate, even though he was really too old for sitting in laps. Watching them, Maddie wondered if Lana was really going to go through with it, if she was really going to leave Marc behind.

Maddie watched as Sage brought a forkful of pancake to her mouth—that mouth that she'd done such disgusting things with. Maddie had already eaten three pancakes but suddenly felt a lurch in her stomach and decided not to eat any more.

She had found it a little easier to sleep and eat again, after Lana had convinced her of the plan. It was a relief, in a way, to have made up her mind. Now Maddie was telling herself she just had to get through this last, worst part, and it would all be over. If she told herself that Sage was already dead, then it all felt a little bit easier. Lana had said she just needed to think about the goal: about the two of them in the house with the porch and the curtains around the beds, with Him protecting them, instead of haunting them.

"I think we should walk to the playground," Lana said when they were done with breakfast.

Maddie glanced at her, but her face gave nothing away. Lana's face was often like that recently, a kind of blank slate.

"My mom said to be home by lunch," Sage said.

"That's fine. We have a couple hours," Lana said.

The girls went back downstairs and got dressed. They all put on shorts and T-shirts, but Lana pulled on an old black wool coat that she had recently started wearing everywhere. Both Maddie and Lana pulled on their backpacks.

"Aren't you going to be hot?" Sage asked.

Lana shrugged, and Sage didn't press her.

They walked down their wide residential street, three abreast. The sun was low and the day was gray, but it didn't matter. The humidity held the heat around them like a clenched fist. Maybe they should have thought more about that, about how hot it would be to walk all the way to the Bay Bridge and then across.

Maddie realized that she was avoiding looking at Sage, was almost ignoring her, but when she glanced over at her now, the other girl's face was placid. It looked like she was having a good time. Sage had been easygoing about everything last night, giving in easily to whatever Lana and Maddie wanted to do, probably because she was so happy to be included, especially after what had happened at the pool.

When they got to the playground, Lana said, "Let's go into the woods. We can play hide-and-seek."

"Okay," Sage agreed.

"Why don't you go hide? We'll come find you," Lana said.

"Both of you?" Sage gave a small frown.

"Hide really good," Maddie said, "and it will take both of us to find you."

Lana whirled around, put her hands over her eyes, and started counting loudly. There was a rustle of pine needles behind her as Sage took off into the woods.

Lana was beside Maddie right away. "Look," she said, pulling back a wing of the black coat to show the knife she had secreted in the inside pocket. It had a black handle and a long thin blade.

"Is He here?" Maddie whispered.

Lana nodded and pressed her pale lips together. "He's here," she said. "I can feel Him." For a moment Sage and the woods seemed to recede, and it was just Maddie and Lana with the knife between them. Maddie swallowed. She was afraid to move her eyes away from Lana, afraid to see Him lurking behind the trees.

"You do it," Lana said, whispering into her ear. "You're bigger than me. You'll do a better job."

"What?" Maddie's voice came out as a gasp. Lana had never said anything about her being the one with the knife. "No, I can't."

"Of course you can. I'll keep it in my coat until we find her, and then you just have to move quickly, okay? Come on."

Before Maddie could say anything else, Lana was bounding off in search of Sage. Maddie followed. She kept her gaze straight ahead of her, allowing everything in her peripheral vision to blur together. She could feel her pulse beating in her ears. Lana had said that after they made the sacrifice, her fear would melt away. After the sacrifice, she wouldn't be afraid of anything anymore.

They found Sage in the clearing, kneeling behind a fallen tree. Although she was crouched low, they could see the slim line of her white shirt above the log. They stopped some distance away. Lana turned toward Maddie and forced the knife handle into her hand, the sharp end pointing down. As soon as her fingers grasped the handle, Maddie knew that she couldn't do it. Not in a million years.

"Take it back," she hissed at Lana. "I told you. I can't."

Lana's eyes were desperate. "I can't do it either."

"What are you guys whispering about?" Sage called from her spot behind the log.

"You're supposed to be hiding," Lana said, composed again, the knife pressed quickly behind her back.

Sage stood up from behind the log. "I know you know where I am."

"Okay, let's make it a game of tag," Lana said. "We're coming for you." She rushed forward suddenly, and Sage squealed and ran from them, away from the playground and deeper into the woods.

Lana started to jog but not run, and Maddie hurried to catch up.

Lana gripped Maddie's arm as she pulled alongside her. "Okay. I'll do it, but you have to tell me when. So we're doing it together. Deal?"

"Deal," Maddie said. Her heart was pounding and her stomach was tight. She had to say when, but what if she never did?

They caught up to Sage at the base of a large oak tree. She had gotten winded and slowed down, waiting for them.

"You guys aren't trying very hard," Sage said. Panting, she bent over, putting her palms on her legs. She smiled.

"Sage?" Lana said. "We're going to play a game. Can you lie down here?"

"Why?" Sage asked, looking back and forth between their faces.

"It's part of the game."

"Just lie down on your back," Maddie said. "And close your eyes."

Sage shrugged. "Um, okay," she said, and she lay down on a bed of pine needles, her arms loose at her sides. Lana took a deep breath. Holding the knife behind her back, she walked over and spread her legs around Sage's hips, the long black coat trailing down past her knees. She looked over at Maddie, waiting.

Maddie squeezed her eyes shut. She felt the presence of the woods around her, all the shadows where He could be watching them, waiting. And suddenly she saw again that moment behind the pool house, Sage on her knees, Ethan's head thrown back with a strange look of concentration and pleasure on his face, the hint of a smile on his lips.

"Do it!" Maddie heard herself scream. "Do it now!"

Violence in real life was not like in the movies. There was no song playing in the background and no camera zooming in. Because of Lana's coat, it was hard for Maddie to see what was actually going on. Sage gasped and then screamed, but they were little screams because she seemed to be putting all her energy into trying to stop the knife, which was the only thing Maddie could see clearly, the knife pumping up and down again and again.

"Hold her arms!" Lana shrieked.

Without thinking, Maddie rushed forward and managed to pin Sage's wrists to the ground, and that was when she saw Lana get two good thrusts into the chest. It was awful, the sound that it made. The knife cut through Sage's T-shirt, and a circle of blood spread quickly across it. Maddie recoiled and Lana lowered the knife, breathing heavily. As soon as Lana's weight loosened over her, Sage pushed her off and stood up, bent with her face toward the ground, her arms wrapping around her chest.

"What did you do!" Sage screamed. "What did you do!"

"Be quiet!" Maddie said, afraid that someone would hear.

"I don't feel good," Sage said. "I can't breathe. It's hard to see."

Sage's arms and legs were covered in blood, and the bloody circle on her chest was growing larger. Maddie couldn't believe she was standing up.

"Lie down," she said. "You'll bleed less if you lie down." She came over and helped Sage to lie back down on her back, just a few feet from where she had been a few moments before.

Lana seemed to have caught her breath. Sage was gasping now, her chest moving up and down.

"Why did you do it?"

"Sage?" Lana said. "Just lie still. Wait here. We're going to go get help."

From the ground, Sage looked up at them. "It's hard to see," she repeated.

"We'll get help," Maddie said. Of course they were lying, but she thought it was kinder for Sage to believe that help was on the way. She didn't want her to be scared.

Then Lana was pulling her by the hand, and the two of them bolted back the way they had come, toward the playground. There was a long tear down the side of Lana's coat. She must have cut Sage through the fabric.

"Take it off," Maddie said. "Look, it has holes in it, and it's covered in blood."

They paused, and Lana removed the sodden coat, but there were still large splotches of blood on the front of her yellow T-shirt.

"I like this coat," Lana said.

"Forget it. It's ruined. And it's too hot to wear it. We have to go fast, remember?"

"I got her, right?" Lana said. "She's going to die?"

"She's probably already dead back there," Maddie said, and as she said it she felt a horrible burden lift off her chest. It had been awful, but it was done. It was all finished.

Lana stripped off her coat and dropped it behind a tree. "We did it!" she said, trying to wipe her hands off on part of the coat. "Maddie, we really did it. That's it. We can be with Him now."

For the first time in a long time, Maddie saw Lana give her a real smile. She reached out, clasped Maddie's hand tight in hers, and gave a small squeal of happiness.

3

She waited until she could hear their footsteps pounding off toward the playground. It felt like something heavy was lying over her chest, and every time she breathed, it was harder to get enough air. There was a loud whooshing sound in her ears. She was lying on her back, looking up into the trees, to where the branches gave way to a glum, gray sky, but the picture was cutting out, like a TV with a bad connection. Black circles were appearing across her eyes, and she blinked, but they didn't go away.

It turned out that all this time, her body had been nothing more than a fragile balloon, and now the balloon had been pierced, and the blood had rushed out. Her blood was rushing out right now, too much of it. They're not coming back, she thought, they aren't bringing any help. All her blood was going to leak out of her, and she was going to die.

When you're lost in the woods, you should stay where you are, but she wasn't lost. She knew that over the ridge there was the bike path, and if she could get herself there, it was possible someone would find her. The bike path was closer and in the opposite direction from the playground, where *they* were headed.

She took a deep breath. Her whole body was pulsing, probably with pain, but it didn't feel like pain, not yet. She rolled onto her stomach. Maybe she could crawl there. She reached out an arm. Something awful squeezed in her chest. She stumbled to her feet, and the trees whirled around her. It would be so much easier to lie back down, but she couldn't let herself do that. She had to get to the path.

She couldn't stand up all the way but instead had to walk bent over. That was okay, though. Walking was still easier than crawling.

It was starting to hurt now, all the places where the knife had entered. The spots were still in front of her eyes, and it was hard to see. She stumbled and fell. She tried to scream for help, but she didn't have enough breath to scream. She couldn't do it. She was going to die here in the woods. She thought suddenly of her mother, who had no idea what was happening to her, her mother, who expected her home for lunch.

With difficulty, she pushed herself up onto her arms and once again somehow launched herself dizzily onto her legs. She weaved unsteadily through the trees. There were pine needles stuck to her everywhere, stuck to the blood on her body. She plodded slowly up and over the small hill.

At the top, she could see the bike path. She half walked, half fell down the other side of the rise. She had made it. Very carefully, she lay down on her back on the gravel. The thing on her chest was very heavy now, and she wished she could shake it off. She closed her eyes and waited.

Kat Davis

IX

1

How does it feel to have committed to your own death? Sometimes it feels like panic. She can't breathe; she can't quiet the stupid thudding of her heart. But at other times, it feels like a relief. I might not live past Friday night, she thinks, and suddenly she has no more problems. Suddenly all her problems are solved.

She used to have to fill out a weekly questionnaire: *Are you thinking of hurting yourself or others? Do you ever think about harming yourself? Do you have recurrent thoughts of suicide?*

Maddie could always honestly answer no. She never thought about killing herself, not even after she heard that Lana had tried, more than once. It seemed to be part of her makeup, just how she was. She suspected it was a reflection of a deep selfishness. Her instinct had always been toward self-protection, to squeeze whatever little advantage out of a situation she could.

She feels that way now, still, even though she has told the Followers that she will be their willing sacrifice. It took over a day for the responses to come in, as if they had for once been stunned into silence.

PraiseSatan69: Wow, I did not see this coming. One of our own volunteers as Tribute!

User89274: I am genuinely stunned at this offer, Mad_as_a_Hatter22. It's incredibly generous of you. What do the rest of you think re would it work or not?

Follower_in_the_Distance: I wasn't expecting anything like this but it would resolve a lot of problems for us. Sacrificing a member of our own group would be essentially what the Founders attempted as well

Fungible_Tokens57: Like everyone else here, Mad_as_a_Hatter22 I say hats off to you for even considering it. Prescott never said anything about the sacrifice having to be unwilling so if we have a volunteer I say all the better!

User89274: If we're all agreed, I say Friday night, in the clearing, at midnight? Will message everyone the street address and a Google maps image

PraiseSatan69: Let's do it!

Perhaps there was some part of her that had believed they would try to talk her out of it, especially Follower_in_the_Distance, that she would be distraught at the loss of Maddie's online friendship. But apparently not. As far as she can tell, Follower_in_the_Distance is the youngest member of the group; the rest are adults, two men and one woman. Do they have any idea what it takes to press a knife into someone's skin until blood rushes out? Or are they the sort of people for whom it will be easy?

She thinks about rescinding her offer. She considers not showing up, but she already knows, somehow, that she will, that she won't be able not to. There's a sense of unreality to everything that happens online. In real life, with her in front of them, they will realize how impossible it is. That's how it was for Maddie, anyway; she helped, but she could never herself have wielded the knife; there was still that one line she couldn't cross.

So she will go to the woods and try to change their minds in person, face-to-face. And if she is not successful—well. She has to be prepared for that. If it has to be someone, it should be her. She is the most culpable and also the most expendable. Who will mourn her? Mom and Steve a little, for form's sake. Omar and Gabriela? Their single night out together does not amount to real friendship, and they are better off without her. The world, she suspects, would be better off without her.

The year she graduated from high school, Sage granted an interview to one of those hour-long network news programs. Maddie knows the video is on YouTube but hasn't been able to bring herself to watch it.

Thursday night she clicks on the link. Sage is easily recognizable, the same short blonde hair and blue eyes, the way that her nose turns upward, giving her a smug look no matter what she says. She is dressed casually for the camera, in jeans and a muted sweater. Maddie's heart beats faster at the sight of her.

The newscaster is a woman in a bright-red suit. She speaks with the put-on sadness in her voice that so many news anchors are gifted at, all the while plowing relentlessly through Sage's worst memories.

"Did you have any idea what the girls were planning?" she asks.

"None," Sage answers, in a voice that is quiet but steady, strangely reassured.

"At what point did you realize your life was in danger?"

"Not until Lana took out the knife and stabbed me with it."

"Yet you had the presence of mind to get yourself to the bike path."

"I knew that was my only shot. The only way that someone would find me."

Maddie remembers Sage standing up after the stabbing, covered in her own blood. Oh, how they had underestimated her.

"And you knew that you were dying?"

"Oh yeah." On the screen, Sage looks almost annoyed with the question, as if she finds it melodramatic. "Someone was either going to find me and get me to the hospital, or I was going to die. I should have died that day."

"Should have?"

"I mean, the fact that I'm alive now is kind of a miracle. I'd be dead if that man hadn't been walking his dog. And without modern medicine."

"I understand you're headed to the honors program at the University of Maryland, where you'll be premed. Did the attack influence that decision?"

"Yes. While I was in the hospital, I got really interested in everything the doctors and nurses were doing. I realized what a difference you can make in a person's life."

The newscaster's face, already serious, turns even graver. "If you could speak directly to the girls now, what would you say?"

Sage licks her lips. Maddie leans even closer to the tiny screen in her hand. Her mouth is dry.

"I know it sounds weird, but I think I would thank them. I mean, they did this awful thing, but up until then, I had just been sort of stumbling through my life. I didn't have any direction. And since then, I know that every moment is a gift. My friends say that I'm intense. I have a lot of drive. I think that's because I know my life is temporary. All of our lives are temporary."

Maddie exits the window and sets her phone face down on the table next to the bed. She lies on top of the blue comforter and stares up at the white ceiling.

For a long time, Maddie didn't think much about Sage at all. When she did, she felt something catch in her chest, as if she couldn't breathe.

It was easier to focus on her own survival. If she thought about the past at all, it was about Lana and Him, not Sage.

Over the years, Maddie has composed several letters to Sage, letters never sent. All of these letters were written at the insistence of others, her lawyer and various psychiatrists, either as an attempt to show the court her genuine remorse or as exercises in "imaginative empathy," and they could not help but sound forced.

> Dear Sage, I am so sorry for what I did. I am really sorry and hope you can forgive me someday. I am so glad you are okay.

Maddie told her lawyers that she was sorry the minute after it happened, that after the stabbing she felt sick to her stomach, but that was untrue. After the stabbing, she felt a strange euphoria, a sense of having transgressed the most basic of human taboos. She felt powerful. The feeling lasted an hour or two and was already gone by the time the police picked her and Lana up by the side of the road. But Maddie would never forget that feeling. That feeling was the strongest proof she had that she had never actually been a good person.

A good person, when told by the officer questioning her that Sage had survived, that she had been found on the bike path by a man walking his dog and been rushed to the hospital and had, just a half hour before, come out of a successful surgery—a good person would have felt relieved, would have felt the burden of her sin lessened. It was a miracle, after all. One minute Sage was dead; the next she was alive. But all that Maddie thought and all she said was, "Does this mean I can go home now?" Her next thought was that she needed to talk to Lana, to find out what it all meant.

Maddie knew as soon as she told the whole story aloud in the presence of an adult that it didn't make any sense, that there was no Him. She was no longer even sure that she had actually seen Him that day in the shadows at Wild World. It had been a regular person, or a trick of the shadows. Perhaps she had even willed herself to see something that wasn't there. Either way, she understood suddenly that what she had done was not just wrong but embarrassing, like believing so much in Santa Claus that she had packed a bag and headed for the North Pole.

All these years she has imagined Sage's rage and contempt. Maddie always knew she would never send any of those letters that other people had made her write. She understood, more and more as time passed, how inadequate any apology must be, that to say "I'm sorry"—to use the same words she would use if she had stepped on Sage's foot on a crowded bus—was somehow ridiculous, could never be enough. But to hear Sage say that she would thank them? That they had done her a favor?

Maddie rolls over onto her stomach, buries her head under the pillow, and screams into the mattress. She perfected this technique a long time ago, back in juvie, though she hasn't used it in some time. You can release a lot of sound into a mattress if you do it right.

PraiseSatan69: I am so psyched for tomorrow!

Follower_in_the_Distance: I won't lie, I'm having second thoughts, but trying to hold on to my beliefs. I know this is for the greater good.

User89274: Stay strong, Follower_in_the_Distance. It will all be clear, as soon as we're all together. We are so grateful to you, Mad_as_a_Hatter22! HE will never forget you, and neither will we.

Mad_as_a_Hatter22: I'll be there

On Thursday afternoon, Miranda looks at her with a frown.

"It's rough, losing a job like that because of your past. Unfortunately, it's not that uncommon, I'm afraid. The important thing is to get back out there—get another one. How's your mental health?"

"Um."

"What about that therapist? Shoot, I was supposed to give her a call. You been seeing the therapist?"

"Well."

"Okay now, Maddie, that is priority number one. I'm going to need you to give her a call this week. ASAP. I mean it. With the job setback, you really need to focus on your mental health. You hear me?"

"Yes, ma'am."

Had she ever believed in Him? She had wanted to believe in Him, to believe the way that Lana believed. It was better to believe in Him, to picture hazy fantasies of running away forever with Him and Lana, than to accept the reality of the next two years of her life within the cracked walls, dirty linoleum, and faded carpets of the local middle school, helpless in front of the uniquely cruel yet perceptive gazes of seventh and eighth graders. So she'd traded one prison for another, traded her chance to grow up for never growing up at all.

She had wanted to believe, but she also knew deep down that believing was not really an excuse. The "not criminally responsible" plea meant that you had lost your ability to discriminate between right and wrong. That was not the case. Though within their delusion their decisions made a kind of sense, they both knew that killing was wrong and that Sage was an innocent. Lana had said it herself—that was what made a sacrifice a sacrifice. But this was all too complicated to explain to people—that she had been deluded, and in her delusion she'd chosen evil.

And yes, Lana planned it, but Maddie did nothing to stop it. Maddie helped her. She doesn't feel angry with Lana anymore, as she did for so long. She pities her. Still, she knows she'll never have the courage to contact her. Lana is just too dangerous—it would be like touching a live wire. When she thinks of Lana, she imagines her, still her twelve-year-old self, short and skinny, her legs pulled up to her chest in a gesture of protection, her back against a painted cinder block wall. Does Lana understand what she did? Does she still believe in Him? Does she blame Maddie, as maybe she should, for not seeing clearly for the both of them, for telling no one, for keeping her secrets, for failing to keep her—her best friend in all the world—safe from herself?

And Sage? She's always had trouble keeping Sage in her thoughts. She can see now that she was protecting herself. Perhaps she had even blocked out that memory of the day at the pool for exactly that reason. To think too much about Sage would be to admit the obvious: That it was Sage who was the true victim, Sage the wronged party. Sage who had done nothing wrong except attract the attention of a boy whom Maddie liked in secret, who had performed a sex act that Maddie now knew was quite common, an act that she had heard others talking about all the time at the state hospital like it was completely normal. Though she had never done anything like it herself, had never done any sex acts at all. Never.

Is she really just a murderer then, one whose victim just happened to survive? Was He just an excuse? Maddie doesn't know. She thinks that the truth is somewhere in between—that she was at once a murderer and a delusional young girl, a person capable of fear and hate and confusion all at once, a young person whose brain was not yet fully able to grasp the inevitable consequences of her own actions, someone who had led such a sheltered existence, in a place where nothing ever really happened, that death was still wholly theoretical to her, something that happened only in a story that she was telling herself about her life. This was all true at once. But how to tell that to the Followers, how to make them understand what she knows now?

She can't fall asleep the night before. Dawn finds her drowsing on the bed, sleeping in short bursts and waking up with a start. She keeps rolling over and going back to sleep, only to awaken with a jerk. At noon, she gets up, showers, and dresses. She checks the website, but there are no new posts to the group chat. Now she really is starting to feel afraid. What will it be like? A knife against her throat? All that blood? She will close her eyes, and it will be over soon. Or maybe they will change their minds. She thinks now that maybe she won't try to talk them out of it at all. Let her human presence solve it for them. They will look at her and decide: Does this person deserve to live?

Perhaps she should have requested a gentler method, though she doesn't know what that would be. And she supposes that User89274 is right: if the cut is deep enough, it is sure to work and work fast. The Followers think that He failed to manifest for her and Lana because Sage lived; they won't make the same mistake.

Mom comes home a little before six with a pizza that Maddie can only pick at listlessly while Steve talks about a work problem. Halfway through, Mom turns to Maddie. "What's wrong? You've always liked pizza."

"Just not super hungry tonight."

Mom squints at her and pauses, as if there is something else she might ask. Then she turns back to Steve.

The two of them usually go to bed promptly at ten, but tonight of all nights they linger in the kitchen, going over some of the paperwork they're getting ready with the lawyer for Luke's next round of appeals.

Maddie looks up from the couch as they cross the living room toward the stairs.

"Going to bed?" she asks, and her voice breaks. She clears it.

"Yup," Mom says.

"Good night," Maddie calls after her. Steve trumps up the stairs wordlessly behind Mom.

It's almost ten thirty. Maddie takes a deep, shivering breath.

What will the Followers do if she doesn't show up? Probably nothing. She imagines them sitting around the fire they've made to keep off the autumn chill. Maybe someone's thought to bring a six-pack. They talk and laugh; they're not surprised that she didn't show up; they knew it couldn't be that easy. And then what? They'll be able to talk face-to-face, to more efficiently plan how to find the real victim.

Maddie swallows. She rises from the couch on trembling legs. She silently lets herself out the side door, turning the key in its lock. As planned, she walks up the block and waits there to schedule the ride. It's only the second time she's used the app, and it hadn't occurred to her that no cars might be available at this time of night in the middle of suburban nowhere. There is a car that's almost forty minutes away, but when she tries to schedule it, the car blinks off the screen. She swears and looks at the time. She has a little over an hour, and the distance is walkable; she'd looked it up and decided it would take too long, but she has no choice now. She can shave a couple of miles off by cutting past her old elementary school, through the woods there.

She forgot to put on her sweatshirt and is shivering from standing still, but after a block she already feels warmer. She's out of shape, was never in shape, her heart rate is already up, sweat slides down her back. Too bad, she thinks, no time to waste. She brings up the map of the neighborhood on her phone so that she won't get lost, checking periodically to make sure that her little blue dot is moving in the right direction. The street is completely deserted. There are no streetlamps, so the only light available comes from the rectangle of her phone. A single car turns up the street and zooms toward her, slowing suddenly as it passes. Maddie looks away. The driver steps again on the gas.

Steve and Mom's neighborhood is a C-shaped street that intersects with one of the major local roads, one of the few that has a sidewalk. After a block, she pauses in front of the elementary school, trying to catch her breath. The empty parking lot is lit by several streetlamps, and the place looks almost ghostly in the dark. It was here that Maddie boarded the bus in fourth grade and took the empty seat next to Lana, produced her library copy of *Scary Stories to Tell in the Dark*. And if she hadn't ever sat next to Lana that day? If she had walked, as she usually did, farther back to find an empty seat?

Beyond the parking lot is a patch of trees, a patch of woods smaller in area but denser than the woods near the old house. Maddie keeps the phone flashlight trained on the ground as she steps over logs and fallen branches. Something stirs in the dark off to her left and bounds away, something bigger than anything she thought could live in these woods.

For the first time in a long time, she feels the chill that she used to feel when thinking about Him, a rush of pure cold fear, unpleasant but also thrilling. Were their thoughts about Him just this, just a childish fear of being alone in the dark? Or was there really something out there, trying to break through? She shivers, shakes her head, and increases her pace. She isn't the kind of person who has those thoughts anymore.

She checks the blue dot on her phone and veers to the left. She emerges through the trees into a cul-de-sac of the old neighborhood, but she's still a mile and a half away from the playground near the clearing. It's past eleven thirty. Her breaths are loud and ragged. The walk back toward her old street is mostly uphill. There are streetlamps here every block, so she turns off her phone flashlight and walks in and out through the small pools of light.

She passes the Newmans' house first, which, she remembers too late, is where Mr. and Mrs. Newman still live. She crosses to the other side and turns her head away. The lights in the house are off, and nothing stirs there.

Her own house she almost walks past. The trees that used to block it have been cut down, leaving an open lawn leading up to the small old rancher. A two-story addition has been tacked on to the back of the house, and Maddie imagines that in daylight, it must look completely incongruous. She remembers Mom saying that the "new people" had put an addition on, and she knew that the house had sold at the time for under its estimated value; they were lucky to be able to sell it at all.

She inspects the Prescotts' house, still standing stately on its corner lot. It has a FOR SALE sign out front; Mom told her that it's passed through several owners over the past decade, that it's considered a "bad luck" house—couples who move in there get divorced, have money problems, or their pets run away—but none of that "bad luck" is as bad as what she and Lana did.

When she finally reaches the playground, she flips her phone flashlight back on and follows the shaft of light almost unthinkingly to the old round-about, where she collapses, her chest heaving. It's five minutes to midnight. She sits, gasping big breaths of air, trying to slow her breathing. She can't look like this when she faces them. For a moment, it doesn't seem strange at all that the playground, too, should be exactly as she left it. It was already in a state of disrepair ten years ago. Mom once told her the community board couldn't decide whether to update the playground or to sell off the lot and the woods to developers. They'd been arguing for years and are still arguing today. Most people want to erase the place where the crime happened in the hope that it will stop people from talking, in the hope that the property values will rebound. Those used to be the things her mother would tell her on the phone once a week, updates on the old neighborhood, as if she cared what happened there.

Her breathing is more normal. She takes one last deep breath and checks her phone: 12:01 a.m.

She rises slowly. She's already starting to feel the cold again through her sweat-soaked shirt. She doesn't want to alert them to her arrival with her flashlight, but it's so dark she has no choice. The little blue light illuminates the path through the trees.

The smell of pine hits her hard. She expects to hear voices, a group of people gathered around a campfire. But when she reaches the clearing, it's dark and empty.

No, not empty. A single figure is seated across a fallen log, jumping to its feet at the sight of her light. Another light flashes on. The figure turns toward her.

She stops, and the person moves closer into the faint cast of light, an unmistakably male figure. Her heart jumps, and for a moment she expects to see Henry, but the body in front of her resolves into a figure too short and slight. A pair of dark eyes peers back at her.

Lana's eyes.

For a moment, Maddie can't speak. Her voice emerges with a squeak: "Marc?"

"Hi, Maddie." He turns the flashlight upward into her face, and she has to shut her eyes. When she can see again, he's aimed the flashlight back onto the forest floor. The silence lengthens, becomes heavy. It should be Marc who breaks it, but instead he stands there silently.

"Marc, what the hell is going on?"

"Well. I mean, I bet you can figure it out now, right?"

Maddie swallows. She glances around them, as if looking for the others.

"No one else is coming. It's just me," he says.

"Just you?"

"I'm Follower_in_the_Distance. Well, I'm all of them actually."

She thinks of the profile pic, the one showing a harmless-looking high school girl. She's been a fool.

"You're saying the whole site is fake? It's all just you?"

"No, no." His tone is annoyed, as if he's disappointed with her for not being able to keep up. "The site is real. But the private group talking about the next sacrifice—that was all me."

"But why?"

"Why do you think?"

Maddie grips the phone. Her fingers are warm in the cold air. All her muscles are taut, and she realizes she's ready to run. Marc was always a strange kid. Mental illness runs in families; everyone knows that. Maybe he came here to finish what Lana started. She thought that she was ready to be a willing sacrifice, but suddenly her body takes over, a simple animal instinct toward survival.

She aims her flashlight up into his eyes, as he did to her only moments before. He puts up a hand, squeezes his eyes shut. "Ow. What are you doing?"

"Why are you here? Did you come here to—complete the sacrifice?"

"Jesus, Maddie, put down the light! I'm not psychotic. I don't believe in Him."

Maddie keeps the beam aimed at his face. "Then what are you doing here?"

Still squinting, Marc puts down his hand, tries to open his eyes. "I'm the one who should be asking you that. Why are *you* here?"

"I'm here to try to stop a bunch of people from hurting somebody else."

"Really? By offering to be their sacrifice? You know how crazy that sounds?"

"Crazy? What about you? Pretending to be all those different people? Just to lure me into the woods?"

"I wanted to be sure. You're lucky I didn't just call the police. There's no way you're allowed to be on that site."

Maddie feels something inside her crumple. Marc is not here to hurt her. He's here to assess whether or not she, the criminal, is still a threat. She's not saving anyone; she never was. She lowers the flashlight, and Marc's face disappears again into darkness.

"It was all a trick," she says quietly. "To see whether I still believed."

"Well, yeah." Again that slightly superior, annoyed tone, as if he were talking to someone exceptionally slow. "You kept changing your story. I couldn't tell which of your lies to believe."

"Marc, I don't believe in Him anymore. I came here to try to stop anybody else from getting hurt, I swear."

"But you shouldn't have been on that site at all. I mean, couldn't they throw you back in jail, just for that?"

"They could send me back to the hospital, yeah."

"So why risk it? What were you thinking?"

"I don't know."

With one hand, she wipes away the tears from her eyes. She is shivering with cold, which Marc seems to notice for the first time.

"You cold? C'mon. We can talk in my car."

Maddie hesitates. Only moments ago, she was worried that Marc wanted to kill her, but she supposes that he's the closest thing she's ever had to a brother, to someone you could fear or hate one instant and forgive the next. She shrugs and follows the trail of his flashlight beam back through the woods.

Marc leads her past the playground and to a small sedan parked halfway up the street that Maddie hadn't noticed before. When he opens the door, the dome light flickers on, and for a moment she sees him in real light—more muscular than she'd thought, like his father, his coloring the same as Lana's and his mother's. There's no trace of the speech impediment he had as a kid, but there is something strangely formal about his speech. When he talks he doesn't make eye contact, but it seems as if this may be a personal quirk, not directed at her specifically. There's no trace of the disgust that Henry showed her.

Marc reaches into the back seat and rustles amid a pile of empty candy wrappers and McDonald's bags. "Here you go." He hands her a tissue, and Maddie blows her nose.

Maddie thinks about how young Marc was when it happened. All the press coverage, the trial. It couldn't have been easy, being her brother. Perhaps that experience is responsible for the self-possessed but strangely intense young man in front of her, so different from the needy, insecure little boy of her memories.

Maddie clears her throat and asks quietly, "How is she?"

Marc shrugs and looks away. "I don't really know. I haven't seen her in like four or five years."

"Five *years*? Don't you visit?"

"My mom visits. Every week. I have school and stuff. I go to college in Pennsylvania. My dad and I moved up there, after our parents split? I'm a freshman at Penn State."

"Shouldn't you be doing your schoolwork instead of impersonating people online?"

Marc shrugs again. "I've done therapy and all that. It's not like I don't have insight into what I'm doing and why. But in the end, I can either try to diminish the harm of what my sister did, or I can sit back and ignore it. I'd rather not ignore it. I have a lot of different avatars—I'm able to influence things, keep an eye on them, even contact local police if I need to."

"How did you know it was me?"

"I knew you were out because Amelia Lawrence posted it all over her social. And you started posting that night. And your username was a real tip-off. You made it easy."

"So you're like some sort of internet vigilante?" As she says it, she realizes that this is exactly what she thought she was.

Marc shakes his head. "Look, I'm not the one who needs to be interrogated here. I'm not the one with a history of violence."

"I thought . . ." Maddie sees that what she thought she was doing and what she was actually doing are not the same thing. The control she thought she had was an illusion. She may not have believed in Him, but she did believe that a group of people she met on the internet was planning an act of violence and that the most logical thing for her to do in response was to offer herself up as a sacrifice. She's done it again, failed to see the clear line between the real and not-real. It must be pointed out to her by—of all people—Lana's little brother. She puts her face in her hands and takes deep breaths. After a moment, she blows her nose again.

"So you really don't visit her?" Maddie asks once she can speak again.

Marc shrugs. "It's just hard," he says. "Seeing her. It's like it's not really her. She was a good sister to me, you know, in her way. She looked out for me. I know she would never hurt me."

Maddie remembers suddenly that day in the clearing. *It could have been Marc,* Lana had said. Maddie feels a chill. But some truths are better left unspoken.

Marc continues, not seeming to notice her unease. "The thing about her diagnosis, the early-onset schizophrenia—it takes hold before the person has developed a sense of what's real and what's not. It's a degenerative disease, you know, and she did not get the treatment she should have early on. She was in juvie over a year before they got her on meds. If we'd caught it sooner—"

He falls silent.

"I'm sorry about a lot of things," Maddie says after a moment. "And that's one of them. Not getting her help, I mean."

Marc bristles. "I just don't know what you were thinking. Why you didn't tell anybody—"

"Because I was a kid too! And I know I should have known better, but I didn't. She was very convincing. I really thought, like, for just a couple weeks, I really thought that He was real. I thought that she knew what we were supposed to do and that if I listened to her, everything would be okay. You know what she's like."

"Yeah, I do." Marc sighs and runs a hand over his face. They sit for a moment in silence. Then he turns to the back seat and rustles around again amid the pile of trash, this time producing a can of Red Bull. He cracks open the can and takes a long sip. "How did you get here?" he asks.

"I walked. From my mom's new place. I tried to get an Uber, but . . ." She shrugs. "You drive all the way down from Pennsylvania?"

"Yeah, I mean, it's my car, so I can do what I want. I'll give you a lift?"

"That would be nice."

He puts the car into gear. The old neighborhood slides easily into the rearview mirror. She directs him toward Mom and Steve's house. She tries to imagine herself back in the blue room, finishing her résumé. No more checking the website, no more mission, no way to make things better.

"Do you think—I've thought about posting something to the site. You know, telling them who I am. That I'm one of the Founders or whatever. I could tell them we made it all up. That I don't believe any of it anymore. That they should shut down the site. What do you think?"

Marc is silent for a time in the seat next to her. He stops for a red light at an intersection where there are no other cars.

"Yeah, WorshipHIM36 will never agree to it. They really believe. I've had that argument with them already. And even if they shut down this site, someone would probably just make another. The people that are into this like having you and Lana as some kind of symbol. You're, like, an urban myth or something now. Even if they believe it's actually you that's posting, people that want to believe crazy stuff are just going to keep believing, you know? I get why you want to do something, like, make some big gesture, but I think it's too late for that. You did what you did, you know?"

Maddie is quiet, deflated. She supposes he's right. The only thing that could help her now is a time machine. There's no heroic act that will redeem her. There's only her guilt and its consequences, only her little life to sort out.

"Turn here," she says dully.

Marc turns into the new neighborhood. After he pulls up in front of the house, he puts the car in park and waits a full minute before he speaks. "I won't tell," he says. "As long as you promise to stay off the site."

Maddie releases a breath. "It's a deal. But I'm wondering if you could do one more thing for me."

Maddie lets herself silently back into the house. It's a little past 2:00 a.m. Quickly, she packs her clothes in the duffel bag she brought with her from Needmore. She takes the wad of cash from the bank account she emptied two days ago and splits it between her wallet and her sock. Gran's pearls she places in the bottom of the duffel, then scrawls a quick note on some paper for Mom and leaves it on the kitchen counter.

She's happily surprised to find Marc still waiting for her outside. His head is slumped against the driver's side window, his eyes closed, but when she knocks, he straightens up immediately.

"You sure about this?" he asks as they drive.

"I've been thinking about it for a while. It just can't work for me, sticking around here."

Marc nods, and she supposes that, of all people, he might get it. It's one thing to atone and another to wallow in your suffering, waiting for a steady string of neighbors and acquaintances to hold you to account for the worst thing you've ever done. To stay is to be trapped in the past, and she needs to move forward; Gran understood that.

It's still dark outside when Marc pulls up in front of the bus station. "Do you want me to wait?" he asks.

"No, thank you, I can take care of myself." She opens the door.

"Bye, Maddie. Stay out of trouble."

She turns to him and says seriously, "You too."

Inside, the bus terminal is deserted except for three people sleeping, at scattered distances from one another, on cold metal benches. She chooses her own empty bench. The first bus for Louisville departs at 6:00 a.m., fifteen minutes before Mom and Steve's alarm goes off. Maddie feels tired now, a deep fatigue that reaches down through her legs and back up into her head.

She types away on her phone for a few minutes. She found an email address for Sage through a directory of the medical school she's attending in Boston. After all this time, she wishes she had more to say, that she could be more articulate, but she can only do the best that she can.

After she sends the message, she hesitates. The phone is still new, so beautiful. She could keep it to pawn or sell, but don't they have ways of tracking phones now, even when they're turned off? She isn't sure. And Marc is right: someone like her shouldn't be spending much time online at all. Eventually, she turns the phone off, walks to the nearest trash bin, and drops it in the empty barrel, where it lands with a thud. She sits back down on the bench.

It's Saturday morning. It's nearly two weeks until her next scheduled meeting with Miranda, but she assumes Mom and Steve will probably notify her that she's missing on Monday morning. By then she'll be across state lines. They can search for her if they want to, sure, but that would cost money and effort—especially if she lies low for a while, uses a different name. She thinks her chances are decent.

An hour later, the ticket booth opens. She buys a ticket and some water and a bunch of candy bars from a vending machine. A little past six, a garbled voice over the loudspeaker announces the bus to Louisville. It's still dark. Maddie picks up her bag and falls into line. As she exits the waiting area into the dim parking garage to board the bus, just for a moment, she thinks she sees something out of the corner of her eye—a large shadow, someone watching her. She starts and turns her head but finds only empty air.

On the bus, she claims a window seat. A few minutes later the bus exits into a gloomy dawn. The driver makes a garbled announcement over the loudspeaker. A little sunshine touches her face, and she can already feel her eyelids growing heavy. She settles in for the long ride, long enough, she hopes, for her to start to become a different person.

2

On Monday morning, when Sage's alarm clock wakes her at six, it's still dark. Everyone told her Boston would be cold, but what she didn't expect was the shortness of the days, the way darkness starts to take hold by 4:00 p.m. The sky is just brightening when she sets out for the gym. She's opted to live in medical student housing for her first year, a dorm-like brick building with twenty-four-hour concierge service. It's only two blocks from the gym, and she has the Mace she always carries on her key chain and the two semesters of self-defense classes she took as an undergrad to get her there safely.

She got looks from several students when, at one of the med school orientation events, she asked for information about crime statistics in the area and whether it was safe to walk around at night by herself. People must have thought she was some small-town girl afraid of the big city, the blonde girl whose questions no doubt betrayed some racialized unease, but people stopped judging once they found out about her. One night early in the semester, one of the first-year med students, Sung-Ho Kim, took it upon himself to google all his classmates, and then everyone seemed to know her story.

It was a little silly, she admitted recently to her new therapist, a little like worrying about being struck a second time by lightning, her fear of being mugged. But of course it happens. In the history of the world, everything has happened.

Sage likes getting to the gym early. She has her choice of machines, and today she chooses the same one she always does, the elliptical next to the window. Over her yoga pants, she wears a long-sleeved cotton top so that the scars on her arms and chest are covered. She places her phone on the stand and the buds in her ears. Her playlist starts out slow, as if to ease herself back into the morning grind. Those first few minutes are always the hardest, the push to get her heart rate up. Then the beat of the music picks up, and so does her stride. She feels the first burst of sweat roll down her back.

The knife missed puncturing the wall of her heart by no more than a millimeter, the surgeon said at the time. If it had, she would have died within seconds. Now there's just a knot of scar tissue resting in her chest, similar clumps on her pancreas and in her lungs.

Sage keeps her eyes on the heart monitor. When it gets up to 180, she eases back, toning down the resistance on the machine and slowing down her speed until she's back under 170.

Gym time is her reflective time. This is the only time of day when she lets herself think about things like the scar tissue next to her heart, lets herself feel sentimental or pitiable. After this, she'll return to her studio apartment and shower, and then her mind will be fixed firmly on the here and now, on this morning's anatomy lab and this afternoon's lectures and, later that evening, studying for finals with David. She hasn't made it this far by allowing herself to wallow in the old trauma.

Still, it asserts itself now that she's started med school, in ways she should perhaps have anticipated. Just two weeks ago during a psych lecture, they had a schizophrenic man in his thirties visit the class, to talk about his experiences. Her fellow first-years acted like he was some exotic zoo animal they were seeing for the first time. They had spoken a lot in the class about the concept of insight, how some patients were capable of having insight into their disorder, where others might not. The man told them that he had schizophrenia, and he told them that once in his kitchen late at night, his spoons and forks had started to sing and dance. But when one of the students asked him if the singing cutlery was related to his schizophrenia, he blinked and said, "No, I don't think so. I think that was a message. I'm not sure if it was a message from God exactly, but it might have been. Sometimes you know something deep down, and it has to manifest itself in a certain way. For me, it was dancing spoons." Some students had to suppress their smiles; others typed furiously on their laptops. After the man left, the instructor said, "So, an interesting case of low insight. He admits the diagnosis—it probably makes life a lot easier—but he doesn't believe that it explains the hallucinations."

Of course the vast majority of schizophrenics are a danger to no one but themselves. Sage tried to adopt this professorial tone a couple of weeks ago when her father called, frantic, because Mom had run into Madeline Thompson working at a nursery across town. Her parents were furious that no one had let them know that she had been released, as her father put it, "back into the wild."

"There's no legal requirement for them to notify us," Sage said. "She was tried as a minor; her slate was wiped clean."

"Well, that's not how we see it," Dad said. "I don't think we'll ever see it that way."

"I mean, in legal terms," Sage said, and sighed. She was trying to keep her voice steady, to pretend it didn't matter.

"I already spoke to the lawyer. He said there's nothing we can do now, but if she reaches out to you in any way, if she initiates contact, we can file for a restraining order. He's already putting the papers together."

"Dad, why would she do that? There's nothing for her to gain. I can't imagine she'd be that stupid." As she spoke, Sage realized she had no idea how stupid Maddie was or wasn't. The lawyers have assured them that there's no way Lana is getting out anytime soon, maybe ever, and Sage felt immensely relieved to hear it. Maddie she is less sure about. She doesn't think that Maddie is actually insane, for one thing. She suspects that if Madeline Thompson had never met Lana Prescott, she might have lived a fairly ordinary life. But Sage doesn't like to depend too much on her reading of a person's character. The only thing she is really sure about is that people are fundamentally unknowable, and therefore untrustworthy. So perhaps that is why she had trouble sleeping for several days after her father's call.

Whatever Sage specializes in, it won't be psychiatry. Psychiatry itself is just so slippery, the criteria and even the disorders themselves mutating with each new edition of the *DSM*. It's barely science, really. Sage wants a field where the answers are clear, where the diagnosis is right or wrong. She doesn't want to have to wonder whether her patients are desperately ill or just evil.

She's been on the machine for exactly thirty minutes. Down on the street, the city is coming alive. People flock toward the nearest T station holding their coffees in their gloved hands, woolen hats on their heads, their work clothes concealed beneath long, puffy coats.

Sage lets her legs come to a stop. Her heart is thumping insistently in the way that it only does when she pushes herself to exercise like this. This is why she exercises like this.

When she steps off the elliptical, her legs feel like putty.

She's drenched, and she walks the two blocks back to her apartment with her coat unzipped, allowing the cold air to freeze-dry the sweat. The sidewalks are busy now, the world is peopled, its threat greatly diminished. On her way into the building, she runs into two other first-year women in gym clothes. They greet her politely.

She showers quickly—anatomy lab starts at nine. Dressed, she pulls a brush through her wet hair, which she wears in the same short cut around her face that she has since she was ten, fixes herself a bowl of cereal, and sits down at the table in front of her computer. She clicks through her med school email, through various updates and announcements. She is just about to exit out when she decides to check her spam filter. Last week Cody sent an email to her account that had been filtered out, and she would have missed it completely if he hadn't texted her to ask about it. Of course it was just another bunch of memes of cute puppies, but Sage doesn't mind cute animals in the morning.

The message is at the top of her spam list. Sender: Madeline Thompson. Without opening it, she can read the first line: Dear Sage, I know you probably are not happy to hear from me . . .

She drops the spoon into her cereal bowl with a clank. Then she slams her hand against the table so hard it stings. Glancing up at the bare white ceiling, she takes several deep breaths. She exits the window, dumps the half-eaten bowl of cereal in the sink, grabs her backpack from off the floor, and locks the door behind her.

She decides to walk the long way to anatomy lab, to give herself some time to calm down and collect her thoughts. But she doesn't really have thoughts yet; she just has feelings, pure physical sensations. The pounding heart, the constriction in the chest. She should have taken a Valium before she left. Her psychiatrist in undergrad took a fairly conservative approach to meds, but the one she's seeing now looked shocked when she said she had only previously been prescribed an antidepressant and nothing specific for the anxiety attacks. "Better to have something on hand," the new psychiatrist said. "Just in case."

By the time her breathing is stable and she's able to take deep, clear breaths, she's about fifteen minutes late. She's never been late before. The locker room is empty as she changes hurriedly into scrubs. Entering the lab, she finds Elena, Taj, and David already clustered around their table. The morning's lesson is projected up on a screen at the front. Dr. Nielsen is circulating, standing with a group at the front of the room and bending over, pointing a finger into the chest cavity of the cadaver on the table.

David glances at her as she approaches, his eyes raised.

"You're late," Elena says.

"Sorry," Sage says.

"Overslept?" Taj asks.

"Yeah."

"You wouldn't forgive yourself if you missed this," Taj says. "We're taking out the heart."

"Want to do the honors?" David asks, motioning to the scalpel on the table.

"No," Sage says, swallowing, "not today. Elena, you should do it."

Elena looks surprised. Since the beginning of the semester, Sage has done most of the cutting. She was nervous about it at first, about picking up a knife and cutting human skin. The first class, the smell of the preservatives made her dizzy; several students vomited and one almost fainted. But Sage just took several deep breaths, and once she got used to the smell, she liked the way the knife sliced so cleanly through the cadaver's skin. The body had been infused with formalin, and all the internal organs had faded to a dullish brown or gray. The blood was coagulated, thick and crumbly. It was nothing like a living, breathing person.

Sage was always gentle, never nicking the organs underneath, unlike Taj, who was still angry at herself for accidentally making a deep gash in the colon. They were all overachievers, perfectionists. That's how they'd gotten here. Perhaps, Sage thought at the time, she might consider becoming a surgeon after all.

Now she stands to the side as Elena picks up the scalpel. Last week they removed the entire breastplate, David using the bone saw to cut out a large panel of skin and ribs, revealing the heart and lungs underneath. They all felt a certain reverence at the unveiling. Here they were at the source, the *lub-dub* of the heart and the *in-out* of the breath, all the components of life, these delicate organs that the body keeps wrapped beneath so many layers of skin and bone.

Now Sage watches impassively as Elena, squinting at the week's handout, attempts to label the major arteries.

"Well, that's the aorta, obviously," Taj says, pointing to a thick spindle of tissue at the top.

"You sure that isn't the pulmonary artery?" Elena says.

"It's the largest one," Taj says.

"The pulmonary artery is also large."

"It's the aorta," David says quietly.

He's been sneaking glances at Sage, and now he turns to look at her, his whole face a question. Usually she'd have rushed in by now to tell everyone her opinion. Her silence is throwing off the group dynamic.

"It's the aorta," she says. "Go ahead and cut it."

Sage watches as David bisects the heart, splitting it open cleanly. He says that it reminds him of a cow's heart that he dissected in high school biology, except smaller.

"You can see the breakdown on this side," Dr. Nielsen says when she stops by their table. "The thinness of the tissue is a direct result of heart disease. The muscle is overworked."

They've arrived, finally, at the thing that killed their patient. Sage glances toward the top of the table, where the head remains covered; she's never seen his face.

She should have deleted it this morning, that stupid email. Instead of leaving it in her spam filter, delaying the decision for later. To read or not to read, that's the question now. As she sees it, nothing good can come of it. There is no explanation, no apology that can make right the wrong that Maddie did. All it can do is disrupt Sage's day, throw off her carefully calibrated equilibrium, give her a panic attack on the way to anatomy lab, and ruin the lesson about the heart that she's been looking forward to all semester. Better to delete it. Pretend that she never saw it, that it was filtered out just like it was supposed to be.

What are the arguments in favor of reading it? Nothing but satisfying her own curiosity. After all this time, what could Maddie want to say to her?

◆ ◆ ◆

By the time they finish at noon, the cadaver's heart lies in pieces, spread out carefully on a small tray. They cover the tray and pull the sheet up over the open chest cavity.

Sage changes quickly out of her scrubs and is pulling her coat on when David appears at her elbow.

"Hey," he says. "Wanna grab some lunch?"

"I gotta head back to my room before lecture." She zips up her coat.

"Is everything all right?" He's a head taller than her, and he bends down slightly as he asks, tilting his whole body.

"I'm fine. I'll see you in lecture."

Back in her room, she takes the bottle from the medicine cabinet in the bathroom and swallows a pill, dry. Then she walks to the kitchenette to get herself a glass of water. She eyes her laptop warily, thinks about going online, and decides against it. She takes a granola bar out of a box she keeps next to her bed and places it on the table. She isn't hungry, but she thinks she should probably eat.

After about twenty minutes, she notices that her heart and her breathing have slowed a little. She feels a little foggy, just a little floaty, but not enough to forget the problem she still faces. Now she supposes that she must read the message after all, because what if she is wrong about Maddie, what if Maddie is actually a crazy bitch intent on finishing what she and Lana started? What if she still believes in Him or whatever bullshit imaginary friend the two of them created to justify their sadism? What if Maddie, who somehow found her med school email address online, is right now headed up to Boston to kill her? Then she'd need to call the police, ask Dad to initiate the restraining order— or maybe Henry, who just started working at a law firm back home. She needs to check herself into a hotel, one with good security. When will it ever end? She was just a little girl who wanted to make friends. She was just a girl in a bathing suit, padding around Wild World in her sandals and a cover-up, laughing with another girl. How is she still living this nightmare?

Self-pity aside, she knows what she needs to do, and better to do it before the Valium wears off. She opens the laptop and clicks on the spam folder.

Dear Sage,

I know you probably are not happy to hear from me, but I wanted to write you as I am about to make some serious changes in my life. I am moving out West and I promise you won't ever hear from me again. I'm sorry if my sending this causes you pain. I really am sorry, though I know you might find that hard to believe. It's hard for me to explain why I helped Lana the way that I did. I still don't understand it myself. I can only say now that I am a very different person than the girl that hurt you. I would never try to hurt you or anyone. I watched the interview where you talked about wanting to be a doctor. I hope that someday I also can find a profession where I can help other people. Anyway, I wish you luck for all your future endeavors and I want you to know that although I cannot change the past I am truly sorry. I still remember the day we had at Wild World. I'm sorry for betraying your trust.

Sincerely,
Maddie

Sage has to read it twice. She feels relief, then a desire to throw something. There's something formal and a little stilted about the letter, though she supposes that shouldn't surprise her. It's actually not that badly written for someone who only finished the sixth grade. The line about Wild World is weird, like something you'd write to a lover you'll always keep in your heart. Weird but not threatening.

She lies down on the bed and takes some deep breaths.

When she opens her eyes, it's 4:47 p.m. and she's slept through lecture. She sighs and sits up. She's sweaty. The heat in the building is centrally controlled, and ever since it came on at the beginning of the month, it's been too hot. She thinks about opening a window but instead reaches for her phone. She has three texts from David.

Saved you a seat!

Still coming?

Everything ok?

She must have been really off in anatomy lab; he doesn't usually deluge her like this. She puts her phone back on the side table, stands up, and opens the window right above the bed, the only one she's managed to crack since she moved in three months ago. A draft of cold air falls on her head. It feels nice for a moment, but she knows she'll soon be cold.

She needs to figure out what she's doing with David. He's been very patient. So far they're just friends, but she can feel him hesitating when he walks to the door at the end of their study sessions, wondering whether this will be the night he goes in for the kiss, if this will be the night she finally gives him permission.

Sage didn't date in high school. After the stabbing, it was like that part of her just dried up. Or perhaps she just channeled all that energy into something else, into the dream of med school. Before the stabbing, she'd thought that blowing Ethan Walsh behind the pool house would be the biggest thing that would happen to her that summer. She worried that he'd tell everybody and that she'd arrive at her new school with a reputation, that people would think she was easy. She'd been strange herself that night at the slumber party, acting a little too silly, a little too young, wearing her Winnie-the-Pooh pajamas, as if she wanted to undo the grown-up thing that she had just done.

She talked to a therapist about that, too, the blow job and whether it was "consensual." She had thought she was going to make out with Ethan. She'd been too naive to conceive of it going further than that. But she never exactly felt coerced. She had felt half disgusted and half like the great adventure of her life was beginning. As far as she knew, Ethan never told anyone. She remembered making eye contact with him once, on one of her first days back at school. He had looked away, as if intimidated. It was as if the thing that had happened to her had placed her on a different plane from the other kids; no one knew how to respond to it.

"Did it feel like those two things were related?" her college therapist asked her once. "Because they happened so close to one another? Like you were being punished somehow for your sexuality?"

"They weren't related," Sage insisted. "It was just a coincidence."

But now she wonders if the therapist wasn't onto something, if she didn't, at some irrational level, believe that the stabbing was a kind of punishment for what she'd done with Ethan, that the universe had punished her for her daring, her desire.

As a rule, Sage kept to herself after the stabbing. She wasn't particularly friendly with girls, though she usually had a few guy friends she hung out with in a strictly platonic way. More than one of these friendships ended when the guy confessed that he liked her as more than a friend. By college, she'd decided that she wanted to lose her virginity. She didn't like feeling that she was so inexperienced, so behind. Sophomore year, she met Zane, a nerdy chemistry major who met her requirements of being attractive in a not-too-macho, not-too-threatening way. They slept together a handful of times, an act that Sage endured more than enjoyed. Self-conscious about her scars, she insisted they keep the lights off and always dressed and undressed in the dark.

After the relationship was finally consummated, Zane became quite clingy, texting her several times a day.

"Wow, you are really perfecting your shitty boyfriend routine," her friend Owen remarked dryly when, once during lunch, she carefully ignored two texts from Zane. Owen was gay, and therefore safe.

Sage couldn't blame Zane when he called things off, saying that he was looking for something different. To Owen, Sage joked that she had found the only college guy who wanted a serious girlfriend, and Owen nodded, tight-lipped, for once biting his tongue.

Sage didn't feel much when Zane went out of her life, but the idea of losing David is alarming. She wishes she could freeze time right now, preserve their relationship forever as a series of study sessions and lengthy discussions about what kind of doctors they will someday become. Lately, though, she's even found herself imagining hugging David, laying her head in his lap, holding hands next to him on the couch, perhaps working her way to a kiss. But she fears a repeat of the Zane situation, her inevitable pulling away. When he gets too close, she'll freeze him out. She's doing it already.

Her phone pings. Another text from David.

I'm starting to worry. Everything ok?

The draft from the window is too much. She stands up and moves two feet over to sit in a chair at her small table. She picks up her phone.

Sorry! Everything's fine. I'm just having a really weird day.

An understatement, surely. The first time Madeline Thompson has reached out to her since the day over a decade ago when she and Lana lured her into the woods to murder her. Yes, a weird day.

It was strange of Maddie to mention that day at Wild World. Sage hasn't thought of it in some time. It got sealed off like all her memories of Maddie and Lana, filed into the Time Before. The Time Before that day she hadn't known who Maddie and Lana really were, hadn't recognized her enemies. That was what continued to haunt her, the thing she spent so many hours talking about with her therapist, how there must have been signs, warnings she had failed to see. How could she trust anyone else when she could not trust herself to recognize the danger right in front of her? She had been, all that time, like Little Red Riding Hood in the belly of the wolf, and she hadn't even known it.

But there's something else about that day at Wild World, some other reason that it doesn't fit with her other memories of that time. She remembers a long slide, being scared of how high up they were. Swimming with Maddie. Playing games with Maddie, walking just the two of them up and down the alley of game stalls. Where was Dad; why wasn't he there? She can see him suddenly, sitting at a picnic table in his red swimming trunks, holding his phone in his hand, frowning. It comes back to Sage suddenly, that woman accosting the three of them just outside the exit.

She feels a lurch in her stomach and shakes her head, as if to banish the memory. Too much, she thinks.

Her phone buzzes again.

We still on for tonight?

She looks out the window, down to the gray street. All she's eaten today is the half bowl of cereal that morning.

She picks up the phone and calls David. He answers right away.

"Hey."

"Hey, sorry for being flaky. Like I said, it's been a weird day. But I was thinking, maybe you could get takeout from the Chinese place, and bring it over? I don't know if I'm up for studying, but maybe we could just hang out. Or whatever."

"Yeah, sure. Definitely. I'd like that."

"Okay."

"Should I come over now?"

"Whatever works for you."

"I'll be there in thirty minutes, twenty if they're fast."

After he hangs up, Sage rouses herself, sniffs her armpits, peels off the sweaty top, and steps out of her jeans. She pulls out a pair of sweatpants and a long-sleeved tee from her dresser, an outfit that is the very opposite of sexy. Then she goes into the bathroom and brushes her teeth.

She knows it's coming, but she still startles when she hears the knock. She stands still for a moment in front of the door, trying to work up the courage to let him in.

3

Tuesday is the best day, the day when Mommy comes to visit. Lana would long ago have stopped paying attention to days of the week if not for Tuesday. The sunlight through the windows in the hallway glints a little differently on Tuesdays, in anticipation of her mother's visit.

At breakfast, Lana is seated next to Samantha, the new patient. They've just upped Samantha's Haldol again, and she moves her arm slowly, as if pushing through molasses. When she knocks over Lana's bowl with her elbow, she stares with an underwater look as the milk runs across the tabletop, threatening to ooze into Lana's lap. Luckily Bettina is on duty, and she spots it right away. She sops up the milk with a cloth before it gets Lana wet and says soothingly, "No problem, right, Lana? Just an accident. I'll get you a new bowl."

Lana isn't happy about the milk, the spilled cereal. It feels like a bad omen for the day. But when she looks at Samantha, she sees no malice, only glazed eyes. That's how it is with the Haldol, especially at first. She remembers feeling as if she had large mittens on her hands that made it difficult to hold things, but the worst of it passed eventually, or perhaps over time she has just gotten used to always wearing that pair of invisible mittens.

Across the table, Mama Val has watched the cereal bowl incident with her usual keen eye. Mama Val is the oldest patient on their ward. Her long gray hair hangs down past her shoulders, and she's missing two teeth: one on the top left, the other on the bottom. Lana has always assumed that the "mama" is a kind of honorific on account of her age, but she's also heard the nurses and techs call Mama Val "Joanne," so it's possible that Mama Val named herself.

For the last couple of years, Mama Val was attached to a younger black woman named Adelphi. Adelphi followed Mama Val everywhere. The two always stood together against the chain-link fence during yard time, whispering, and they sat together at meals, whispered over cards during free time. No one messed with either Mama Val or Adelphi because they were understood to be a pair, and there's strength in numbers. Lana always kept clear of them, but three weeks ago, Adelphi got out, and now Mama Val stands alone against the chain-link fence. When Samantha showed up, Lana thought that perhaps she would become the new Adelphi, but so far all Samantha has done is fall asleep everywhere. She fell asleep yesterday during group, her mouth hanging open and slack as Kayla droned on about her anger issues.

Lana doesn't like the look in Mama Val's eyes, so she averts her eyes. She takes her small paper napkin and blots the last few drops of milk as Bettina places another bowl of cereal in front of her. Blanca and Missy look at her over their empty bowls, probably calculating that Lana has gotten extra cereal as a result of the mishap. Lana worries about Missy the most, the way her eyes glitter at Lana over her own empty bowl while Lana eats the new cereal.

Lana swallows and remembers that today is Tuesday. She doesn't want to let anything ruin her mood on visiting day.

After breakfast, she asks for her art supplies. They keep her things in a separate plastic bin in one of the supply closets, including the special acid-free paper that Mommy buys for her. She's gotten very good over the years at doing portraits in crayon. They're realistic drawings, nothing like the fantastical stuff she used to draw in her notebooks back home. She starts with a simple line and lets the line guide her to other lines, until a face emerges.

The last couple of years, she's done portraits of everyone on their ward and given them out as Christmas gifts. Sometimes some of the nurses and techs from other floors will even come sit for her, to get their portraits done. Dr. McCullough tells her he's happy that Lana has found a healthy outlet for her creativity.

This morning, she starts to sketch, slowly, her first portrait of Samantha. It's always nice to have a new face to work with. For now, Samantha's face is droopy from the new drugs. It lacks the spark that Lana tries to capture, the reason that her portraits are so popular with those who value them—the sense that she has captured some aspect of the sitter's being. But that's okay. For now, Lana will practice capturing Samantha's features, with tracing the lines. And then later she'll be ready to capture the spark when it comes back to Samantha's face, as the other woman gets better.

Visiting hours are after lunch. Mommy is always waiting for her at the table when she arrives. For many years, ever since they established this routine, her mother has never missed a Tuesday, and she has never been late. Her boss at the large box store where she works knows that she always takes Tuesdays off.

Today Mommy is waiting for her as she always does. Mommy takes her in as she approaches the table, trying to see if Lana's week has been good or bad. They are allowed to hug at the beginning of the meeting and the end, and sometimes they can get away with holding hands if one of the nice guards is on, but today it's Frank, and Lana knows he won't allow it.

Lana takes a deep breath when she hugs Mommy, taking in a whiff of her shampoo and some other smell as familiar as childhood. The smell of their old house has faded over the years, but something of it still lingers in the folds of skin along Mommy's neck, maybe just the smell of Mommy herself.

Daddy lost his job with the federal government after Lana was arrested. It turned out her parents' finances were overextended, and they lost the house. And not long after that, for reasons Lana has never been able to understand, her parents separated, then divorced.

"How are you, my love?"

Lana shrugs. There is nothing special to report this week. She tells her mother how Samantha knocked over her cereal bowl that morning, but it was all right; they let her get another.

"Is Samantha giving you trouble?" Mommy asks, her brow furrowing. Over the years, Lana has often been bullied by the other patients, an easy target because of both her diminutive size and her youth.

"Samantha isn't a problem," Lana says, thinking of Missy's eyes at the breakfast table that morning.

Mommy starts to tell her about her week, and Lana listens with a slightly distracted air, pulling at the long ends of her hair. After the trial, Mommy's hair went white, but she dyes it now and it looks almost natural, though it fades week to week, from a dark chestnut to a reddish brown, until she gets it redone. She does that on her other day off.

Mommy moved a couple of years ago into a two-bedroom apartment near the highway. The second bedroom is for Lana, for when she's released. Mommy showed her photos when she first moved in so Lana could picture it for herself.

It's not time yet, but in a month or so Mommy will bring in the Christmas card from her father and Marc. It's been years now since Lana has seen either of them in person, but she's allowed to post that year's Christmas card above her bed, and she carefully replaces it year after year. Her father and Marc moved to Pennsylvania years ago for Dad's new job. Her father's face is recognizable, though he has put on weight and his hair has grayed. Marc looks like a stranger, a young man with a thin smile. In the photo still hanging above her bed from last year, he is taller than their father now and wearing a T-shirt from Penn State.

When she looks at this photo, it appears to Lana as if someone has replaced the family she once knew with these imposters. After the trial, Daddy never looked at her the same way again. The man who came to visit her then was her father, but he was not Daddy. After a time, he stopped coming at all.

"How's Maddie?" Lana asks suddenly, and Mommy startles a little, as if dreading the question. Mommy has a funny look on her face, something she doesn't want to say.

"Honey, Maddie's gone," she says.

"Gone?" Lana swallows. "Is she dead?"

"What? Why would you say that?" Lana blinks at Mommy, not answering. "No, I heard from some of the old neighbors. She left a note. They think she got on a bus, but even her mother doesn't know where."

Lana tries to keep her face neutral, but she can feel her eyes widening.

"What did the note say?"

"I don't know exactly. Just that she was leaving town, I guess."

"Are the police looking for her?"

"I assume so."

Lana plants her hands on the table in front of her as if to steady herself.

"I'm sorry, honey, I know that you were hoping she would come for a visit."

Lana brushes this off. "You should check in the woods—where it happened."

Mommy blinks. "What are you talking about?"

"Someone should check in the woods, you know, near the old house, just in case."

"In case what?"

Lana sighs and pushes her glasses back up to the top of her nose. She can see that she's alarmed Mommy.

"I just think . . . someone should check in the woods. You know, just in case she went there."

"What are you talking about? Why would she go back there?"

Lana shrugs. She shouldn't say anything more.

The clock hanging above the wall over Mommy's head tells her that the forty-five minutes have already gone too fast, the way they always do. Apparently seeing her anguished look, Mommy turns to look at the clock too. She reaches out and takes Lana's hands in hers.

"I'll be back next week," she says. "And we'll talk on Thursday and Saturday. Remember I'm doing an extra shift Saturday, so don't call until after eight."

"Hands," Frank says, and Mommy draws her hands back, but not without giving Frank a scowl. Mommy gives her an extra squeeze at the end of the visit, and then Lana is walking down the hall, back toward the common room, and that's it: seven more days until she sees Mommy again. It's up to her to call on the right days, and sometimes she does, and sometimes she doesn't. She'll have to remember this week—so she can ask Mommy for any news about Maddie.

Back in the common room, everyone is already cleaning up in anticipation of yard time. Samantha is snoring quietly on the couch. Blanca is sitting next to Samantha, her eyes intent on the TV, which is muted, with only the closed captions turned on. Mama Val is surveying the entire room from her chair in the corner. Missy and Kayla are clearing the checkers off the table.

The techs have fetched their coats and have laid them down on one of the round tables, ready to dress each of them as if they were preschoolers. No one greets her when she enters, but she knows that the nurse behind the desk has marked her off, entering another X into the day's spreadsheet.

There's a sense of excitement as they put on their coats, though most of them will be bored and cold after fifteen minutes outside and will start talking about how they wish they could go back in.

Amira has been working here less than a week, and when she hands Lana the wrong coat, she thinks about pointing it out to her, but Amira has already pulled Missy's coat up around Lana's shoulders, and she decides to accept it, the other woman's coat, which is black. When Amira tries to put Lana's green coat on Missy, Missy protests, but Amira doesn't believe her because Lana's accepted the black coat and Missy is a troublemaker, while Lana is generally sedate and does what she's told. Missy shoots a look at Lana, and Lana knows she'll have to pay for this later.

Outside it's cold and overcast, with only about an hour until sunset. They can walk around the whole enclosed yard. Some worn exercise equipment that nobody touches lies in one corner. Samantha, groggy, is shuffling her feet along the stone walkway. Blanca has started her laps around the perimeter. She'll walk around and around for the whole hour, until they blow the whistle. Kayla hurries to catch up with Blanca, though Blanca shows no sign of wanting company. Missy stands fixedly by the door, staring at Lana.

Lana turns and makes her way warily across the yard. Mama Val is leaning against the chain-link fence, watching her.

"You got the wrong coat," she says. Lana shrugs. "Trouble," Mama Val says. "You're looking for trouble."

"Tech gave me the wrong coat," Lana says.

"What are you aiming at, crossing Missy? You know what she did?"

"You know what I did?" Lana asks, shoving her hands in the coat pockets.

Mama Val waves a hand. "That's nothing," she says. "You were just a kitten when you did that. What were you, ten?"

"Twelve."

Mama Val shakes her head. "See, they're willing to take something you did when you're twelve and lock you up for life. It's more subjects for them. More data."

Mama Val believes that all of them are the victims of a government conspiracy. The government will find any reason it can to lock people up and then observe them, carefully collecting and sorting the data. This happens to anyone who steps slightly out of line, who gives them the slightest excuse, but eventually the government will take the data it's collected and use it against everyone, all of society, to try to find a way to control them.

Mama Val has shared this theory with Lana several times over the last few weeks. So far Lana has remained agnostic.

"Missy is a low whore," Mama Val says, "not to be trusted."

Lana, wearing Missy's coat, shrugs again. Missy is still watching her from across the yard.

When they line up to go back inside, Mama Val goes to the end of the line. Lana falls in behind Kayla, but Missy comes over and grabs her by the arm. Lana is ready and spins away. Before Missy can grab her again, there are two techs pulling Missy off her and dragging her, struggling, through the door and down the hall. They can all hear Missy shouting as they head in to dinner.

"She stole my coat!" Missy shouts. "She stole from me!"

Missy isn't back for dinnertime. Lana's eyes flit across the table, and Mama Val gives her a wink.

Lana's favorite time of day is after the lights go out. She has about fifteen minutes until the evening meds kick in, carrying her off to sleep whether she wants it or not, but those fifteen minutes are often the only fifteen minutes she gets to herself.

Tonight she thinks about Maddie. If the Followers had gone through with the sacrifice, she supposes she would have heard by now; they would have found a body. No, she corrects herself, if they had gone through with it, He'd be here now, in the flesh.

Something happened. Something went wrong.

She squeezes the phone out from between the mattress and the bed frame and checks the site again, but there have been no new updates to the private group. The battery is getting low; she'll have to slip the phone to Mama Val at breakfast tomorrow morning. Mama Val charges it for her every few days—she doesn't know how—in exchange for a steady supply of pudding cups. It was Adelphi who smuggled the smartphone in for Lana several months back, in exchange for three months' worth of commissary money.

Perhaps she should have told Maddie who she was when she had the chance, not hidden behind her role as WorshipHIM36. But it was too risky. She didn't know how Maddie felt about her after all these years. It had taken some time to remind Maddie about Him, to draw her back into the fold. She was shocked when Maddie offered herself up, had even thought about saying something on the chat, but then she remembered that day at her house with the knives spread out on the counter, and she realized that He had always been interested in Maddie. And wasn't it better for it to be someone like Maddie, who actually believed, not an innocent like Sage?

But what happened? Is Maddie dead, or did she escape somehow? What if she really has left? What if she never logs back on again?

Lana rolls over in her bed, facing the wall. She can't be too focused on Maddie. This isn't about Maddie, she reminds herself. This is all much bigger than Maddie—it's about Him.

He left her for years, just disappeared. Then one day last fall, at bedtime, after lights-out, He returned. This time she didn't feel afraid. More than anything she felt relieved, after all that time alone, all that time doubting herself. Finally, she had a friend again, and this was her second chance to get things right—to help Him cross over so He could be with her always.

Once she was able to get online, she knew what she had to do. By now, she has amassed a considerable group of Followers, of believers, whom she monitors and communicates with as often as she can. Their numbers grow every day.

She was so close this time. At least she still has the site and all her Followers. She'll log back on again soon and start another thread, build off the good work that Follower_in_the_Distance has done. And if Maddie is still out there somewhere, she's sure they'll find one another again, someday. She doesn't doubt that now. They are connected forever. That's what it means to be best friends.

Lana blinks in the darkness. Now the walls twist around on themselves, patches of greater darkness alternating with the lighter ones. It seems like something is trying to break free, something like a face pushing through the glowing plaster of the walls. The face is pale white, and its eyes and nose have been wiped away. Slowly something tugs at the bottom half of the face; slowly the black cavern of the mouth starts to form, the gray lips begin to part, and she leans forward in the dark, the better to hear Him.

ACKNOWLEDGMENTS

Special thanks to my agent, Hillary Jacobson, who understood and believed in this book from the beginning. Thank you to Jessica Tribble Wells and Angela James for taking on this project and for the excellent editorial guidance.

I began this book during the unlikely summer of 2020, and it is thanks to the support of many people that I was able to finish it. Linda Solomon provided childcare, enabling me to write and rest during a global pandemic. Jennifer Close and the participants of Catapult's Online Novel Generator in the fall of 2020 gave generous guidance and feedback on an early draft. Annie Hartnett has been a source of both editorial and practical advice. Carl Hurvich read and discussed with me. Kieran Dieter has been a loyal friend and first reader for many years now—thanks, dude. Special thanks also to Alice Stevens and Dr. Andy Smyth.

Finally, thank you to Anne and Michael Davis, who encouraged me to follow my dreams and whose love and support ensured I had a very different childhood from the one I have imagined for the characters in this book. Thank you to Eliza who, by limiting my time, helped me to focus my energy and my love. Thank you to Isaac for believing and for accompanying me on this journey.

ABOUT THE AUTHOR

Photo © 2023 Sharona Jacobs

Kat Davis has an MFA in fiction from Washington University in Saint Louis and currently resides in the Boston area. Her fiction has been published in *Wigleaf, Juked, Cosmonauts Avenue, New Orleans Review,* and *Monkeybicycle.* Her work has also appeared on the longlist for *Wigleaf*'s Top 50, and her essays and literary criticism have been featured in the *Chicago Review of Books* and on the *Ploughshares* blog. Kat's most recent piece of flash fiction, "The Babysitter," was selected as a finalist for the Mythic Picnic Prize for Fiction and appears in *The Best Small Fictions 2022.*